Minutes BEFORE Sunset

By: Shannon A. Thompson

Minutes Before Sunset
Copyright ©2015 Shannon Thompson
All rights reserved.

ISBN:978-1-63422-104-7
Cover Design by: Marya Heiman
Typography by: Courtney Nuckels
Editing by: Cynthia Shepp

For more information about our content disclosure,
please utilize the QR code above with your smart phone
or visit us at

www.CleanTeenPublishing.com.

Dedicated to Kristine Andersen and Megan Paustian, for the timeless memories and unfailing support.

ONE

H E HADN'T SMILED SINCE MOM DIED. I WASN'T ALLOWED TO either. In fact, our whole community didn't smile. At six years old, I didn't understand, because I couldn't, but I would later. I knew that much.

It was Independence Day, and I stood with my family on Willow Tree Mountain. They called it that, but, in reality, it was Willow Tree Hill, and the town denied that reality. I didn't care that a famous Civil War battle took place on it. It was a hill, and the only exciting part was the tree.

Wrapping my arm around a loop in the trunk, I peered over the valley. Beneath the fireworks, the entire town was celebrating, dancing, drinking, and even odder, smiling. I wanted to smile.

"They're just bursts of useless fire, Eric." My father folded his arms and glared at the scene. "Nothing more."

I kicked my tennis shoes against the torn-up dirt and dried grass, not able to look at my father like a son should've been able to. The fire didn't look useless. Fireworks, all red and blue, illuminated the darkening sky, and deafening bangs echoed through the valley. The fire seemed powerful—something that hissed from the ground and exploded into the air, defying gravity. They were magnificent.

"You have more important things to worry about than blasts of colored sparks," he said as shadows crawled over his

legs. The darkness whirled around his body, and his glare dissipated with his form. He was gone, back in our shelter, and I was alone. Kind of.

"Eric." Camille, a girl three years older than me, grasped my hand. Her white hair glittered beneath the light, and she spread her fingers into the dark. "We have to go."

I moved my foot closer to the edge of the hill. I wanted to ride the wind down to the crowd. I wanted to celebrate and dance. I wanted to throw my arms in the air and listen to the exploding fireworks. I wanted to run around in endless circles until I fell down from exhaustion. I wanted to enjoy everything.

But that couldn't happen. It was impossible.

Instead, I turned to her and nodded. She was my guard, for life, and I had to listen to her, even if I wasn't listening to my father. "Let's go," I said, and she knelt down to meet my eyes.

"Are you all right?"

No.

"I'm fine," I lied, and her eyes searched mine before she stood up. Without another word, her powers flowed through me, and the dark engulfed us, leaving the fireworks and the happiness behind.

TWO

"CAMILLE," I CALLED, GRUMBLING AS I MOVED THROUGH THE LIFEless forest, leaves crumbling under the pressure of my feet. I hated it when she played stupid games.

It was cold, really cold, and I was wandering through the woods, trying to find my guard. Despite being twenty-one, Camille hadn't changed from the day she was assigned to me. She loved annoying me.

It didn't matter that she was my guard. We were supposed to be together whenever possible. However, after twelve years, Camille was annoyed with responsibility. If she were assigned to an average shade, she'd be free during daylight, the only time we were allowed to be human, but she wasn't. She was assigned to the first descendant.

I gained my powers at my naming, at the age of thirteen. The next four years passed quickly, even though everything had changed.

My father married a naïve woman. The Dark was our life, yet she didn't even know what the Dark was. Mindy was oblivious that she'd married a practical king, and she never would know. It was a secret for a reason. We protected the humans from evil, because they weren't capable of determining evil for themselves.

The Light was malicious, and it always had been. Forget archetypes. They were completely wrong, and they always

would be.

In our history, the Light and Dark accepted one another until the elders decided separating our energies was the smart thing to do. *Idiots.* We turned on one another and the power was taken away, only to return when the true descendants were born. Thousands of years later, that was exactly what was happening, and, lucky me, I was one of them.

Our prophecy was in the making, and the only thing the Light had to do to gain power was prevent the rest from happening. It seemed simple enough until everyone realized only the descendants held the power. In turn, only they could fight the battle, and killing one of them would define who won.

No worries. No pressure at all. Shaking my head, I stomped through the only forest in our small Midwest town. I only had to save my kind or die myself. At least I was aware.

I was raised with three simple rules:

Fight defensively and offensively.

Under no circumstances is it safe to reveal your identity. (Unless it was Urte, Pierce, Camille, or anyone else the elders deemed an exception.)

Win.

The last rule was my favorite, because of the dishonesty. Win didn't mean win. It meant murder. It meant I had to kill the second descendant, the power of the Light, and I had no choice. I would get blood on my hands.

Brushing my hand along the shivering trees, my gaze darted around the darkening forest. I rarely had time to leave our underground shelter and use my powers, and I didn't feel like wasting my night chasing Camille around in the dark.

I threw my senses out around me. The forest reeked of evergreen and pine. I could feel every prickly leaf and see every shadow. From stump to stump, I searched the darkness for Camille's body heat. No one could avoid my radar.

Bingo. I grinned as I locked onto a girl by the river. Sprinting through the thicket, I pushed past scraping branches and leafless oak trees. As I neared the forest's opening, my body sank into the shadows and my skin tingled as it morphed into

4

the chilly air. It was the greatest feeling—other than flying, of course—and I relished in the moment. The blackness of night flowed with me as I floated along the trees, the leaves, or snow. I was enveloped in silk.

I only solidified when I reached the forest's edge. Just as I thought, a girl stood on the river's guardrail, but she wasn't Camille.

She didn't have Camille's white hair or mischievous dark eyes. In fact, this girl didn't even look Camille's age. She was my age, and she had the dark hair, bright eyes, and pale complexion that our sect had.

She was undoubtedly a shade, but I didn't know her.

My fingers gripped my jacket as I moved backward, trying to conceal myself in the darkness, but the girl spun around and stared at me. She was perfectly still when her purple eyes met mine. She didn't budge. Instead, she pointed at me, and the dark magnetically trailed her fingertips.

"Who—" She stepped off the railing, and her eyes widened. "Who are you?"

I put my hands in front of me and stepped out of the forest. This must be one of Camille's illusion jokes.

"Who are you?" she asked again, backing up against the guardrail.

I didn't respond. Instead, I flew through the shadows and reappeared in front of her. My body heat escaped me, and she froze, completely petrified by my closeness. I laid my hand on her cheek, expecting her to disappear like any of Camille's illusions, but she didn't. She was real, and we were centimeters apart, teetering over the edge of the river.

She didn't move. I had the ability to hypnotize any shade, but I hadn't used my power. She was shaking—shivering—beneath my touch, and her heartbeat thundered her energy through my veins.

How odd. She was powerful, yet fear suffocated every bit of her being.

"Shoman!"

A shout split the air, and I sensed a body rushing through

the forest. Camille was coming for me. "Where are you?"

Reflexively, I released the girl and turned to the forest, waiting for Camille to appear. *"Over here,"* I said, sending her a telepathic message. Immediately, she appeared in a beam of light.

Her dark eyes were ablaze as she picked sticks and dried leaves from her glittering hair. "What the hell, Shoman? At least tell me where you are going if you want to be alone."

"I was with—" I closed my mouth as I waved my hand toward the nameless girl, but the ground where she once stood was empty. Nothing. No marks or anything signifying her leave. She was gone.

Impossible. No shade had ever been able to stay off my radar, yet I hadn't felt her leave. It was as if she had never been there.

"With who?" Camille asked, trudging up to me.

"Shh." I held up my hand and threw my senses out.

Camille tensed, and her black eyes darted around. "What are you looking for?"

"Be quiet," I said, spinning in tight circles. My senses were useless. Nothing was there. Not even a bat or a plane. I was being blocked.

I grabbed my guard's boney shoulders. "Camille, who else was out here tonight?"

"No one. Everyone is at the Naming," she said, rolling her eyes. "If you haven't forgotten, you're supposed to be there."

"I don't care," I said, ignoring the ceremony of the last harvest. It was hard to forget. A thick layer of frost coated the dying grass, and I knew that the first layer had fallen yesterday morning. The Naming always followed. As the first descendant, the Dark expected my attendance, so I abided. My father hadn't shown up in years, and I was beginning to forget the point.

Camille touched my arm. "Is something wrong, Shoman?" she asked, her eyes widening. "Was someone here?"

"No," I lied, patting her palm. "Let's go," I said as I dissolved into a shadow.

———— ◆ ————

The elders created the shelter after my mother died. I was five years old when my father bought Hayworth Park and closed it to the public. In six months, it was converted into an underground safe house, and, naturally, the forest protected it. At first, the shelter was made up of two offices, a nursing room, and one training room. Since then, it had grown remarkably, and I couldn't even guess where it ended.

Without a word, I walked through the dim hallways, avoiding the thirteen-year-olds as they ran around in their Naming excitement. Blue, white, and green sparkles littered the floor. Boys snapped their fingers, testing out their powers before they settled, while girls modeled the silver crowns they received. It was exhausting.

"Shoman." I felt a small tug on my shirt as I met eyes with a young boy. He reflected the average shade: dark hair, light eyes, and pale skin. "I passed."

I patted his head. "What's your Dark name?"

"Brenthan," he said, grinning behind his long bangs. "You have to teach me everything you know."

I chuckled and knelt down. "It takes time, Brenthan."

An older boy ran up to us, and he glared at his younger brother. Both of the boys shared dark hair and green eyes, and they acted in the same manner. "The elders are waiting for you," he said, pushing Brenthan toward the short hallway behind us.

Brenthan already received his basic powers, but he still needed to vow to the Dark. Only then would he learn about the prophecy. He would learn who I was, who my family was, and what would come in the near future. For them, it was an exciting promise for a magnificent future. For me, it was a death sentence.

"I'll be back," Brenthan said, his ceremony robe dragging behind him as he bolted away.

Pierce turned to me and bowed his head. We were the same age. We went through the Naming together, and his fa-

ther, Urte, was my father's guard. Pierce's family supported mine after my mother's death and my accident two years ago. He was my best friend—my only friend outside the Dark—yet he was expected to bow to me. I was the first descendent, and he was merely a shade.

"Those kids, eh?" Pierce grinned. "They get so excited for something that seems so natural now."

"Isn't that the truth," I said, watching supportive parents follow their children around. My father hadn't shown up to mine.

"I only hope Brenthan realizes this isn't all fun and games," Pierce said, his eyes focused on the elders' door. "I don't want him to make my mistakes."

"We all do, and we all get through it. Controlling power is a learning process," I said, sighing. "Don't worry about Brenthan. He's a smart kid."

With a trace of a smile, Pierce agreed. "Wanna get out of here? I can't stand it any longer."

My insides tingled at the idea of flying through the cold night air. Images of swerving between trees and clouds engulfed me. Our little town actually looked important from the sky, all lit up and alive.

But the girl. Our rules directed I inform an elder of any unnatural or unsuspected appearance, yet I hadn't even told my guard. She was a secret, and I wanted her to remain that way. Didn't I?

"Getting out sounds great," I said, ignoring the fact that I'd already defied the Naming by leaving.

"Shoman!" My father's telepathic scream tore through me. *"Get home now."*

I cringed at Pierce, and he whistled low. "Bracke?" he asked, referring to my father's Dark name.

I nodded. "I'll have to take a flight with you later," I said as I dissolved, transporting.

My father's office was golden, and the lit room was filled with the same musky cologne he wore for the past decade. He stood by the bookshelf, and his weary, brown eyes shifted

over my shade appearance. "I'd prefer you change when you're home," he said, and I fell out of myself.

My black hair lightened to brown, and my crystal blue eyes dimmed to a mossy green. I lost height, and my facial features shifted. Even my clothes had changed. Suddenly, I was human again, and Eric Welborn was my identity. It didn't matter how many times I watched the unnatural transformation in the mirror; I'd never get used to it.

I slouched in the nearest chair as he returned to his desk and said, "You missed the ceremony."

"You always do," I said, knowing he'd locked himself in his office since the day I was Named. Even the leader of the Dark was unsure of his prophetic son.

My father sighed, shifting his thin hair onto one side of his head. "I wish you would have gone, Shoman."

"Eric," I corrected. After all, we were at home now—our human home—and my human side had the right to hate who I was expected to be.

My father glanced over the leather book in his hands. "Eric," he began. "Where were you tonight? Camille told me you disappeared when the ceremony was about to begin."

She was the one who disappeared. My jaw locked. We left the shelter together, but I couldn't rat on my guard. But that girl. Who was she? How had she gotten there?

"Eric?" My father tapped his desk. "Can you at least pretend to listen to me?"

I shrugged. "I was thinking about Pierce," I lied—one of my only talents—and kicked my feet up on his desk. "His little brother was Named this year."

My father grinned. "He was?"

"Do you even talk to your guard anymore?" I asked, thinking of Urte.

My father's face fell, and his brow furrowed as he sat down. "I'm glad that you could calm Jonathon down."

Jonathon Stone was Pierce's human form. We knew each other's identities and went to high school together, but we rarely talked to maintain that secret. In fact, I rarely talked to

anybody at school. I was kind of a loner. Who was I kidding? I was a loner.

"Actually," I began, leaning forward as I considered my words. "I didn't get a chance to calm Jonathon down. I promised him a flight soon—"

Light flooded my father's brown eyes. "You guys should go tomorrow night."

I raised a practiced brow. "Tomorrow?" I asked, already knowing my next move. "But Camille isn't available."

With his hand, my father waved the idea away. "You can go one night without a guard. It'll do you some good."

I agreed quickly and stood. "Thanks, Pops," I said, knowing I had no intentions of seeing Jonathon on my one night of freedom.

THREE

Jessica

I FLIPPED OVER AND OVER IN MY BED, WRAPPING THE COVERS TIGHTer around my shaking torso. My curly hair fell around me as I shoved my face into my pillow, trying to force the nightmare out of my mind. The man—he had gotten so close to me—and I couldn't move—I couldn't get away. I placed my cold hand on my burning cheek, and I could still feel his touch.

Trying to fall asleep was impossible. I was too nervous about starting my spring semester in an entirely new school— let alone school at all. My parents' jobs forced us to move around, and, because of that, I was homeschooled. Now my mom was jobless, and we were living in our hometown in the middle of Midwest nowhere. I was born in Hayworth, but I didn't remember it. Not at all.

I knew I was adopted, and my family moved us before I could walk, but I didn't know anything about my biological family except the fact that they were dead. My adopted parents avoided the topic like they avoided settling down. Hayworth wasn't particularly pretty, but I liked it. Only now, I couldn't stop thinking about my biological family. How exactly did they die? Who gave me up? Did I have any siblings? Any information gave me control over my life, and now I was having nightmares. How much more complicated did my life have to get?

The stress was too much. I wanted to ignore the world, fall

back into sleep, and escape into my dreamland.

"Wake up," my mother sang as she burst into my room, bubbling with energy.

You have to be kidding me. I rolled over, pulling the pillow over my head. She was a morning person, as was my father. I was not.

She opened my curtains and basked in the morning light streaming through my window. "Jessie, I know that you're dressed and ready to go under those covers," she said, and I groaned. She was right.

"So what?" I mumbled.

"Aren't you excited?" she asked, spinning around until her blonde hair escaped her loose bun. Ever since she gave up her job for the move, she was more of a friend than a mother.

"Not really."

"Come on, Jessie." She pulled my covers off and pouted. "You have ten minutes to get in my car before I go to your school without you."

"When can I start driving to school?" I asked. I was sixteen, not ten.

"When you know where you're going," she said. "The sooner you get in the car, the sooner you'll know where the school is."

I rolled my eyes, pushing myself out of my warm bed. "Okay. Okay. I'm coming."

I was off to start my new life, psychotic nightmares or not.

————◆————

The car's heater blasted hot air into my dry eyes as I stared at the soft, falling snowflakes. For the past two years, we lived in Georgia, and I missed the snow. Winter was ending soon, but I was thankful we'd moved in time to see a snowfall. It was my favorite kind of weather. It reminded me of the hope I held in my biological parents—even more so in Hayworth—but I didn't know why.

We stopped in front of the school. Freshmen and sophomores trudged inside, their cheeks rosy red from the bitter cold. I didn't move from the car, even when I saw the parent behind us roll her eyes. These kids were lucky to know who gave them life, yet they didn't appreciate it. Because they didn't know what it was like without the luxury.

"Mom?" I said and took a deep breath.

"Yes, sweetheart?" she asked, turning down the roaring heater.

I didn't respond; instead, I tapped the window, thinking about my restless night—my dream. It had been on my mind since I woke up, but why? I had more important things to worry about.

"Something on your mind?" she asked, interrupting my thoughts.

My gaze dropped to my shoes. "Mom." I paused, choking at the idea of saying it aloud, but then blurted it out. "Would you and Dad be okay if I looked for my biological family?"

My mother sucked in a breath, and I knew her heart had collapsed. My parents argued about moving back to Hayworth, because I had been born here. They moved away immediately for a reason. They wanted to leave my past behind, but I couldn't. Not anymore.

"This is where I was born," I said, locking my blue eyes on her brown ones. "This is where my biological family was from—"

"But, honey." Her softened voice was barely audible. "They died. I thought we went over this."

"I might have relatives."

"You don't," she said. "The adoptive services showed us the death certificates and explained the situation in detail."

"But they could've missed something," I said, gripping my backpack.

My mother's lowered brow placed shadows over her gaze. "They didn't," she said firmly. "Hayworth is a small town. You'll come to see that."

I dug my nails into my palm, swallowing tears as they threatened to crawl up my throat. "I still want to try."

She put the car in park, and the car behind us honked before reversing and driving around us. Sighing, Mom leaned against the steering wheel and peered at me from behind her straight, blonde hair—another physical trait opposite of mine. "Sweetheart—"

"I could at least find someone who remembers my biological parents," I persisted. "I want to know who they were before they died. You've never even told me how it happened."

My mother placed a hand on her wrinkled forehead and breathed into her arm, hiding her face as she shook her head in silence. I slumped in my seat as curious freshman began to stare at our parked car. "Mom—"

"If that's what you want, Jessie," she finally said, swiping a tear away. "I'll support you every step of the way—as long as you keep your grades perfect. Research is a lot of work, and if one grade slips, then the deal is off until you can pass again."

My lips stretched into a wide grin. "Thank you." I reached over and wrapped my arms around her neck. "No matter what, you're still my mom. I'll always love you."

She stroked my back before pulling away and smiling. "We'll worry about your father later, just have a good day."

Grabbing my backpack, I opened the passenger door. "You, too, Mom," I added as I shut the car door, watching as she sped away. Her car weaved between the others. The engine's white smoke curled toward the tires. It was only the beginning of the day, and so much had already happened. I hugged myself, enjoying the cold, and rushed toward the school in delight. A lot could happen in twenty-four hours.

———◆———

The high school was smaller than I expected, but the hallways were smothered with people. Punks, gothics, cheerleaders, dorks, and teachers crowded the entrance, and more flocked to the cafeteria at the end of the hall. I stood in silence, clutching the handle of my small backpack, and my eyes flew over hundreds of new faces. Where was I supposed to fit in?

Shaking my head, I was saddened and petrified. How could my parents expect me to fit in? I was starting as a junior, and I'd never even been in a high school.

"Heads up!"

I heard the warning at the last minute and stepped to the side. A McDonald's coffee cup splattered on the ground, missing the trashcan by a good yard. The light brown liquid soaked into the blue carpet, and the sickening sweet smell of morning filled the hallway.

What had my parents gotten me into?

Seconds later, a tall boy stood next to me, shaking his head as he ran a hand through his dark brown hair. "Sorry about that," he said, tilting his face as he met my eyes. Before I knew it, his chestnut-brown gaze slid from my face, to my body, and then a grin plastered his face. "Hey, there."

I stepped back in disbelief. He hadn't even tried to hide his interest.

"What's your name?" he asked, showing off a set of perfectly white teeth.

"Don't answer that." A girl interrupted him as she shoved her way in front of the boy. She had dark eyes, pale skin, and nearly white hair despite the black roots. Her lip curled when she looked at the flirtatious boy. "Can't you back off for one second, Robb?" She smacked her gum, and her lip piercing sparkled.

He threw his head back and laughed. "Not when there's a pretty girl around."

"Believe me, I've noticed." The punk girl rolled her eyes before focusing on me. "Hey," she said, smiling and showing her nice side for the first time. "So, you're the new girl." So maybe it wasn't exactly her nice side.

"I'm assuming that's obvious in a town like this," I said, smirking, and Robb whistled.

"New girl got spunk," he said, practically drooling. "But, if you had to ask me, you stand out for reasons other than not being one of the dimwits we went to kindergarten with." He winked.

"For my stomach's sake, Robb, it's seven in the morning," the girl said before turning to me. "Ignore him. I'm Crystal."

"Jessie."

Robb leaned forward. "Jessie—?"

"Jessie Taylor," I said, taking the time to study them. Neither had backpacks or notebooks. Instead, Crystal carried a small, black purse. Her painted nails were chipped and black. She wore tight jeans and a white jacket that matched her discolored hair. Robb, on the other hand, was a mess.

His brown hair stood in a hundred different directions as if he just woke up, and his blue T-shirt was crinkled and worn. He was wearing short sleeves and shorts. It was January.

"Jessie Taylor?" Crystal asked, and when I nodded, she opened her purse. "Your new name is Jess. I don't need another Jessie or Emily in this school."

"But—" I began to argue, but she shook her head.

"No exceptions, Jess," she said, pulling out pen and paper before jotting down my name.

"Don't be surprised." Robb laughed at my dropped jaw and widened eyes. "Crystal's a journalist like her mother, and she runs our student rumor column." He patted her on the head. "She knows everything about this school."

Crystal rolled her dark eyes at Robb. "Maybe because my best friend is the biggest man whore in the school," she said, pushing his hand away before meeting my gaze. "Don't be intimidated. He forgot to mention the fact that my mother and I despise one another, and I'm not nearly as good as her." She grinned. "But I will be."

I nodded slowly, taking in all the information. Robb was Crystal's best friend. Crystal was a journalist, same as her mother, but they hated one another. *Got it. I think.*

"So what's your story, Jess?" Crystal asked, chewing her gum.

"I don't have one."

Crystal's eyes squinted. "Not yet, anyway."

"Right," I said, looking away, and she sighed as she put her interview materials away. I grabbed my schedule from my bag

16

as a teacher warned us to get to class.

Robb leaned over his short friend and grinned. "Can I see your schedule?"

I was surprised he wasn't asking for my cell phone number as well.

I shrugged, handing it over, but Crystal snagged it from my hands and glared at Robb. "Don't you stalk this girl down," she said. "She's nice."

"Exactly why I want to get to know her." Robb looked at me. "You, I mean," he said, stuttering. "I didn't mean to talk about you like you weren't here. Right here."

"It's okay," I said, and Robb hung his blushing face before walking away. As he disappeared into the crowd, I shook my head. "He never gives up, does he?"

Crystal groaned. "He's disgusting," she said. "Believe me, I've known him since birth. There are better guys in Hayworth than him."

I laughed. "Don't worry; I'm staying away," I said. "But thanks for the warning."

"No problem. It's my job to make it crystal clear—no pun intended," she joked as she skimmed over my schedule. "Well, Jess, I've got some good news and some bad news."

She handed my schedule back, and I raised my brow. "What is it?"

"The good news: we share homeroom, and you'll be stuck there for the next two years, so you'll learn to like it."

I gulped. "What's the bad news?"

She cringed. "We have the crazy science teacher, and she'll force us to have a second chemistry class." Her eyes lit up, and she hit herself on the forehead. "Oh, and Robb just happens to be in it, too."

I sighed. *So much for escaping his flirtation.*

"Can't wait," I said, and Crystal linked her arm with mine.

"Jess," she began. "I think this is the beginning of a beautiful friendship."

My heart beat with excitement. "*Casablanca?*" I asked, recognizing the famous movie line.

She spun us in a tight circle. "I knew I'd like you," she said, and I grinned.

"It's my favorite movie."

"Mine, too."

Maybe this high school thing wouldn't be too hard after all.

FOUR

"ERIC WELBORN?"

My teacher, Ms. Hinkel, reached the bottom of her attendance list and called my name. *Always at the bottom.* I raised my hand, and then laid my head on the desk. My head thundered from all the lights and sounds. I was sensitive to everything, but so was every shade, whether they were in their human form or not. School was practically torture.

"Well, at least everyone is here," Ms. Hinkel said, tapping her manicured nails against her clipboard.

"Not everyone." Crystal—a girl I'd gone to school with since kindergarten—dragged a girl I'd never seen before up to Ms. Hinkel's desk. "We have a new student."

Great. I turned up my iPod. *More loud students to get through the system.*

If I could just make it through this class, I was out of here. I'd had the same homeroom for three years, and I was mentally done. The teacher was crazy, the class was unnecessarily long, and it was fifth hour—my last hour in the day. Unlike the other students, I got to leave every day at the end of fifth hour for work leave. I hated to admit my father had used his connections, but he had, and I was thankful I didn't have to stay any longer than I already had to.

As long as I had books, I could teach myself. School was pointless nowadays when knowledge was so easily accessible. I didn't need the institution of education, and it didn't need me.

Homeroom lasted two hours with a lunch period in between. After lunch, class passed quickly, and I hadn't listened to a single word of it. Sadly, I doubted I missed anything. When the bell rang, I gladly followed the crowd of students into the hall.

I hated the hallway—it was loud and crowded—but it was my pathway to freedom, so it ranked above the cafeteria. Cranking my music over the noise of the students, I knew the teachers wouldn't lecture me. Nobody did. Instead, they pitied me—or they were scared of me—I still hadn't decided.

I was Eric Welborn, son of the richest asshole in town, and we had everything but happiness. That became obvious the minute my mother passed away, even though I blatantly ignored it until my freshman year.

The accident would always haunt me.

I pushed through the crowd until I reached the front door and went outside. At the end of the sidewalk, a silver BMW was parked, engine still running. Within a minute, I had the car door open, and I was staring at an older girl with short black hair and light eyes—Teresa Young, Camille's human form, and she had the most ironic appearances I knew.

Camille was a half-breed. Her father was a light, and her mother was a shade. They hadn't even known they were in different sects until Camille was born. After that, Camille's mother gave her to the Dark, and her parents fled town, leaving her to be raised in the shelter. She was enrolled in class to meet other struggling half-breeds, but she hated the constant reminder that she wasn't a full-blooded shade. We never talked about it, other than the fact that her appearance and abilities helped me.

At night, she looked like a light, and she retained the light's abilities of illusion. She could intercept their signals, sense them coming, and fight them with their own strength. She saw this side as a flaw. In reality, it was her most powerful gift. Still, we never talked about it.

After I sat down, Camille twisted her nail polish cap closed and pulled away from the curb. "How was school, Shoman?"

"Eric."

She rolled her light eyes and tapped the steering wheel. "So how was school, Eric?"

"I don't appreciate the sarcasm," I said, glaring out the window. "You don't see me calling you Teresa."

"That's because I hate my name, and you know it."

And what if I hate my Dark name?

She sighed, "Sho—Eric," she paused. "Are you having anybody over tonight?"

"No," I said, hoping she wasn't planning on busting my plans. I had freedom—no guard—and she wasn't going to ruin my only opportunity to figure out what was happening.

"You never have friends over anymore," she said.

Maybe because I don't have any.

"Ever since Abby—" she continued, and I shook my head. "We're not talking about this, Camille."

"I'm sorry," she said, biting her lip as she focused on the road. "But I feel like we used to be such good friends—you, Jonathon, and me—and now you barely talk to us."

"I have other things on my mind," I said. *Like that girl I saw last night.*

Camille immediately raised her eyebrows. Her job was to guarantee I made it to the Marking of Change alive. If I was up to something, she was supposed to know and tell my father.

"What happened last night?" Camille asked, and my throat tightened.

She hadn't seen the girl. She would've freaked out.

"Nothing," I said, and she squeezed the steering wheel.

"Then why were you acting so strange?"

"Camille—"

"I'm concerned, Eric," she said, and I groaned, lying backward in the seat.

"You sound like my mother," I said, and she shook her head. My mother was dead. I didn't have to remind her of that.

I gripped my hair and dug my nails into my scalp. "Sorry, Camille," I muttered, searching for a complicated lie. "My father and Mindy are getting to me." Personal information would distract the conversation away from last night. "I don't enjoy having a stepfamily. I never have, and I never will. Especially a human one."

"Mindy and Noah have been around for two years, Eric."

Right. Noah. I had a stepbrother.

"They aren't even shades," I said. "I can't be myself in my own house."

"To be honest with you," Camille hesitated, shaking her head. "That's probably for the best."

I crossed my arms, but she was right. The Marking of Change was prophesized to happen on my eighteenth birthday. The battle was almost exactly a year from now, and I wasn't even ready. On top of that, the Light wanted to know anything about me—my name, my identity, where I lived, where I went, what school I attended, anything—just as long as they could kill me before the prophetic battle.

I was constantly hiding, even from myself, and the only time I had exposed myself, Abby died. Other than Camille and Pierce, she was the only shade I had known in both of my worlds. Now she was gone, and it was my fault.

"Eric?" Camille leaned over to catch my eyes, and I realized we were parked in my driveway. I was home.

I picked up my stuff and opened her car door. "Thanks for the ride, Camille," I said, ducking outside.

"Are you sure that you're okay?" she asked, and I nodded.

"Have a nice night off," I said, shutting the door before she could continue the worst conversation of all time.

"Shoman." Her resonant voice shuddered through me. *"Be careful. I love you."* She was my best friend, my sister, and my mother figure, yet she couldn't trust me to be alone.

"Love you, too." I sent a message back, knowing our love was meant for siblings. We weren't infatuated. That would practically be incest.

Camille's BMW backed out of the driveway as I burst through the front door. I shut it behind me and listened to Mindy laugh away at my father's jokes in the kitchen. Our kitchen was on the second floor, next to my bedroom. It was perfect when I was hungry, torture when they were in it.

I tiptoed upstairs, hoping to avoid the situation, but it was impossible.

"Eric, you're home," Mindy said, still chuckling at whatever my father had said.

Damn.

My father raised his brow. "Why don't you come prepare dinner with us?"

Mindy smiled wide behind her bright red hair. "Noah should be home soon, and he'd just love to spend some time with you." Noah, my stepbrother, was her ten-year-old brat.

"No, thanks," I said before she could suggest something dumber. I finished walking down the hallway and disappeared into my bedroom.

Crashing onto my bed, I looked at the small, blue nightlight on my wall. *Stupid thing.* I closed my eyes, enjoying the silence. Nothing was better than a few hours alone in my bedroom, shunning myself from the family.

"I'm home, Mom!" Noah's high-pitched voice shattered the silence.

"Hi, Noah," Mindy screamed with enthusiasm. "How was school?"

"It was great."

Thud! Noah always dropped his backpack in the middle of the entrance hallway.

My father cleared his throat. "Anything interesting happen?"

"Yeah—" Noah spoke again, but I drowned him out with my stereo—hoping to drown my family out with him. My phone vibrated against my leg, and I jumped up, yanking it out of my jeans.

Text from JStone: Hey, man. Bracke told my father we were flying tonight?

My eyes glided over my phone's screen, and I gaped at the text. I wanted to go out without Camille tonight, but not to see Jonathon. I wanted to see somebody else—the girl who caught my attention.

"Eric." My dad knocked on my bedroom door and opened it without permission. He walked in, tossed a dinner plate on my desk, and folded his arms. "I brought you dinner since you don't want to join your family."

"Thanks," I said, continuing to stare at Jonathon's words. *Now what?*

My dad rubbed his hands together. "How was school?" he asked, and I shrugged.

"Okay."

"That's good."

I nodded without meeting his eyes. I knew I was being rude, but I just didn't care.

"Are you going out with Jonathon tonight?" he asked.

"Yeah," I lied. "That's exactly what I'm doing."

"That's great," he exclaimed, Mindy's attitude rubbing off his tough exterior. "You boys better be careful, Eric."

"I always am." *Another lie.*

He left my room, and I was alone again. Mindy's food suffocated my sense of smell, and I lifted my hand, using my abilities to carry the food through the air until it landed on my bed. I bit into my sloppy Joe and typed in my text.

Text from EWelborn: Change of plans. The old man is forcing me to bond with Noah and Mindy tonight.

I waited for a second, and my phone binged.

Text from JStone: Dang. Well, plan on it soon, because I'm getting sick of hanging out with humans every night.

Text from EWelborn: You're telling me. I'm with the brat all night.

Text from JStone: Have fun with that.

Text from EWelborn: Ha. Yeah right. See you later, Jonathon.

I flipped my phone over and powered it down. I might not be seeing Jonathon, but I told my father I was. Camille wouldn't show up at the house, and I was free. At least I was doing something productive.

I was still seeing someone; it was just someone they didn't know about.

FIVE

Eric

S HE STOOD EXACTLY WHERE I SAW HER LAST—BY THE RIVER. HER purple eyes widened as she dragged her fingers through the shadows, dissolving into smoke before reforming again. At first, she frowned, but then she smiled as she found a fluid motion in the darkness.

I leaned against a tree and threw my senses out, letting her know I was near. She froze, and I stepped out, raising my hands up. "I'm not going to hurt you," I said, and she squinted.

"How do I know that?"

"You don't," I said.

She bit her lip, and the air filled with nervous electricity. She had no control. "How'd you know I was here?" she asked.

I shrugged. "Lucky guess," I said. "I haven't seen you anywhere else, so I figured this was my best bet."

She leaned her back against the guardrail, folding her arms. "Why would you want to see me again?"

I gaped at her. How could she not know? I'd never seen her in our shelter, and that was against our ways. She was breaking our basic laws, and I wanted to know why before I turned her in.

"I want answers," I said, and her face tilted.

"I thought I was the one who wanted answers."

"About?"

"What is this?" she asked, raising her hands and waving the shadows around. Her voice was high, and her cheeks flushed as she rambled. "What the hell am I?"

My gut fell. She didn't know—but how? That was impossible. Every shade was raised from birth with basic knowledge, and, looking at her age, she should've already had her powers and the prophecy memorized. This had to be a joke.

"What do you mean?" I asked, stepping forward, and she pointed at my feet.

"Stay there," she said. She didn't want me any closer than I had to be.

"Okay," I said, holding my stance as I looked over her face. Her lips were bitten, and her eyes were red from tears. When she used her powers, her fingers shook, and she held them close to her body afterwards. She was scared.

"Is this a dream?" she asked, her voice trembling. "It's happened before, but it was a dream, just a dream—"

I shook my head. "You're not dreaming," I said, unable to comprehend how she could be so oblivious. She had no clue what she was.

She turned away. I could hear her breath shift, shaking in the wind. Her shoulders hunched, and her face twisted.

"I can help you," I said, hoping she'd let me approach.

Her purple eyes looked me up and down, and then she dropped her head. "Are you like me?" she asked, and I nodded, mirroring her staggered movements. Her eyes widened. "You are like me."

"You're a shade," I said, searching her face. "Do you know what that is?" She shook her head, and I stepped forward. "Can we talk like civilized people?"

"Are we people?" she asked, and I chuckled. "It's not funny," she said, glaring, and I stifled my laugh.

"You're right," I said, stepping toward her again. She tensed, and I stopped, but then she waved me forward. Her violet eyes watched my every move until I leaned against the guardrail a yard away. She still needed her space.

I breathed in the frigid air and shoved my hands into my pockets. "You don't know anything, do you?" I asked, meeting her eyes, but her expression was blank.

"Am I supposed to?" she asked, fiddling with her clothes, like she wasn't used to them changing during the transformation. "I only learned this was real last night—when I saw you."

My jaw dropped. "Last night?" My voice strained against my throat. "You're supposed to know about this your entire life."

"What?" she whispered, her breath stolen by the wind. "This has only been happening since—"

"Since what?"

She shook head, and I stepped in front of her, trying to meet her eyes. "Every shade is raised in the Dark and by the Dark with their mentors and their parents," I said, hoping to spark a memory. Maybe she'd been separated or attacked by the Light. But she didn't respond.

I ran a hand through my hair. "We're given our powers at the Naming, and we're waiting for the prophecy." She blinked, and I fought the urge to shake her. "You have no clue what I'm talking about?"

She tilted her head and squinted. "You think?"

This was not good. If she was a shade, she was a part of the community. If she didn't know the information she needed to, she wouldn't understand the difference between the Light and the Dark, the lights and the shades. She would be easily influenced. She had no idea what kind of trouble she could be in.

"Who's your mentor?" I asked.

"I don't have one—"

"You have to," I said, shaking my head. "Somebody—anybody must know you're a shade."

"I doubt my parents even know."

"It runs in blood," I said. "They're shades."

"No," she said, her purple eyes burning into me. "They're not."

"They have to be—"

"They're not like me," she screamed, and I stepped backward, lifting my hands in front of me. I didn't need her shouting at me; my ears were sensitive enough.

"It's okay," I said. "We'll figure this out."

She raised her thin brow. "But this is normal?" she asked, staring at her foggy hands again. "These powers?"

I nodded. "They're normal for shades, not humans."

Her eyes widened, and her powers rose around her. "I'm not human?"

"Yes, you are," I lied swiftly, calming her down. She couldn't control her powers or emotions. I had to watch what I told her. "Shades are human, just in different forms."

"And you?" she asked, her eyes fluttering over me. "You're one of these shades?"

I nodded again, my black hair brushing against my forehead. "I'm Shoman."

What the hell? My entire body froze. I never gave out my name. The prophecy already did—telling the naming of the first and second descendant: Shoman and Darthon. I can't believe I just told her that. I wasn't supposed to give it away so easily. Actually, I wasn't supposed to give it away at all.

She smiled, completely unfazed by my information, and spoke, "My name is—"

"Don't tell me," I interrupted. "I can't know your real name. Your identity is everything."

She frowned. "Shoman isn't your real name?"

"Of course not," I said, bewildered by her reaction. She knew nothing of the prophecy. "I was Named—and you should've been too."

She smirked. "By a prophecy?" she asked, fighting a fit of giggles. "This has to be a dream."

I touched her arm, and she whipped around automatically, latching her nails into my wrist. I winced, and she glared, her powers vibrating through my blood. "I wasn't trying to hurt you," I said, cringing, and she threw my arm away.

"Then don't touch me," she said, stepping backward, and I glared back at her.

"I was trying to make a point," I said, laying my hand out. She stared at my palm. "Go ahead; touch it."

"Why?" she asked, and I groaned.

"Just do it."

She bit her lip, stepped forward, and, slowly, she laid her shaky hand on mine. I exhaled, concentrating. Soon, my power flowed through her veins. I could feel it—her—and all her fear, panic, and rage. She truly was oblivious. In turn, I exposed myself to her—showing the serious honesty I felt. If she was an abandoned shade, she was in danger, and she needed my protection.

She yanked her hand back and hugged herself, shaking her head. "What was that?"

"Proof you're not dreaming," I said. "You can't deny touch."

"I can deny anything I want," she said, and I shook my head.

"Not this." I leaned over and caught her gaze. "You need to trust me, or you could end up dead; do you understand that?"

Her face twisted. "No one's going to kill me for hanging out by a river at night."

"A light will," I said, knowing how dangerous it was to be a shade, let alone an abandoned one. Her kind was in the middle of war, and she had no idea she was a target.

She paled. "There are more of us?"

"Lights are nothing like us. They're our enemies." I strained through the conversation. "But, yes, there is a whole community of shades—"

She lit up. "Can I meet them?"

"No." *Because they'll kill you for being an intruder.* "Not yet."

Her chest sunk beneath her black sweater. "I don't understand."

"You will," I promised, grabbing her hand and allowing the energy to flow between us. She was electrifying—more powerful than any other shade I knew—yet she was naïve, and her lack of knowledge made her dangerous. How could she be so strong?

She gaped at our touch but didn't move away. "I don't know how I can learn without meeting others."

"Because you don't need them," I said, my heart pounding against my ribs. "You have me. I'll be your mentor."

SIX

ONE WEEK PASSED WITHOUT MUCH CHANGE. IN HOMEROOM, I tapped my pencil against the black lab desk and waited for lunchtime. After that, I'd go home and train, but today I only wanted to sit outside in the warming weather. Last week it had snowed, yet it felt like spring outside today. Midwest weather was completely unpredictable and probably the most change I got on a day-to-day basis.

Staring at the clock, I felt like fifth hour would never end. It was the beginning of second semester, and the teacher was already changing all her rules and lab partners. Personally, I enjoyed the lab system that she had: work alone and work quiet. Then, she started watching *Dr. Phil*, believed children's communication skills were dying, and felt the need to force us all to become the best of friends.

How adorable.

To get us to bond, she assigned a partner project—with a science theme, of course—and it had to be completed in a month. No exceptions. Ms. Hinkel passed out an array of notebooks, full of rules, and then she called out the groups' names.

"Christina Hutchins and Robb McLain, Lab 5," Ms. Hinkel said, and a thin girl with thick, white hair stood up in protest.

"My name is Crystal," she said between smacks of her gum.

She changed her name before she even got into first grade. I remembered, because she hated the fact that her mother named her without permission, even though Crystal couldn't talk. I could talk when the Dark named me Shoman, and I still had no say. I envied Crystal's abilities to fight, but her stubbornness caused a lot of disciplinary trouble.

She and Robb stared at the station only a few feet away from me, and Ms. Hinkel moved on to the other students. No one was allowed to move from their seats until the teacher finished.

"Annie Lockman and Justin Paul, Lab 8," she said, causing a boy behind me to jump out of his much-needed sleep. He had started to snore, and his breath on my back was definitely not appreciated.

"Jessica Taylor and Eric Welborn," she droned on, and I didn't bother looking for my lab partner.

She was the new girl, and I already knew what she looked like. She had thick, curly brown hair, light blue eyes, and she was always trailing after Robb or Crystal. Instead of staring, I concentrated on my hearing and opened it up to the room. I could hear everything—texting, breathing, gum chewing. The little noises were the ones that bothered me, which was why I used music to drown it all out.

Crystal was easy to signal out. She was always chewing on her gum, and she smacked it as she tapped my partner's shoulder. "That sucks, Jess," she whispered, and Jessica's hairspray crinkled as she turned her head.

"Why?" Jessica Taylor—or Jess—had a higher voice than I expected. "He looks nice."

Robb laughed. "He's not."

Crystal hummed in agreement. "He's a freak."

Jessica gulped. "He doesn't seem like one—"

"That's because you don't know him," Crystal said, explaining the truth. She and Robb had been my best friends since birth, except I hadn't talked to them since freshman year—not since the accident.

"Now he only talks to Teresa Young," Robb finished, and Jessica turned her face, looking around the room.

"Who's Teresa?" she asked, and I felt her eyes on my back.

I looked the other way. I didn't want them thinking I was eavesdropping, but, then again, I was halfway across the room.

"Some family friend," Robb said. "She's always around him; it's weird."

"Maybe they're dating," Jess said, and I cringed, fighting the urge to shake my head. *Gross.*

Crystal laughed hysterically, covering her mouth to smother the sound. "They're definitely not dating. I already looked into it for a possible rumor piece, and there's no way."

"Then why would he only talk to her?" Jess asked, and Crystal inhaled, her breath whizzing past her lip piercing.

"She's been stuck on him since his mother died," she said.

Robb huffed. "Both of them lived with me for a while after, but we were just kids."

"What happened?" Jess asked, dropping her voice.

Crystal's nails ran along the lab desk. "Have you heard of Hayworth Park?" Jessica didn't respond, and Crystal sighed. "Of course not."

I heard her shift in her chair, and I knew the group was staring at me again. "His mother committed suicide there, and his father bought the land afterward," Crystal explained. "He shut the whole thing down; he won't let anybody in."

Jessica gasped, and I couldn't help but turn around. Her blue eyes met mine, and she turned away, completely scarlet. "Why?" she asked, not specifying whether she was asking about my mother's suicide or my father's actions.

"Because he wants us to be miserable like him?" Crystal guessed, choosing which way the conversation would go. "Who knows? He's crazy."

"But what does his father have to do with him?" Jess asked, and I gripped my legs beneath the table. No one had asked that before. Instead, they looped us together, and I didn't stand a chance.

"I guess he doesn't," Crystal said, allowing her words to linger. "But Eric doesn't have the best track record with sanity either."

Robb's chair scraped against the tile floor as he pushed it

against Jess' desk. "When we were freshman, Eric was dating this girl—Hannah Blake—right?" he began, and my entire body froze. *No one talked about it. Not even me.*

"Well," Robb continued. "She was in a car wreck with him and died. He walked away scot free."

"And," Crystal added. "The accident happened under suspicious circumstances."

Jess held her breath and whispered, "What kind of suspicious circumstances?"

"Hell if I know," Crystal said, hitting the desk. "Suspicious is enough for me."

"It should be for you too, Jess," Robb said, and Ms. Hinkel cleared her throat, glaring in their direction.

"Are you all done or should I wait?"

They apologized, and I zoned out as all the students rushed to their new lab assignments. I didn't need to move. I was already in my spot.

The chair next to me scraped back, and Jess sat down, tossing her bag onto the table. Her cheeks were red, and I could practically hear her nervous heart beating. "Hi," she said, turning briefly toward me to smile. "I'm Jess."

She offered her hand for a handshake, and I pushed my chair against the wall. "I heard your name when Ms. Hinkel assigned you," I said, opening the chemistry book left on my desk from the previous period. I was not interested in small talk.

"Right," Jess said, letting her hand fall into her lap. She had small hands. "So, Eric—"

"Call me Welborn." *Even though you stood up for me, I am not your friend.*

She nodded, raising her brow. "If that'll make things easier for you, Welborn, then fine."

I fought a grin. At least she had attitude.

She adjusted her chair, and my eyes shot to the class clock. "So, Welborn—"

Ring. Ring.

Lunchtime. Right on time.

I rushed out of the classroom to the outside lunchroom as quickly as I could. I did not need to talk to Jessica Taylor. She'd give up trying soon enough. Everyone did.

I climbed up the hill and leaned against the willow tree, placing my hands behind my head as I listened to the leaves brush against one another. The warming weather glided across my skin, and birds were actually outside today. It'd only be a few more months until school ended and summer came. Normally, I'd look forward to the prolonged freedom that came with summer, but this time I'd be too busy training to have any free time.

I peered down at the outside cafeteria. Students were everywhere, yet I didn't see my new lab partner. Maybe I was a little harsh. I fiddled with my headphones and put them on, but kept the music off. She hadn't associated my dad's madness with me—but, then again, she had pried into my life, and I didn't like that. And she wasn't the nameless shade.

I thought about the night before. The girl was so innocent, so oblivious to everything, and she was afraid. I would have to be careful around her. I needed her to trust me, not to turn against me, and if she really was abandoned, she needed my help.

The idea of being raised outside the Dark community intrigued me. If I had been separated from the Dark, the prophecy would be different. I wouldn't be Shoman. I would be Eric. Just Eric. And no one could tell me what I was expected to do.

"Shoman." Camille's voice dimmed my thoughts, and my eyes popped open. *"Turn around."*

I took off my headphones and spun my torso toward the valley. A girl with short black hair waved as she trudged up the hill toward me. "Teresa?" I asked. "What are you doing here?"

"That's a nice way of saying hi," she said, leaning against the willow with her arms crossed. She laughed lightly, and her eyes darted across the valley, staring over the entire town. Willow Tree Mountain, even though it was a hill, was the tallest point in Hayworth.

"Nice view," I said. "Do you remember watching the fireworks up here?"

"The willow tree was smaller then," she said, running her hand across the bark. "It was healthier, too."

"It's almost been twelve years," I said.

"I know." She pushed off the tree and pointed at the nearest street. "We have to go."

"But—" *Was I seriously arguing?* "I still have school left."

She waved a piece of pink and yellow paper. "I already got you a pass."

"I can't argue that," I said, grabbing my bag and taking the pass. "Let's get out of here."

SEVEN

Jessica

"I TOLD YOU HE WAS WEIRD," CRYSTAL SAID AS WE WALKED TO LUNCH. Robb rested his arm on my shoulder. "Your grade is over, Jess."

"No," I said, glaring at Eric's back as he rushed outside. "My grade is going to be perfect, whether he likes it or not."

After all, my grades needed to be perfect, if I had any chance at finding my biological parents. I didn't care if Eric Welborn had a rough life or not. His problems weren't mine, and I wasn't going to let him impose them on me.

"Good luck with that, Jess," Crystal said, looping her arm through mine as we walked outside. Strangely, it was nice out, and we sat at the first table we passed. The outdoor lunchroom was squared-in by brick walls. On one side, the front of school teased our desire for freedom, while the other side stretched into a large hill.

The hill was huge, and an enormous willow tree loomed over the side. As the wind blew, branches swayed, sprawling dancing shadows over the dying grass. The tree was remarkable—breathtaking even—but it was secluded, aside from the boy leaning against it.

Crystal rolled her eyes in his direction. "He always sits up there."

"By himself?" I asked. She nodded, and I bit my lip, unable to look away.

Eric Welborn, with his eyes closed and his headphones on, leaned against the tree as if he were a part of it. His brown hair matted against the bark, melting into the color, and his eyes fluttered as he opened them, staring at the shadows. Even from a distance, I could see his shoulders tense, and I fought the urge to go to him.

For the first time, I actually felt sympathy toward him.

"It looks cold," I said. *He looks lonely.*

"Who cares?" Robb shrugged, barely looking over as a girl appeared from the other side of the hill. Immediately, the two began talking, and I peered at the unfamiliar face.

"Who's that?" I asked, tapping Crystal's arm.

Crystal's dark eyes squinted. "That's Teresa Young—the girl we told you about."

"They're obsessed with one another," Robb said, pulling his lunch out of his backpack. "I swear they have something going on."

"They don't," Crystal said.

Robb bit into his sandwich. "I bet they do," he said, singing as he leaned into Crystal. He was just trying to annoy her.

I turned away from my friends and kept my gaze on my homeroom partner. Both Eric and Teresa looked downhill, and then Teresa waved a piece of paper at him. He spoke, and he grabbed his stuff, disappearing down the other side.

He did not just leave me to handle class on my own.

I gripped the table, and Crystal sighed, leaning her entire torso on the table. "Did you guys want to do anything tonight?" she asked. "I'm about to go crazy."

"Not at my house," Robb said.

Crystal cringed. "Don't worry; I wasn't planning on it." She turned to me. "My mom should be home late. You guys could come over."

"Sounds good to me." Robb's eyes lit up. "I'm sure I could get away from the 'rents for a while."

"Your parents are way too strict," Crystal said, smacking her gum. Apparently, she didn't eat lunch.

"That's exactly why we don't go to my place," he said, allowing his gaze to land on me. "You coming?"

I shook my head. "I can't," I said, trying to ignore the pressures of my school project. "I have plans."

Crystal flipped a pen around her fingers, a nervous habit. "With who?"

"Me, of course," Robb said, winking his brown eyes.

Crystal punched his arm. "You wish," she said, and I laughed.

"It isn't with Robb," I clarified. "I have family stuff I have to figure out." Like my biological parents.

"I thought you were going to get a head start on your project," Crystal said. "You know you'll have to do it all by yourself, right?"

Robb straightened up. "I could help you."

"It's okay," I said, standing up as the return bell rang. "I'll get Eric to talk to me."

Crystal laughed but ultimately nodded. "Good luck with that, Jess."

"Thanks," I muttered. *I'll probably need it.*

EIGHT

Eric

TERESA WAS LYING ON MY BED, HER BLACK HAIR SPILLING OFF THE side. She tapped her painted nails against her stomach, and I watched her, unsure of why she dragged me out only to read Mindy's magazines in my room.

"What's this about, Camille?"

"A lot." She sighed and flipped the page. "The elders have me practicing my Light powers." She cringed. "I'm really uncomfortable with it."

I frowned. Camille never talked about her Light side. "Why's it uncomfortable?"

"I'd rather not talk about it," she said, changing her mind as she stared at me upside down. "But there is something I wanted to talk to you about."

I laid my chin on my hands. "So talk about it."

"Jonathon told me your father forced you to bond with Noah and Mindy last night," she said, sitting up to catch my eyes. "How'd that go?"

"Okay," I shrugged, relying on my remarkable lying skills. "I still don't like them though."

She lifted her thin, black eyebrows. "Anything else you want to tell me?"

Did she know? I locked my jaw. *There was no possible way. She couldn't.*

"No."

Her expression fell, and she shook her head back and forth. "Eric," she sighed. "Your father told me you went out with Pierce last night, but it's obvious you didn't go."

I tensed. "Did you tell him?"

"No." She glared and waved her hands in the air. "But why'd you do it? Don't you know how dangerous it is for you to go out, let alone by yourself?"

She didn't know about the girl.

"I know, Camille," I said, nodding slowly. "I'm sorry."

Her lips thinned. "Did you activate anything?"

"You would've felt it if I did," I said, unable to make eye contact. By being the first descendant, I inherited stronger, more reliable powers. My favorite one was my sword, but I could never use it unless I was in a secure room in the shelter. The Light could track it, and they would kill me when they did.

I hadn't used my descendant powers outside the shelter in years.

"I stayed out of sight last night," I said, dragging my fingers through my hair. "I promise."

She widened her blue eyes. "They'd blame me if you got killed."

"But I didn't get killed," I said, grabbing the edge of the bed. "And nothing happened. I was safe. I wouldn't do anything stupid." *Except talk to a nameless shade.*

Camille—in Teresa form—flickered from her emotions. "I don't know if I can trust you anymore," she said, and I groaned, staring at the ceiling.

"I just need to get out more," I said. "At home, I'm stuck as a human, and I'm stuck in the prophecy at the shelter."

"Because you're the first descendant, Shoman," Teresa yelled, using my shade name without thinking. "You need to be able to handle it."

"How can I when I'm protected all the time?" I asked, glaring at my guard. "I can't even practice my powers without the Light tracking me. I have a year until this battle, and, at this rate, we are going to lose."

Camille quieted, and I hung my head, shaking it back and

forth and regretting my honesty. "In my mind," I said. "I have a year to live."

Silence spilt between us, and I lifted my head as my guard laid a hand on my shoulder. She managed a smile. "I'm doing my best to understand you—you're like a little brother to me—but I don't want you to get hurt or killed."

"I know."

"That being said," she continued, winking. "If you want a little more freedom, I won't follow you around as much."

I shot up. "Are you being serious?"

Her small smile spread into a grin. "I'll only come when you call me."

I squinted at her. "But why?"

She shrugged. "If it means winning the Marking of Change, then I don't have much of a choice," she said. "But—" She shook her thin finger at me. "You have to promise me something."

"Anything," I said.

Camille held up a necklace with a black tree pendant swinging on the bottom. "There's a remedy inside this," she said, twisting the top before pulling down the stump. A dark liquid waved inside the branches.

"It'll heal any Light spell," Camille said, closing it. "Luthicer and I made it last night."

Luthicer was the only half-breed elder in the Dark, and he taught Camille everything she knew. Personally, I hated him. He was a prick—always trying to make me look incompetent as the first descendant. In his opinion, surely, there was a mistake.

I grabbed the pendant from her and stared at the black liquid inside. "What do you want me to do with this?" I asked, and she straightened up, beaming.

"Wear it at all times," she said, and I nodded instantaneously.

"It's a deal."

NINE

"WHAT'S THAT?"

I gazed past Camille's necklace and met her violet eyes. The nameless shade had been silent for an hour, but I didn't mind. She had a lot to take in.

"My guard made it for me," I said, shrugging as I tucked it into my black T-shirt.

She tilted her head, causing her long hair to cascade over her shoulder. "A guard? Like a security guard?"

"Kind of." I chuckled, thinking of Camille securing an outlet mall. She'd be too busy shopping to get anything done. "But you don't have to worry about her," I said. "She won't be around tonight."

"Her?"

I looked over, and my eyes flicked over her face—the nameless shade, the only girl I talked to outside the shelter, let alone after Abby's death. I had to turn away.

"She was assigned to me years ago," I said, hoping to distract the conversation away from Camille.

The girl shifted, pulling at the wet grass. "Does everyone have a guard?"

I shook my head. "You're a warrior unless you decide to denounce your title," I said, leaning forward on my knees. "Then you're a guard."

"So you're a warrior?" she asked. I nodded, and her expression didn't budge. "What exactly are you fighting?"

"A war."

Her shoulders rose, and I stood up, offering my hand. "Come on," I said. "Let's talk about something else."

Instead of taking my hand, she frowned. "I thought you were going to teach me, not avoid the subject."

I ran my hand through my hair. "Not tonight."

"Fine." She grabbed my hand, and I pulled her up. "You don't have to talk about your war, but you better teach me something," she said, brushing the dirt off her pants. "I didn't come out here for nothing."

I smirked. "Hanging out with me isn't good enough?"

"Not yet."

I laughed. "This should be good."

She stepped back. "Why do you say that?"

"Because you have no clue what you got yourself into," I said, mirroring her steps. "I have a lot to teach you, but you have to be ready."

"I'm ready," she said, digging her shoes into the park ground. She beamed. "Teach away, mentor."

"Teach?" My cheeks hurt when I smiled. "I'm not teaching you anything yet."

Her expression fell. "You're not?"

I shook my head and grabbed her arm. I winked. "I'm going to show you."

She screamed as her feet left the ground, and we shot into the sky. Her petite hands tightened on my jacket, and I twisted us into circles, shadows spiraling at our flying feet. The air spun around our bodies, winding our clothes with every moment and change in the atmosphere. I hadn't flown in so long, and I had forgotten how alive I felt when I did.

"Shoman!" She wriggled against my grasp. "Put me down. Let me go!"

"If you say so," I said, dropping her.

She plummeted, falling from my grasp and through the clouds. Guess she couldn't fly. In an instant, I shot after her trail of shadows, grabbing her before she even neared the ground.

Abruptly, she silenced, and her echoing scream pierced the air. As she hung in my grasp, her purple eyes blinked up at me.

"What the hell, Shoman?" She gasped as I pulled her up, steadying her against my chest. She dug her nails into me and glared. "I did not mean literally."

"I know." I fought back laughter as she continued to glare. "But I thought you'd be able to."

"Be able to what?" She hit my chest. "Fly? Are you crazy?"

I spread my free arm out and gestured to the world around us. "What do you call this?"

Her purple eyes strained away, and her gaze flickered over the lit town below us. We could see for miles. The river flowed past the high school, the willow tree swayed in the wind, and the highway stretched on for eternity. There were so many places to go. But I couldn't go anywhere. I had a battle to win.

My jaw locked, and I held onto her wrists, slowly pushing her away. She tensed. "What are you doing?"

I forced a smile. "You can do it too."

She shook her head. "Did you not see what just happened?"

"That was my fault," I said as I straightened her out in front of me. "I should've warned you. Guess I'm a bad mentor."

She giggled, her cheeks rosy, but her expression withered when she looked below her. "Will you catch me if I can't?"

"Of course."

"Okay." She bit her chapped lip and spoke past it. "I'll try."

I grabbed her hands, holding her up, and concentrated on her energy. She seemed ready. "Whenever you want to," I said.

She hesitated, tapping her fingernails against my palms, before she let go. Her body dipped, and I mirrored her, but she remained in the air, gaping. "I'm doing it," she said, shining. "I'm flying!"

"You're flying." Her accomplishment felt like my own.

Slowly, she spun around, staring at the ground beneath her. "I can't believe it," she whispered, and I tapped her shoulder. She looked up, her eyes met mine, and her cheeks burned red. The shadows faltered, slipping beneath her feet, and she started to drop. She yelped, shocked by the sudden loss of control, and I grabbed her.

"Don't," I emphasized, "lose your concentration."

She nodded, and I held her in my arms again. Except, this time she didn't seem mad about it. She lightly held onto my jacket, relaxing as she stared across Hayworth. Her violet eyes glittered with reflections. "I never realized how pretty Hayworth looked at night," she said. "It seems bigger up here."

I froze, forcing myself to look away from her in order to study my hometown. Flying had always been what I concentrated on. Not the beauty. Why didn't I look at it that way before? When I looked back at her, she was staring at me.

"Is something wrong, Shoman?"

I shrugged, shaking my head. "I'm fine," I said. *I feel strange.*

Without much thought, I laid my arm around her petite shoulders, tracing basic calming spells along her arm. They weren't hurting her, and they weren't evil. They were more like comfort food. My mother had always used them to relax me before bed. I loved them, but I hadn't used them in a long time.

Her purple eyes wavered, but she smiled, pushing her black hair back. "It's soothing up here, isn't it?"

I nodded.

"So much better than my real life."

My hand tightened around her shoulder. "This is your real life."

She held her breath and peered up at me. "It is, isn't it?" Her tone had dropped. At least she had the right to leave if she wanted to.

"Can I ask you a question?" I asked, listening to my words as if I wasn't the one who spoke them.

"I don't see why not," she said, and I dropped my eyes.

"How'd your parents separate from the Dark?" *Because I want out.*

"I told you," she said, moving away as she folded her arms. "They don't know about this."

"But—"

"I'm adopted," she said, and I inhaled, my lungs burning against the midnight cold.

"That explains things," I said, and her lips thinned.

"It happens." Without another word, she floated away and spread her arms out. Slowly, she descended to the ground, her black hair flying above her, shadows sparkling behind her. She was a natural. It had taken me two weeks to perfect a landing, and I was the best in my class. She mastered it in minutes.

What was she?

My heart slammed into my gut as I followed behind her. My feet met the ground, and I steadied myself, unsure how she could handle herself so well. As natural as she was, it was unnatural for a shade who hadn't even gone through the Naming.

"I should be going," she said, avoiding eye contact. "I have school in the morning."

With my night vision, I stared at my wristwatch. It was two in the morning.

"Right," I said. "Me, too."

"See you tomorrow then?" she asked, and I nodded.

"Can't wait."

TEN

J ESS SLAMMED HER CHEMISTRY BOOK AND GLARED. "YOU KNOW we have a science project due soon, right?"

Of course I did. She'd been on my case all week.

"So what?"

"So I think we should plan a time to meet up," she said, her lips pressing into a white line. "We need to work on it."

"Why would we want to do that?" I asked, scanning over our current, and painful, lab.

She tied her curls into a ponytail so aggressively I was surprised the hair tie didn't snap. "Because we have to finish this project," she said, tapping her nails.

The sound was deafening. I cringed. "Why don't we work on it now?"

"We can't," she said, leaving her mouth hanging open. "We're in the middle of a lab."

"So what?"

"So we can't work on our project right now." Her blue eyes turned to slits. "The project is homework—meaning we do it out of school."

Her attitude made me smile. No one talked back to me. I hated to admit I was impressed, but I was.

I laid my chin on my hand, covering up my grin. "I do homework in class." *Or not at all.* It wasn't like I'd get to graduate if I was dead.

Jess blinked, her face reddening. "Well, I do it at home."

I shrugged. "Then whose problem is this exactly?"

She gripped the table with her tiny hands. "Look, Eric—"

I laughed. "You call me Welborn, remember?"

She groaned and laid her forehead on the black desk. "This is impossible."

"Welcome to high school," I said, and she pushed her chair backward, scraping the metal legs against the tile floor. Goose bumps crawled over my skin, and I turned away. "I'm busy outside of school anyway." *With a girl.*

I also had a meeting with the elders tonight. I didn't have time to worry about my human life. I needed to prepare to deal with Luthicer and Eu, two of the fiercest Dark elders. They expected a lot from the first descendant, yet I had nothing to show them.

"Maybe I'm busy too, Welborn," Jessica said, leaning over to catch my gaze. She was persistent. "Did you ever think of that?"

My lips pulled into an uncontrollable grin. "I can't take your anger seriously."

She hit the table and stood up. "Whatever, Welborn," she said, collecting her bag. "If you stop being a selfish prick, I'll be with Crystal and Robb."

This time, I was the one to glare. "So you can ask them more questions about me?" I asked, knowing I was revealing my eavesdropping.

She paled. "I don't know what you're talking about."

I rolled my eyes, ignoring her denial. "I'd prefer you ask me about my problems instead of gossiping," I said. "It isn't a good look on you."

She froze, but she didn't redden. Instead, she raised her brow and leaned down, whispering. "And being an asshole isn't a good look on anyone."

Then, she turned and walked away. I watched her sit next to her friends, struck with the peculiar urge to stop her. *I'm not an asshole.* I wanted to say it, but it was too late. She was gone, and I couldn't even distract myself with our science lab.

I was already done.

ELEVEN

Jessica

"PEANUT BUTTER AND CHOCOLATE IS THE BEST MEDICINE," Crystal said, dropping the sticky mess in front of me.

I stared at it, unable to feel hungry. I was too angry. Eric was so conceited. He only cared about himself, and my grades were going to drop because of it. I'd never find information on my parents.

Robb reached over me, dipping a pretzel into the peanut butter. "Don't mind if I do."

Crystal swatted his hand. "Rude much," she said. "Lola would have a fit if she saw you do that."

Lola was Crystal's mother, and she wasn't going to be home all night, despite the fact that Crystal had school tomorrow. We all did.

"Lola doesn't have to know," Robb said, chewing with his mouth open. "It's the best medicine, after all. I'm sure she'll understand."

"Medicine for Jess," Crystal's pierced lip banged against her teeth, and she winced. "We're here to make Jess feel better," she mumbled. "Not you."

Robb chewed on his pretzel and stared with his big, brown eyes. "How's that science project going for you anyway?"

I moaned, collapsing on Crystal's bed. "Horribly."

Crystal sighed. "Reminding her of it is not how you make a girl feel better."

Robb waved his arms in the air. "How was I supposed to know that?"

"Maybe from all the girls you've dated," she said, raising her black eyebrows. Robb shrugged, returned to his food, and Crystal rubbed her temples. "No wonder none of them worked out."

"Hey!" Chewed pretzel spewed from Robb's mouth. "Some of them worked out."

Crystal nodded. "The drunk ones."

My mouth hung open. "You two drink?" I asked, reminding myself that I barely knew my two closest friends. "Like alcohol?"

They turned to me and grinned. "What else can you do here?" Robb laughed. "The parties are the best."

"The clubs are even better," Crystal agreed.

My cheeks burned. "I didn't know you had any."

"We don't," she said. "But the next town over does."

"My friend, Zac, makes fakes," Robb said, leaning back with his arms behind his head. "We can get in anywhere."

I swallowed my nerves. "But aren't you a little young?"

Crystal waved her hand in my face. "You're never too young for journalism."

Robb rolled his eyes. "I got her a fake, so she could beat her mom's news stories."

"And if you want the best stories, you have to go to the best places," Crystal said, beaming behind her bleached hair.

"That's when she realized how much fun clubs could be." Robb laughed, his chest rising beneath his red shirt. "Alcohol is better than sweets any day."

I cringed. I generally avoided alcohol. Warping my mind didn't appeal to me.

"Relax, Jess," Crystal said, pinching my arm. "It's not a big deal; we'll take you sometime."

I ignored her and stared at Robb. "I thought your parents were strict."

He raised his brow. "Who said they ever catch me?" he asked, suddenly checking his watch. "But I should get out of here before my parents freak."

My heart pounded. "What time is it?"

"Eleven."

"What?" I leapt from Crystal's bed and grabbed my things. "I'm late."

Crystal blinked. "So call them."

I searched my pockets, and my entire body sank. "I left my phone at home." That explains why they weren't blowing up my phone.

"Weirdo."

I frowned at her. "It's a bad habit."

"Relax," Robb said, stepping between us. "I can drive you."

Before I knew it, I wrapped my arms around him. "Thank you," I said, shying away before he could reciprocate my touch.

When I looked at him, he was grinning. "Let's go."

I threw on my jacket. "See you at school, Crystal."

She waved, not even bothering to walk us out, and we rushed to Robb's blue Chevy Suburban. As soon as we were buckled in, Robb took off, and I gripped the seat.

"Sorry if this is a burden," I said, knowing he knew where I lived. He already drove me to school twice, yet I was oblivious about where he lived. "I hope my house isn't out of the way."

"You're not a burden, Jess," Robb laughed, pointing to Crystal's neighbor. "But I live right there."

My stomach sunk. "I'm sorry."

"Don't be," he said. "My parents can't mind if they're asleep."

I watched his unlit house disappear behind us. "Why are they so strict anyway?" I asked, hoping to find someone to relate to. "Grades or something?"

Robb chuckled. "My grades are perfect. Believe me, they make sure of that."

Our conversation stopped, and Robb fiddled with the radio controls on his steering wheel. He briefly looked away, but quickly returned his focus to the main road. Then his hand pushed against the console, and his radio turned off. "They're strict, because they're paranoid."

"About what?"

He shrugged, but it was stiff. "Stupid teenager stuff."

Clearly, he didn't want to elaborate.

"Mine are too," I said, attempting to lighten his mood. Ever since my mother told my father I wanted to look for information on my biological parents, they hadn't been the same. They tiptoed around the subject as if I'd leave them the instant I found a long-lost uncle, twice removed. Like that was going to happen. I was beginning to believe an extended family didn't even exist, yet I hadn't bothered looking. Because I was afraid and didn't want to find out I was born practically alone.

"I'm barely let out on weekend nights," Robb said, suddenly breaking the silence again. His brow was furrowed. "I normally study. Isn't much of a life for a player," he joked.

I bit my lip, curiosity bubbling in my veins. "How many girls have you dated?"

"Quite a lot," he said, winking. "I'm addicted."

"You're going to get screwed over one day," I said, and he smirked.

"And I'm looking forward to it."

We laughed for a few seconds but spun into silence quickly afterwards. I leaned my head against the passenger window and watched the streets fly by. His truck sped past a drug store, and long lampposts stretched light over the street in a blur. We passed our school, and, even in the darkness, I could make out the willow tree's looming shadow.

Eric. I remembered how he met Teresa beneath it and frowned. I had no clue what I was going to do about my incompetent homeroom partner. Clearly, he wasn't going to help me, but I couldn't do the entire project by myself. It was due in three weeks, and Crystal and Robb had already begun theirs. They weren't even close to done yet.

Robb leaned over and tapped my leg, breaking my enraged trance. "See that mansion over there?" he asked, and my eyes adjusted in the darkness.

Somewhat hidden in a thick mass of trees, a house peered out. A few lights shined through the thorns and lit up the contorted driveway. It was dark and eerie—the kind of house neighborhood kids would only approach on Halloween.

As we passed it, Robb's lip curled. "That's Welborn's house."

My knuckles tightened into a fist. "He's so rude," I said. "I tried so hard today, and he doesn't care at all—"

"Jess," Robb interrupted me quietly, and his eyes fogged over. "He used to be a really great guy. Awesome, nice, smart, funny, you name it. He was even there for me when my dog died," he spoke through a struggled laugh. "He was my best friend until Hannah's death."

"I'm sorry."

"I wasn't asking for pity," he said, briefly meeting my eyes. He sighed and gripped the wheel. "That Eric is still in him somewhere; I'm sure you can talk him out of it."

I held my breath. "Do you really think that?"

He nodded, but didn't elaborate, and I didn't push it. Who was I to judge them? I'd never lost anyone, aside from my biological parents, and I didn't even remember what they looked like. I knew nothing of death, and, for some unexplainable reason, I was beginning to feel guilty for that.

"It'll be okay, Jess," Robb said, pulling into my driveway minutes later.

"Thanks," I said, forcing a grateful smile. "For everything."

Before he could continue our night with more conversation, I shut the door. I watched him back out of the driveway, and then I turned to my house. All the lights were on. *Fantastic.*

When I opened the front door, my parents met me with folded arms.

"Jessie Taylor." My mother's blonde hair was ruffled. "Where have you been? It's a school night."

I sighed, dropping my bag on the floor. "Studying."

"Studying?" She raised her voice, and my father placed a hand on her shoulder. "It's almost midnight."

"It's eleven."

"Don't argue with me, young lady," she said, jabbing a finger in my direction. "We've been worried sick."

"And who was that boy who dropped you off?" my dad asked, peering behind his reading glasses, and my shoulders dropped.

"His name's Robb," I said. "And I was with Crystal and him—studying. We were working on our science projects."

"That's funny, because your teacher called," my mom said, raising her brow. "She said you haven't even started."

My mouth hung open. I was ready to argue.

"My partner won't help me," I said, and my father waved my excuse away.

"You're failing, Jess," he said, shaking his head back and forth. "We made a deal; if you don't keep your grades up, then you can wait to research your—"

"My parents?" I finished, and they tensed. "I haven't even had time to start researching yet."

"Whose fault it that?" my mother asked. "Maybe if you spent less time socializing, and more time studying, you'd be able to."

"But—"

"No 'buts', Jessie." She didn't even let me speak. "We made a deal."

I bit my lip, avoiding their eyes. They didn't understand. They'd never understand.

"You get your grade up, and you can start searching."

"Fine," I said, climbing my stairs to my bedroom and ending the conversation.

Welborn was going to get it tomorrow.

TWELVE

MY EARS WERE RINGING. NOAH CHEWED WITH HIS MOUTH open, and his sticky slobber glued food to the roof of his mouth as he slurped his dinner. Across from him, Mindy filed the first layer of her nail off, and my father tapped his foot, humming. He only hummed when he was anxious. Still, he smiled at his new wife, and my stomach churned.

How could he be so happy with a human? If it wasn't for his wedding, the accident wouldn't have happened, and Abby would be alive. But she wasn't.

"How was your day, Eric?" Mindy asked, her high-pitched voice tearing my sensitive ears like a razorblade.

"Fine," I said, shoveling food into my mouth to avoid a discussion. My father's glare burned my skin, but I'd never acknowledge his human life. It was only a distraction. In fact, I often wondered if he married a human to throw off the Light, hoping they'd write him off as a human as well. But he wasn't. And if I couldn't deny it, he shouldn't either.

Noah kicked the table's legs, shaking our dinner. "My day was amazing," he said, spraying meatloaf across his plate. "Billy and I scared the substitute."

"That's nice, Noah," Mindy said, patting her son's head. She hadn't even paid attention; she was too focused on us. "You two are acting strange."

No. Really?

"We're just practicing our poker faces," my dad said, beaming.

As far as I had been told, we couldn't have our meeting in the shelter. Security was breeched, and the elders weren't risking exposure if a light decided to attack. Instead, my father was holding it in his office. We told Mindy it was a father-son poker tournament. She wouldn't interrupt—not when we had been fighting so often.

"We lost the last one from getting too excited," I said, pushing my meatloaf around. "We don't want that happening again."

She grinned, lighting up at the opportunity to talk to me. "I really hope you win tonight."

Me, too.

The front door rattled with knocks, and then it opened. A man waltzed in, peering into the kitchen from downstairs. "Hello."

Mindy shot up from her chair and waved over the railing. "Hey, George. How are you doing?"

"Great," he said, scaling the stairs with his son behind him.

Pierce barely resembled his human form of Jonathon Stone. Instead of pale skin, green eyes, and dark hair, Jonathon had light brown hair and eyes. He wore thick glasses, but his right eye was fogged over with a thick, white cloud. He was partially blind.

At school, he was an artist, and he was easily picked on, but his bullies would shake if they ever saw his Dark side. He was strong, capable, and had the best endurance I'd seen from a trainee. He could easily kick any human's ass. Too bad they would never see him like that.

I stood from the table and shook my friend's hand. "Hey."

Jonathon avoided my eye contact. I'd known him since birth, but he was never secure about his human identity. "How's the family?" he asked.

"Don't force small talk," I said, dropping my voice. "You sound like our parents."

He laughed. "Isn't that a scary thought?"

I nodded, and his telepathic thought shot through me.

"You ready to talk to the elders?"

"It's not like I have a choice," I said.

Jonathon pushed his glasses up his nose, and my father waved sodas in our direction. "Come on, boys," he said, forcing an awkward, chipper tone. "Let's start."

We followed our fathers down the hallway to the office. George opened the door, ushering us inside, and then he spun around, surveying the golden room. "They should be here any second," he said, locking the door.

Without a word, my father laid his hand on the wall, and we watched as a thick layer of shadows spewed over the room. Gliding around the room from the floor to the ceiling, they twisted into oblivion and the room spun in a tight circle. He'd used a silencing spell.

George smiled. "That should help," he said, enveloping his body in blackness. When he reappeared, his long black hair was shortened, and thick bristles grew along his formerly smooth chin. His black eyes burned green, and I recognized him for who he was after transformation, Urte—my father's guard and fellow elder.

In seconds, my father morphed as well. In his shade form, he was taller, thinner, and had a lot more hair. "You two stay human," he said, shaking his limbs as he solidified. "I don't want these elders pushing you around."

"I'd like to see that," I said, and Urte glared.

"Don't be ignorant, Eric."

I shrugged, and my arm hair spiked up. I tensed, watching the office floor unfold into a whirlpool. Jonathon and I stepped back, and two men sizzled to the surface. Luthicer's patchy white beard stretched to his collarbone, while his blond hair curled at the nape of his neck. His pitch black eyes wavered from side to side, but Eu stared right at us.

He had silver irises and the whitest pupils I'd ever seen, and they contrasted harshly against his thick, mangled black hair. He was three feet shorter than Luthicer, making him about a foot shorter than me. I had only met him once before, but he always seemed to be out of place. He hovered behind

Luthicer like—well—a shadow, and Luthicer shined like he was more of a light than a half-breed.

"Will Camille be joining us tonight?" Urte asked, and Luthicer's forehead wrinkled.

"She's resting," he said, dragging his dark eyes over Jonathon and I. "Her training has been rigorous, but it'll help our descendant."

I hid my fist behind my back. *What'd he do to Camille?* I didn't care if he was her trainer or not. He didn't have the right.

"Which one is he?" Eu asked, and I raised my hand as he stepped forward. His white eyes flickered. "It's hard to recognize you in this form."

I raised my brow. "Isn't that the point?"

"Eric." My father's tone dropped. "You must excuse my son. He's very—"

"Nervous," Luthicer finished, dragging his eyes over me.

I smirked. "That's your opinion."

"And it's right," he said, tilting his head. "If you aren't nervous, why would you still be a human right now?"

"Luthicer." Urte stood between us. "This meeting is strictly going to be a conversation."

"A conversation won't get Eric anywhere," Luthicer said, stepping around Urte.

"No," my father said, sitting on the edge of his desk. "It's up to Eric."

I changed before anyone even realized I had decided. I didn't hesitate. I had to be Shoman, the first descendent, and hesitation was weakness.

Luthicer smiled, slowly pushing Jonathon aside. "You're weaker than I expected," he said, waltzing around me as his fingers grazed my skin.

A pain shot up my arm, through my shoulder, and my skin burned. I sucked in breath and grabbed my arm as the pain thundered through me. What was this? I felt hot and dizzy, like I'd collapse at any moment. *Why can't I move?*

"What are you doing?" Urte's voice wavered through my foggy hearing.

"Testing him," Luthicer said, leaning in to stare at my pupils. His breath was hot against my cheek. "You can't even handle a little Light energy."

Light? My body trembled. *Is that what this was?* Light energy could kill a shade—easily—but it could also poison us.

"I can handle it," I said, forcing my voice through clenched teeth.

"I'm not so sure," he said, digging his nails into my shoulder, and, as if to prove his point. I lurched over in pain, gasping.

Urte slammed his hand against the wall. "Elder or not, you have no right to hurt this boy."

"He isn't hurting him, Urte," Eu said.

Urte shook his head. "I'm an elder just like you, Eu," he said, and I stumbled back, leaning against the wall for support. "Eric doesn't need this sort of a test yet."

I held my hand up, silencing them. "If they think I need it," I said and sucked in a breath. "I'll believe them." *I will not be weak. Not in front of them.*

Luthicer hummed. "You're either brave or very foolish."

"What's the difference?"

The room silenced, and Luthicer knelt in front of me. "That kind of talk can be used against you, Shoman."

My lip curled. "They can't use anything against me," I said, and Luthicer squinted.

"What about love?"

Abby. "I have no love," I said, shoving the loss away. "I haven't had love in a long time. Not for anybody."

Luthicer's face turned, and he focused on my father. "You, at least, raised the boy right." Then, he stood, pointing at Urte. "But you," he said. "You haven't begun his training."

Urte straightened. "I was planning on starting soon."

"Planning does nothing," Luthicer said. "You start soon. Understand?"

"Don't forget we're equals," Urte said, his chest rising.

Luthicer's brow scrunched. "So act like it then."

My father stood and pushed himself between the men. "This isn't about you two," he said, his black hair springing into the air. His eyes radiated as he glowered at Luthicer. "Shoman will start training with Urte soon—as long as Eric agrees."

Everyone turned to me, and I winced. My spine was squeezing. "I can do it," I said.

"This is a serious decision, Eric," he said. "If you do it when you're not ready, you'll only injure yourself."

I hesitated for the first time that night. In the corner, Jonathon was pale, his working eye widening behind his thick glasses, and I knew he realized what I had. Our fathers were just as capable as Luthicer, and Darthon—the second descendant—was worse than them. He was more powerful than our elders, just as I was supposed to be, but I wasn't even close to meeting that power. If I was going to survive, I needed to be stronger.

"I will try," I said, wincing as my voice strained against my throat. Whatever Luthicer had done to me resonated. The pain was worsening.

"Then it's decided," Luthicer said, stepping back and clasping his hands together. "Eric will begin his training."

I clenched my teeth together, while my father guided the men to the middle of the room. "So this meeting is over," he said, and both men nodded.

"We'll be within calling distance," Eu said, and then they were gone—without even bothering to say their goodbyes to me. The shadows spiraled and dissipated. When I was positive they were long gone, I collapsed.

"What the hell did he do to me?" I asked, grabbing my scalp.

My father shoved water in my face. "Drink it," he said, and I gulped it as he explained. "It's a torture illusion; you're okay."

"You mean," I choked, hitting my knee as I caught my breath. "That wasn't even happening?"

"It attacks your nervous system," he confirmed, shaking his head. "It's probably the most commonly used spell. You're not hurt."

I lay back, groaning. "I hate that guy."

"Roll up your sleeves," Urte said, and I fell out of my shade form as I obeyed. Urte ran his fingers across my bruising skin, glowering at the red marks Luthicer left behind. "He had no right."

"The power he used," I breathed. "Does Camille—"

"She's capable of it," my father said, cringing. "I'm afraid she knows much more than that."

"And she's nothing compared to Darthon?"

Their silence answered my question.

"It's going to be okay, Eric," Urte said, helping me sit up.

I shook my head. "Lying is my forte, Urte, not yours."

Slowly, I stood up on my shaking feet and walked across the office. I leaned against the desk, ran my hand over my father's paperwork, and picked up a pen. Turning around, I shoved it in my father's hand.

"What's this?" he asked, raising a brow.

"You'll need it to sign my death certificate," I said, pain vibrating my veins against my muscles and bones. "Are we done now?"

THIRTEEN

"**W**HAT ARE YOU GOING TO TEACH ME TONIGHT?" THE GIRL spun in a circle, her black hair flowing around her in a wave. "Flying?" she suggested. "Sword fighting? Maybe even dodging death-threatening blows?"

I laughed and walked a few steps behind her. For once, we had taken most of the night off and talked—just talked—and I dreaded the fact I was actually enjoying myself.

"I could teach you most of that," I said, nearing the forest's end. "But not the sword fighting—that doesn't exist." *Except for the two descendants, and you're not one of them, but I am.* I locked my jaw, preventing an explanation of who I was.

"No swords at all?" she asked, stopping.

I stood at her side. "Of course not."

"Dang," she sighed, her breath fogging out in front of us. "I was hoping I'd get to swing something at people."

"So pick up a stick."

She hit my arm. "Aren't you the funny one?"

"Your words; not mine," I said, laughing to conceal a wince. She'd hit Luthicer's mark. "What do you want to do tonight?"

"Can we fly again?" she asked, widening her purple eyes. "We haven't flown in three days."

"That's because it's tiring," I pointed out. "And you won't impress any of the elders if all you can do is fly." *Except you'll never meet them.*

She frowned, shook her shoulders, and forced a smile. "So teach me something new," she said. "I want to impress them."

My gut wrenched with guilt, but my mind raced with my twisted logic as I tried to justify myself. She was an outsider, we were in the middle of war, and I could've abandoned her or helped her—neither of which involved the elders for a reason. I didn't want her killed over old laws not adapted to modernization. Especially with Luthicer around. He'd kill her to make a point with me.

I wasn't allowed friends, and I was definitely banned from relationships. *But this girl*—she reminded me of what it was like to believe in something. Her hope was naïve, but it was real, and I hadn't felt something real in years. Nothing positive anyway.

"Shoman?"

She leaned over and blinked her purple eyes when she caught my gaze. She smiled. "Are you okay?"

"You have to learn something new," I said, repeating myself as I moved away from her. I couldn't let her affect my feelings.

"Like what?" Her gaze flickered over the empty space where I'd been standing. Pathetically, I had to concentrate from moving back over.

I dug my feet into the ground and shrug. "Dodging would be a good place to start." *Dodging this friendship would be even better—expected even.*

"Dodging what?"

Without a word, I smacked my palms together and slowly pulled them apart. A cloud of energy, bright blue and electric, collected between my hands, and I shot it toward her. The air flashed, barely shoving against her, and she fell backward, her mouth hanging open.

I burst into laughter as she folded her arms. "That's not funny. That really hurt."

"I'm sorry," I gasped through my laughter. "But that's the simplest power to dodge; it doesn't even hurt." I walked over to her, offering my hand. "You only had to move, and it wouldn't have knocked you over."

A purple light slammed into my chest, and I fell, slamming against the ground. Air filled my lungs, and I wheezed as she stood over me, brushing purple dust off her hands. She'd retaliated.

"You only had to move, Shoman." She used my words against me and winked.

"How did you do that?" I asked, springing to my feet. I hadn't even shown her how to create it. How did she know what to do? She was too accurate.

She flipped her dark hair over her shoulder. "I watch and learn."

"You're a natural," I said, studying her. First, she avoided my radar, and now she was using Dark energy. What'd she have that others didn't?

Even though I'd be the strongest shade in less than a year, it took me weeks to learn a new power or spell. I couldn't teach myself—especially from watching—yet she'd perfected her energy in one sitting.

"Something's wrong," she said, wrinkling her brow. "I didn't hurt you, did I?"

"No," I said. *You only startled the first descendant. No big deal.*

"Then why are you so quiet?" she asked, lowering her tone, and I stepped forward, leaning out to rub her arm.

"I'm fine," I said, and she bit her lip. "Let's take a break." *To distract you.* "We can fly."

She lit up. "I actually wanted to show you something."

"Okay—"

Her fingertips sparkled like a lake reflecting the stars, all silver and purple. When she swirled her hands back and forth, her nails shone, and her palms glittered, dipping in and out of the misty shadows. I'd never seen anything like it.

"Isn't it beautiful?" she asked as little droplets of energy fell from her hands and splashed across the grass like morning dew. The light never dissipated. Instead, it illuminated the grass, and I stepped back.

"What is that?"

It disappeared, and I caught her eye. She raised her brow. "I thought you could tell me."

I shook my head. Something wasn't right with her powers. "Energy is only used for defense; that didn't do anything."

"Why can't you use it for other things?"

I opened my mouth, but closed it when I realized I had no argument. "I've only been taught to use it for the war."

A slow smile pulled at her lips. "You can't relax, can you, Shoman?"

Not with you around.

"You've been stiff all night," she said. "Spill."

"It's nothing."

"So there is something."

I rubbed my temples; she was relentless. "I wish I could tell you," I said, mentally surrendering. I could feel my guard dropping around her, yet I couldn't report her to the elders.

"Why can't you?" she asked.

Because I'm the first descendant, you already know too much, and it's my fault, because I stopped thinking. I'm not thinking.

"Because I can't," I said, hoping she'd linger in silence, but she sighed.

"I'm sorry if I was rude," she said, sitting on the grass, small, purple lights waving around her. "I'm just worried about you."

My throat tightened. *Worried?* "I'm okay," I said, sitting next to her.

Her gaze shifted over my arm. "Then what's with the bruises?"

My hand shot up to cover Luthicer's marks, but my clothes already did. I gaped at her. "How'd you see them?"

She shrugged. "Your sleeve moved when we were walking earlier," she said. "I see everything at night; it's crazy."

I kept my face blank, but my heart was sinking. Her extreme senses weren't supposed to develop until years of training. She was either lying to me, or something was severely wrong. I needed to report her.

Could I turn her into the elders? I doubted it.

"So—" She leaned against her knees and blinked her purple eyes. "Did you get into a fight or something? Is that why you didn't show up the other night?"

I nodded, knowing I'd left her alone in the forest for two days. I was too busy to train, and I couldn't get away from the Dark. I hadn't even gone to school. But I couldn't tell her that. Not yet.

"Talk to me," she said, bumping her shoulder against mine. "Be human for a minute."

"If you haven't noticed," I said and laughed. "We aren't exactly human right now."

She narrowed her eyes. "You're avoiding the subject."

I groaned, laying my forehead on my knee. "I worked with an elder," I said, and, when I looked up, she was smiling.

"That wasn't too hard, was it?"

I chuckled and shook my head. "But you aren't my therapist."

"No," she agreed. "But I'm your friend, and friends help each other."

Friend? I gaped at her. *She considered me her friend?*

I tensed as she scooted closer to me. "So tell me about it already."

"The elders—" I paused, clearing the nerves from my throat. "They tested me the other day. That's it."

She leaned back and stared at the bruises. "And they hurt you?"

"It was necessary."

Her purple eyes flickered. "How is pain necessary?"

"There's a war coming, remember?"

Her already white skin somehow paled. "And you're a warrior."

I nodded. "The elders think I need to know what it's like to be attacked by a light."

"The Light." She let the word linger in the air, and she hugged her knees against her chest. "Those are the bad guys, right?"

"Depends on who wins, I guess." I smirked, but she didn't smile.

"When will someone win?"

I sighed. "There's a battle," I said, hesitating. I shouldn't be telling her so much, but I hadn't talked to anyone in so long, let alone someone my own age. And a girl. "It'll happen this December."

Her thin eyebrows scrunched. "It's scheduled?"

"It's based on the first descendant's birthday." *My birthday.*

"That seems really odd," she said, and I shrugged before she pushed her shoulder against mine again. "Especially with these cranky elders dictating it all."

I chuckled. The prophecy was dictating it. The elders only wished they had that kind of power. "It isn't their fault," I said. "Really."

"But you have to fight in it?"

My gaze darted away until I could control my expression. "I choose to." *Lie.* "Defending my kind is the honorable thing to do."

"You're eighteen," she said. "You're not supposed to care about honor."

"I'm seventeen."

"What's the difference?" she asked, and I opened my mouth to tell her, but I couldn't—not because I didn't want her to know, but because I still didn't want to accept it.

"There's a big difference," I said.

She huffed. "One year."

"Yeah," I agreed. *The one year I had left to live.* "A lot can happen in that amount of time."

FOURTEEN

I SLAMMED MY BOOK ON OUR DESK AND GLARED AT THE MISTY-EYED boy who had skipped school for almost an entire week. He jumped, but his expression remained starkly neutral. "What's wrong, Jessica?"

I shuddered. *Did he just use my full name?*

He leaned forward, and his green eyes flew over me. "Jessica? What's wrong?"

"What's wrong?" I collapsed into my chair, my hair whipping against my face. "Are you joking?"

He smiled, and anger flooded my veins. *Why the hell was he smiling?*

"You could tell me what's wrong," he said. "Then I'll start joking."

I held my hand up in his face. "Quit the bullshit," I said.

He raised his brow. "You still haven't told me what's wrong."

"Give me the chance."

"I already have," he said, lowering his voice. "But I'd calm down if I were you. The entire class is staring."

He was right. Everyone lifted their eyes from their labs to gawk at our table. Even Robb and Crystal were watching.

I gripped the table and turned my back to them. At least there was one positive thing about sitting at the front of the classroom. "Maybe if you were listening to me, you wouldn't have noticed what others were doing," I said, and he leaned back, raising his brow.

"I've been under the stare radar for a few years now," he said. "I think I can sense when it's happening."

Because you're an asshole. "Can you try to talk to me like a normal human being for a minute?"

His shoulders rose, and his face flushed. In a second, he turned his torso away and leaned his elbows against the table. *Had I said something?*

He sighed, running his hand through his brown hair. "Just tell me what's bothering you already." He was no longer the witty Welborn he was a minute ago.

I bit my lip, shoving my guilt away. "I need to get this project done," I whined. "Please." *I want to find my parents.*

He studied me, and his face twisted. His dark brown hair fell dangerously close to his eyes, yet their green color pierced me. I was completely transfixed, my eyes locked with his, and I felt a twinge of familiarity dig into my soul. My stomach churned, and my cheeks burned.

"Why?" he asked, breaking our eye contact. My chest sunk.

"What's that supposed to mean?" I snapped, feeling my illogical emotions take over my words. *Why was I feeling this way?*

He raised his brow and flipped his pen through his fingers. "Why do you want to finish it so bad?" he asked. "It's one grade."

"One grade that's important to my family—"

"So it isn't important to you?" he asked, and I lost all capability of responding.

What was going on here? Something was wrong with me.

"It's important to me," I said curtly. "It's ridiculously important, and I can't finish it without you." *Unfortunately.*

He turned away. "I guess I can help."

"What?" I asked, expecting him to crack a sarcastic joke. There was no way he was suddenly agreeing.

"You're acting as if you were expecting me to decline," he said.

"I was."

He sighed, leaning on his hand. "Helping one person can't be that big of a deal," he said. "Plus, I'm assuming you have a reason behind this irrational need to conform to this institution." He leaned over, yanking a stack of papers from his backpack. As the bell rang, he shoved them into my hands. "I typed up our lab report last night."

Who was this guy, and where was Eric Welborn?

"Uh—thanks," I said, skimming it. He'd done extra work.

"Turn it into the teacher," he said, standing as kids rushed for the door. "See you later."

He threw his bag over his shoulder, brushing past without another word. I stared at his back, awestruck, and found my voice at the last second. "Welborn!" I called out to him before he disappeared into the crowd, and he spun around, meeting my eyes. "Where are we meeting?"

Everyone stopped to stare, but he ignored them. "There's a new coffee shop in town," he said. "Meet at seven."

"How am I supposed to know where that is?" I asked, and he tilted his head toward Crystal and Robb.

"I'm sure your friends can help you," he said, waving over his shoulder as he walked away. "See you around, Jessica."

I was still frozen at my desk, my heart thundering in my ears, when Crystal grabbed my arm. "What the hell was that?" she asked, and I blinked.

"I have no idea."

"He took a shot at us," Robb said, shoving his hands into his pockets. "I don't like that guy."

"You're the one who stood up for him," I said, and Crystal hit his arm.

"Don't ruin her accomplishment anyway," she said. "I thought she'd never get that boy to talk; he doesn't talk to anyone." She flipped her purse open, and her pen came out. "How'd you do it?"

I grimaced at her potential rumor column. "I have no idea." The last thing I wanted was Eric to stop talking to me, because my gossip about him was printed in our school newspaper.

Robb rolled his eyes. "So he's in a good mood," he said. "He's probably has a new girlfriend."

"Yeah, right." Crystal giggled, but Robb ignored her, leaning over to scan the papers in my hands.

"Isn't that the lab from last week?" he asked, and I stared at it again, somehow unable to comprehend how much Eric had changed.

"I guess so," I said, planning to talk to the teacher about the late assignment after I checked off my next task. "Do you think you could drive me to the coffee shop tonight?"

Robb's dark eyes lit up. "Of course, Jess."

"Thanks," I said, pushing past them to turn it in. Maybe this project wouldn't be so bad after all. Even better, maybe Eric would be a good person, and his friendship with Crystal and Robb could heal. But I doubted it.

As much as I wanted to believe in Eric's nice side, I'd only seen it once and didn't trust it. All of a sudden, he was kind and—normal. But his eyes. His resonating stare fluttered through my memory, and I shivered. I hadn't seen kindness in his pupils. I only saw intensity, and, I hated to admit it, but he was beyond intimidating. He was overwhelming.

FIFTEEN

MY EARS WERE RINGING, AND MY HEAD THUNDERED WITH EV-ery single sound. Fingernails scraped across key-boards, lips hissed in whispers, and machines roared, steaming with hot liquids. Weren't coffee shops supposed to be quiet?

I pulled on my headphones and cranked my music to drown out the little noises. Two elderly women glared as I disturbed their peace, and I fought a cringe. If they only knew what their bickering did to my ears, they'd smile with sympathy.

Sweet smells and warm air circled around my skin, but I chilled. After the sun set, it was draining to be a human. I was constantly fighting the urge to shift, and my human skin felt like solitary confinement—something the elders enforced when a shade broke the law. *Which they'd do to me if they knew what I was doing.*

The nameless shade flickered over my closed eyelids, and my lips pulled into an uncontrollable grin. She was mystifying. Just her presence affected me. When I was around her, I actually felt like an average shade—not Shoman—and I relaxed. Even when she was upset with my attitude, I was happy. In fact, her frustration delighted me. I'd always reacted that way with girls. They looked so adorable when their cheeks flushed. I couldn't help grinning, and they'd only get madder, which made my grin spread. It was a lose-lose situation. Just like the one I had with Jessica.

My partner's aggravation grew so easily, and I couldn't help but enjoy it. She got angrier, and my sarcasm enhanced— only when it wasn't serious.

I actually felt bad for her when the classroom gaped at her, but that wasn't my fault. *Correction: It was. I should apologize when she gets here.*

My responsibilities had truly clouded my judgment. Just because I wasn't human, didn't mean I could discount human life. The shade girl had taught me that much. In fact, she made me want my human life again.

In only a few days, I was opening up to Mindy and Noah more—not a lot, but more than I ever had before. I stopped ignoring them completely, and my father relaxed, lecturing me less.

Being a human wasn't as bad as I thought.

A memory of Abby flashed through me, and my senses dipped into the day of my father's wedding. My entire body spun with the screeching tires and smoke. Glass shattered, and pain slammed through my temple. I'd smacked my head against the car door, but my hand remained wrapped around my friend's. I prayed for the Dark to save us, but no one came.

I remembered every little sound, every single movement. The noise damaged my hearing for weeks, but the damage was nothing compared to the days afterwards. I could still taste the gasoline and smell the blood. I always saw her death.

"Eric."

Someone tore through my memories by yanking off my headphones. I leapt into the air, spun around, and, automatically resorted to a fighting stance.

Teresa and Jonathon stepped back, and the entire coffee shop silenced. I froze, darting my eyes around, and dropped my shoulders. "What are you guys doing here?" I hissed, and their eyebrows rose.

"We were hoping you could hang out, jumpy," Teresa said, letting her eyes flicker over me. "What's gotten into you?"

I ignored her. "How'd you find me?" I'd never been here before, and I hadn't told anyone where I was going. Not even my father.

Teresa grinned, and, immediately, I knew. My muscles stiffened.

"You tracked me?" I asked, realizing Teresa—as Camille—used her Light powers to zone in on my energy.

"Does it really matter?" she asked, sitting at my table.

"It's dangerous," I spat, falling back into my chair next to her. "What if the Light sensed you?"

"It's more dangerous to speak about it," she said, waving her arm toward the customers who'd returned to normal. "What are you doing here anyway?" she asked, toying with my stack of notes.

I yanked them away. "I'm meeting someone." *So get out.*

Jonathon raised his brow as he pulled a seat over. "Jess?" My grip tightened, and Jonathon rolled his eyes. "The whole school was talking about it."

I groaned, and Teresa leaned toward him. "Who's Jess?" she asked, whipping toward me. "Do you have a new girlfriend?"

"No," I said, fighting my past again. "I'm not allowed; remember?"

She whistled low. "Don't get so defensive."

"I'm not being defensive," I argued, and Teresa fiddled with her short hair.

"It's not like you're not allowed to have friends," she said, raising her brow, and I glowered at her. She was testing my emotions.

"I don't have any," I said.

"You have us," Jonathon said.

I laid my head on the table. "Why are you guys here?" *Please leave me alone.*

"Saving you," Jonathon said, shooting up from his seat. "We're going out for a flight, just us three."

"We haven't done it in ages," Teresa added, and I shook my head.

"I can't," I said. "I have plans."

Jonathon adjusted his thick-rimmed glasses. "With a human."

"So what?"

Teresa slammed her hand on the table. "She is your girlfriend."

"No, she isn't, Teresa," I said, forcing my guard's human name on her.

She frowned. "I don't like this, Eric," she said. "You never do homework."

"And you never talk to anyone, let alone girls," Jonathon added.

"It doesn't mean anything," I said, dreading their suspicions. I did not need them studying my every move when I spent most of them helping an unregistered shade. "I'm completely focused on training."

"Then why didn't you show up today?" Jonathon asked, reminding me of Urte's training sessions. They were supposed to start today, and I avoided them like I avoided the elders.

"I needed a break," I dismissed my actions, and Teresa grabbed my arm.

"So come out tonight," she coaxed. "And don't hesitate, or I really will think you're into this girl."

"Let's go then," I said, collecting my things before my current situation threatened exposure. I wasn't about to risk my freedom for Jessica Taylor's homework. I had priorities, after all. *Even if my priorities involved lying to the Dark.*

I rushed out of the coffee shop before they could further their interrogation, and they skipped behind me. The door rang as it slammed shut, and the streetlamps blurred against my night vision. Beside me, Jonathon took his glasses off, revealing his burning green eyes, and Teresa's black hair slowly grew. My blood began to simmer, and I fought the urge to morph completely in the street.

"Good luck, Jess."

My feet dug into the pavement as I heard Robb's shout fly over us. I turned, leaning against the brick wall, and watched as my partner jumped from a blue Chevy. Robb waved out the window, and Jess waved back, clutching her purse with her free hand.

"See you around, Robb," she shouted, running into the coffee shop.

"Is that her?" Teresa asked, grazing against my arm.

My jaw popped as I turned away. "It's fine," I said, leading her toward the nearest alleyway. We could change and leave from there. "Let's go."

I had the weekend to avoid Jessica anyway.

Sixteen

"**E**RIC JAMES WELBORN.**"

My father burst into my room in a cloud of smoke. He hadn't even bothered to walk down the hallway as a human. He was pissed, and I was in trouble. A lot of trouble.

"My office, now," he said, and then he was gone.

The blood in my veins froze, and my heart seized. *What was this about?*

I shook off my nerves, shifting so rapidly that my skin felt like it was ripping. In seconds, I transported to his office, and gaped at the situation in front of me. Luthicer was standing in the middle of the room, arms folded, and my father, along with Urte, stood by his side.

"What now?" I asked, hoping they hadn't seen my body tense. "Another test?"

Luthicer's white hair tingled with electricity. "Where were you last night?"

My muscles stiffened as I locked my legs. I'd spent all night flying with Camille and Pierce, soaring and dodging one another's powers. I knew we weren't supposed to be out, let alone using our powers so openly, but we'd done it before and never got caught. Ever.

"I didn't realize you were my secretary," I said, locking glares with the half-breed elder.

Luthicer's lip curled. "Apparently, someone needs to fill

that role, since your guard isn't good enough."

Camille. "What's this about?" I asked, suffocating from fury. *Where was she?*

"Why don't you tell us," Luthicer said, and I lowered my tone.

"I don't know what you want me to say."

My father stepped between us. "I'd prefer you accuse my son, so he can defend his innocence rather than prolong unnecessary guilt."

Luthicer's black eyes turned to slits. "With all due respect, Bracke, I'd prefer to do things my way," he said. "Your son needs a chance to admit to his deeds first."

My father ignored him, turning to me. "Have you gone against any of the rules?"

"No." *Aside from the girl.* "I have nothing to admit to."

Urte sighed, grabbing his bristled chin. "Are you sure?"

"Positive."

My trainer closed his green eyes. "This meeting is pointless, Luthicer," he said. "Shoman is telling the truth; there isn't an ounce of hesitation in his face or doubt in his eyes."

"He could be a good liar," Luthicer said, running his black eyes over me.

"My son wouldn't lie to his trainer or me," my father said, and guilt seeped into my veins.

"I don't believe him." Luthicer remained rigid.

"Yet you haven't even told me what I'm being accused of," I said, glaring.

Luthicer returned my glower. "Someone was outside the shelter last night, and they used a large amount of power. They risked our safety."

I froze. He knew that we'd been out, but how?

My father pointed at the half-breed. "My son wouldn't risk his life so foolishly; he values his descendant responsibilities just as much as the rest of us."

Luthicer's face reddened as he spoke, "How could you think your son is so worthy of being the first descendant?" he asked, shoving a finger against my father's chest. "He isn't even an adult."

I grabbed my father's shoulder and yanked him back, taking his place. "You have no right—"

"I'm an elder," Luthicer said, his nose twitching. "I have more right than you ever will."

"Not when I'm the one saving your ungrateful ass on the battlefield."

"Eric." My father pushed his way into the fight and shoved us apart. "Don't speak to Luthicer that way; he's higher than you."

"Only because of age," I spat.

"Which you'll never reach," Luthicer retorted as Light energy waved off him. I felt nauseous. "You'll die before you can ever become an adult."

My hands tightened into fists. *And you could die right now.*

A hand grabbed the nape of my neck, and I knew Urte was holding me back. He was the only one who could sense my actions, even before I did. "Fighting won't get us anywhere."

"Eric doesn't respond to anything else," Luthicer said, dwelling on my human name, before he faced my father. "And I can see where he gets it from."

My father tensed, and I half-expected Urte to abandon my side in order to hold my father back. Instead, my father held his ground, and he grumbled, "What's your point, Luthicer?"

"Shoman needs to take responsibility for his actions—"

"What actions?" I screamed, and Luthicer chucked a piece of metal at me.

In reflex, my fingers snatched it from the air, and I looked down. The dark circle was engraved with a willow tree, and I knew the dark liquid held inside was meant for me.

Camille. My free hand slapped against my sternum. My necklace was missing.

"I found it by the river," Luthicer said, folding his long arms.

My father's eyes lingered on my hand. "Tell me it isn't yours," he said, but I couldn't speak. It must have fallen off in flight.

"Of course it is his," Luthicer exclaimed. "I'd recognize my student's work anywhere, and Camille wouldn't give that to anyone but Eric."

Urte shook his head. "Camille could've dropped it."

Luthicer laughed. "Why would Camille need a remedy? A little Light power doesn't affect her," he said, gloating in my silence. "If you don't remember, Urte, that's why she was assigned as Eric's guard in the first place. She can stand up to either power. Eric cannot."

"Camille could've been delivering it," my father said, and Luthicer shook his boney finger.

"You're missing the point, Bracke," he said. "If she was out delivering it, she wasn't guarding your son, and his presence is unaccounted for."

"That's not Camille's fault." I broke through the conversation, but Luthicer wouldn't silence.

"She's your guard," he said. "It's her fault if you get attacked and she isn't there to help you." Suddenly, Luthicer was inches from my face, his Light energy pulsating against my skin. "Do you understand what would happen to us if you died?"

"I won't die."

"According to whom?" he asked, tilting his face. "The prophecy? It only promises our kind's survival if you live up to the battle, let alone make it to the battle." He paused, and his dark eyes flashed white. "Even you have to know that the Light is searching for you, hoping to kill you before you even get the chance to defend yourself."

"I can fight, Luthicer."

He shook his head. "How do you expect to defeat Darthon when you can't even withstand my powers?" he asked, referring to his previous test. "I'm a half-breed, Shoman. A half-breed! I'm not even close to Darthon's power level—"

"Darthon's my age," I said, relying on facts. "He can't be much stronger than me."

"Is that what you're depending on?" Luthicer's voice tore against his throat. "Is that the first descendant's battle plan?"

Even though I was stronger than any shade my age, I'd

always be hopeless to the elders. I was still weaker than the Light, and I knew it. Lights could practice their powers all day long, while shades were constricted to night. I had less time to master my strength, and Darthon, undoubtedly, would use time against me.

Luthicer sighed shakily and stepped back, dusting off his shirt. "Now," he said. "Just tell us who you were with, so we can carry out the necessary punishments."

I locked eyes with the ground. "I was by myself," I said.

"Camille's already in solitary," Luthicer said, and my heart slammed against my ribs. "Your lies won't protect her."

"I'm not lying," I said. "Your punishments are for nothing."

Luthicer's black eyes waved over me, and he opened his mouth, his lip curling, but he turned away. "I'm done here," he said, lingering in the shadows that grew around him. "I'll be spending my last living months studying the prophecy; maybe there's another hero who will prevent our doom."

With that, he was gone, and Urte slammed his hand against the wall. "Don't listen to him, Shoman," he said, panting. "Luthicer is stuck in his own world; he always has been."

I didn't respond, and my father's blue eyes searched mine. "Were you out with Camille and Pierce last night?" he asked, and I sighed.

"I've already told you I wasn't."

My father looked away, and Urte grabbed his beard. "Did you just lie to us?" he asked, and I gaped at them before Urte hung his head. "They already told us, Shoman. I knew you'd lie to Luthicer to protect them, but—"

"You can't lie to us," my father said. "And you can't be so irresponsible."

"It was my fault," I managed, holding my expression steady. "I convinced them to go out last night. I needed a break. I didn't mean to cause problems."

My father's blue eyes glided over every curve of my face, every line and freckle. His forehead wrinkled, exposing a vein. "What kind of father am I to not be able to read my son's face?"

"A good one," I said. "You've trained me well, and I will

prove it to Luthicer."

He shook his head. "You need to prove it to everyone."

"So I will," I said, pocketing my remedy. I'd find another string for it. "I'll wear my necklace, so I'm safe."

"You're safe as long as Camille is with you," my father said, tearing my recent freedom away. Camille would never leave my side again.

"But I won't get hurt—"

My father held his hand up. "I don't want you to speak; I want you to listen," he said, pacing through his office. "I know this is a hard time for you. With all the stresses—Luthicer, Camille, Mindy, the prophecy—I would rebel too," he paused and shook his head. "But it's my job to lead you to success, and, if you fail, it's because I failed, not you."

"But—"

I got the hand again. "The Marking of Change is inevitable, and to expect a seventeen-year-old to fulfill such a destiny is treachery in itself," he said, rubbing his forehead. "Know that you're my son, Eric, but don't forget that you're Shoman as well."

"And which one comes first?" I asked.

He sighed. "I think you know that answer."

"Shoman?" I guessed, rage suffocating my leftover energy.

Urte and my father were silent.

"Of course he's most important," I said, stomping toward the door. I shifted and fell into my human form, yanking the door open.

Urte grabbed my shoulder. "Our lives depend on that prophecy, and our future depends on you. I wish there was another way, Eric—I really wish there was—but there isn't."

"You better hope Luthicer proves you wrong," I said, shrugging past him and out the door. I didn't want to come back. I wouldn't.

Seventeen

Eric

MY POWERS SIZZLED AS IF BLOOD COULD BOIL. SHADOWS clung to my arms and legs, and blue sparks escaped my curled fist. I punched a tree, and the bark broke my skin. The injury healed before I even pulled away, shaking my hand.

"Shoman!" The nameless shade leapt back.

I'd met her in the forest, even though the elders were probably watching me. It didn't matter. They'd taken my chances of freedom away. I wouldn't be able to see her anymore, and she'd get caught eventually. We both would.

"What is wrong with you?" she asked, and I shrugged her off.

"We have to stop this," I said, and her worried expression crumbled into a glare.

"What are you talking about?"

"You heard me," I said. "We can't do this anymore."

"Why not?" She jumped next to me and grabbed my arm. "What happened?"

My jaw rocked back and forth. *Could I tell her?* It wasn't as if I could lose anymore. They'd even taken Camille away from me. She was my guard, and she was in solitary because of me. I knew what solitary entailed. Your powers were stripped, and you were left to insanity. A shade—not even a light—couldn't handle being completely human for very long. It was too unnatural.

"Something happened," I said, feeling the words as they slowly fell off my lips. "And it wasn't good."

"Did the elders test you again?"

"The elders," I growled, desperately trying to control my anger. "I despise them—all of them."

"Let's walk," she said, and I nodded, stomping by her side as she moved through the trees. We wouldn't be flying tonight, and, at this rate, we'd never fly again.

In silence, we walked through the forest, curling past the darkness, and strolled along the river. The full moon reflected off the trickling water, and I gazed at the nature that had become home to me. The shelter was no longer comforting and home definitely wasn't, yet the place we met every night soothed my rage. My emotions—that weren't allowed to exist—were alive again here.

"They don't think I'm good enough to fight," I said.

"But you are."

"It doesn't matter."

"Don't take this the wrong way," she said, stringing out her words. "But if you're this stressed out, why don't you become a guard?"

Because I don't have a choice. "I can't."

"Why?"

I groaned, falling backward to sit. "It isn't that simple."

"Make it that simple," she said, slowly sitting next to me. "Explain it to me." She laid her hand on my knee, and I stared at her petite fingers. They seemed so familiar—then again, we'd been seeing one another for weeks now. She was familiar. She was my friend.

"I can't."

She tapped her nails along my knee. "When you started training me, you told me I couldn't be afraid—of anything," she said. "Yet you're afraid to speak."

My neck nearly snapped as I turned to stare at her. She smiled, but the ends of her lips twitched. She was nervous. "You'll have to tell me eventually," she said, and I shook my head.

"I won't ever get the chance."

Her hand returned to her lap, and her shaky fingertips fiddled with the ends of her hair. "Why do you keep saying that?" she whispered.

My shoulders tensed. "Because it's the truth."

"I can help—"

"You're weaker than me," I grumbled, unsure of my words. She was more powerful than any shade I'd ever met; she only needed to control it. "How do you expect to help?"

"With your training—"

"My training is nothing compared to theirs," I said, ignoring her timid tone. "Everything we've done is useless; don't you see that?"

Her face scrunched up, and her eyes became glossy with unshed tears. "You're just being mean now," she said. She shook her head and her black hair matted to her face as tears slipped over her eyelashes. "You said I could meet the Dark. You said I could be somebody."

I reached out to touch her, but she moved away. My chest sunk, and I sighed. "I'm sorry," I said. "But I lied."

She blinked, barely meeting my eyes. "About what?"

"You," I said, knowing I had to admit to my faults. "But mainly them—they don't accept outsiders; they kill them."

Her tears ceased. "What?"

My jaw ached. "They'll figure you were abandoned for a reason," I said, sickened by the ways of my kind. "They wouldn't even give you a chance to explain."

"But I can explain—"

"You haven't even explained it to me," I pointed out, and she opened her mouth, but I stopped her. "And I don't want you to. It won't make a difference now."

She shook her head. "I don't understand this."

"You don't want to," I said. "Trust me."

Her lips thinned into a white line. "Fine," she said, jumping to her feet. I mirrored her, but she stomped away, turning around abruptly. She walked back as I conjured up words, but she lifted her hand and smacked my face.

My neck twisted, and my cheek burned. Her coarse breathing filled my ears, and I turned back, stunned. "What the hell was that for?" I asked, my voice wavering.

"You're like everyone else," she said, pressing her finger against my chest. "I'm trying to help you, and all you do is blow me off like I'm nothing."

I grabbed her hand, and she tried to pull away, but I wouldn't let her. "You aren't nothing," I said. "You're the only one who's helped me—"

"Yet you gave up on me!" Her face flushed, and she squirmed beneath my grasp. I wasn't even holding her that hard; she could get away if she wanted to. "I thought I finally had someone I could count on," she said, dropping her face as she stilled. "You're not the only one going through a hard time right now, Shoman; you never are. Why can't you understand that?"

My fingers loosened, but hers spread over my chest. I couldn't breathe.

"I didn't even know what I was until I met you," she said. "You told me I was okay; you helped me realize who I was again—what I was—and now I'm trying to repay you, and you won't let me."

Her words pummeled my stomach, and my eyes squeezed shut as I bent my face away. She was right, yet I couldn't tell her. I couldn't even stand up to her. I had pushed her away, just like everybody else, and she didn't deserve it. No one had.

"I should go," she said as her body heat dissipated. She stepped away. "I won't be back, so you don't have to worry about that."

I won't be back. Her words shuddered through me as she turned to go. Her footsteps along the ground felt like I'd fallen in the river and begun to drown. *No.* I wasn't ready to give up yet.

I raced behind her, but she quickened her speed. "Don't go," I said, leaping in front of her.

"Why not?" she spat.

"Because you would've been gone by now if you really wanted to," I said, knowing she could transport away and avoid my radar. After all, she'd done it before. "And I don't want you to," I added.

Her arms folded across her chest, and she dropped her gaze. "I wasn't the one ending it," she said.

"I know." I laid my hands on her small shoulders and bent down to catch her purple eyes. "And I'm sorry," I said, knowing she could feel my hands shake. "I really am."

Her lips quivered. "How do I know you mean it?"

"Trust me."

She shook her head. "I don't know if I can anymore, Shoman."

My chest fell. "Then I'll earn it again," I promised.

The words flew out of me in a way they never had before. They were uncontrollable and desperate, yet I didn't regret them. The emotions had taken over, and I knew why I was thrown off guard. For once, I was speaking the truth.

Her hand raised, and she wiped the tears from her eyes. They sparkled against her white skin. "You have an entire community, Shoman," she said, unable to speak loudly. "You don't need me—"

"I do," I said, and she stared. "I need you more than anything; you're the only one who's been here for me." My throat tightened. "And you're the only one I've wanted to be there for in a long time. I do need you."

I didn't care about the elders or the danger they said I was in. I didn't want to let her go. I couldn't let her go.

"Please," I said. "Try to understand that."

"I do, Shoman," she said, and her hand touched mine. My heartbeat slowed. "I feel your pain, even when we're not together; I feel everything you go through." Her fingertips swayed over my cold skin. "I don't know why, but I'm always worried about you." She bit her lip and sighed. "You told me never to lose my concentration—and I haven't—but it's nearly impossible not to when I'm around you."

"But—"

She slapped her hand over my mouth, but she smiled. "I'm not an elder, and I may not be a great shade, but I know you're capable, and the Dark is ignorant if they think otherwise," she said. "I don't know everything about your situation, but I believe in you, Shoman—even if I don't want to." She smirked, and a half-laugh escaped her. "I only want you to believe in me too."

I froze as she wrapped her arms around my neck and pulled me into an embrace. She smelled like the sky. "Let me help you," she whispered against my neck. "Let me be here for you like you are for me."

"You already are here for me," I said, slowly hugging her against my thundering heart. Could she feel it? I couldn't feel anything else.

I didn't know what it was that I felt, but I knew one thing. She felt—right—and the only thing I wanted was to feel right for her.

EIGHTEEN

Jessica

I T WAS MONDAY MORNING, AND I KNEW EXACTLY WHERE HE'D BE. I walked up the steep hill, and my eyes glided over the willow tree as I approached. The narrow-leaved branches swung in the wind, and I tied my curls into a ponytail before I reached the top. I wasn't in the mood for a fight, but fights weren't always conveniently scheduled.

I trudged over the grass, hoping my adrenaline would appear, but I froze when I saw him. Eric sat beneath it, his body leaning against the trunk like it was his personal La-Z-Boy. His arms were propped behind his head, and his hair was matted to the bark as he closed his eyes and listened to his music.

"Welborn!"

He didn't move, and I hesitated stepping closer. He was asleep.

His shaggy brown hair blew against his forehead, and his chest rose slowly as he snored beneath his breath. His fingertips twitched in his lap, and his eyelashes batted as his eyes moved beneath his eyelids. He was dreaming.

I sighed and sat in front of him, unable to leave. I'd come this far, hadn't I?

My gaze shifted above him, and I studied the elongated shrub. The branches were slender, but the trunk was toughened from years of weather. Even in the unusual climate, the leaves were vibrantly green, and I wondered why it was the only willow tree I'd seen in the Midwest, let alone Hayworth. The plant was out of its usual environment, yet this one showed no signs of dying.

It thrived.

"Beautiful; isn't it?"

I startled, gaping at Eric as he tilted his face, staring at me with his emerald eyes. "You're awake," I said, and he smiled.

"Looks that way."

"I didn't mean to wake you up," I said.

"Better you wake me up than stare at me," he said, and my cheeks burned. He chuckled, gathering his things. "It was a joke."

"Right."

He glanced over, but he was no longer smiling. "I'm sorry I didn't show up Friday," he said. "I honestly tried, but something came up."

My fingernails dug into the grass. "I didn't show anyway," I lied, and he turned his face away, but not enough. I saw his smile.

"Whatever you say, Jessica."

He used my full name again, and I tensed. *What was with this guy?*

"When do you want to reschedule?" he said. "It's due next week."

My heart stopped. "Reschedule?"

He turned to me and raised his brow. "Unless you didn't want to."

"No," I said quickly, practically spitting on him. "I want to."

"Are you available tonight?" he asked, standing as the warning bell rang. "We can meet at my house."

His house?

"Unless that's intrusive—"

"It's not," I said, unable to stand with him. I was afraid I'd fall over in shock.

He nodded, reaching into his bag to pull out paper. I stopped him. "I know where you live," I said, and his brow rose as he smirked.

"Maybe you were staring at me," he said, chuckling.

"Robb showed me." The words left before I could stop them.

He looked away. "I see."

"So how about seven?" I asked, hoping to change the subject. This time, I sprang to my feet, and Eric's eyes glided over my every move. He was so intense.

"Sounds good."

"Jess!" Crystal's shout shattered over the courtyard, but only Eric turned to look toward her.

"Looks like you have to go," he said.

"Yeah," I agreed, but I was unable to tear away from him. "I guess I do."

He turned away from the school and started toward the street, but I shouted after him. "Where are you going?" I asked, pointing behind me. "School's that way."

He walked backward downhill as if he practiced it. "I need to get stuff done, if I'm going to be able to help you tonight," he said, spinning back around and ending the conversation.

Stuff?

"Jess," Crystal panted as she finished her climb. "What are you doing up here—" Then she stopped and raised her dark brow, watching Eric as he neared the street. An old BMW pulled up, and he got in the passenger seat, driving away before I could fathom his absence.

"That was Welborn, wasn't it?" she asked, apparently as shocked as I was.

I nodded. "And I'm going to his house tonight."

Crystal dug her manicured nails into my arm. "You're joking."

"No," I said. "We made plans."

"What kind of plans?"

"What do you think?" I pulled away from her and stormed down the hill. Her gossip was beginning to bother me.

"Eric Welborn doesn't make plans with anybody," she said, sliding over the morning dew after me. "I wouldn't go."

"Why?"

"Because he's weird—"

"Let it go, Crystal," I said, rolling my eyes. "I'm going whether you like it or not; he's my science partner."

She folded her arms and glared at the school. "Good luck with that."

"Thanks," I said. "But I don't need it."

Nineteen

S HE WAS REALLY PRETTY, AND HER HEAD CAME UP TO MY CHIN. HER hair was nearly the same length as mine, but it was lighter than the average shade. She'd always hated it, but I envied her unusual appearance in our Dark world full of practical clones. I'd been attracted to her since the Naming, despite knowing her for years. Abby—or Hannah in her human form—was my girlfriend, and she had been for two years.

"Can we go back to the shelter?" she asked, following me through the forest. "It's cold."

"I know," I said, scraping my new tennis shoes through the mud. "But I want to show you something."

She sighed. "Can't you show me inside?"

I turned around and grabbed her freezing hands. "I learned something new today."

Her blue eyes squinted. "So? We learn something new in training every day."

"I didn't learn this in training." I said, grinning. "I learned this all by myself."

"What are you talking about?" she asked, tilting her head, and I dropped her hands, so I could step back.

"Just watch," I said, clenching my hand into a small fist.

Between us, air ripped and hissed, and wind spun around my torso like Saran Wrap. My eyelids shuddered as an electric blue sword lurched from the shadows and into my grasp.

Abby leapt backward as I gripped the handle, the blade spiraling into a jet-black color. My feet dug into the soft ground as the weight pushed me down, and the tip quavered as I supported the heavy sword in my fifteen-year-old hands.

"Is that—?"

"It's the first descendant sword," I said, gazing at the power in front of me—the only power that was unique to me. "Beautiful, isn't it?"

———◆———

My dreams fluttered away when I opened my eyes. The morning burned my eyes, and I sat up, freezing my movements. Beneath the shade of the willow tree, Jessica Taylor's bright blue eyes blinked as she stared at me. "You're awake."

"Looks that way."

"I didn't mean to wake you up," she said, and I breathed. *How long had she been here?*

"Better you wake me up than stare at me," I said, and her face went scarlet. I couldn't help but laugh. "It was a joke." *Kind of.*

"Right." Her voice was strained and quiet.

I looked up, fighting a frown. Guilt consumed me. Between how I treated her and the nameless shade, I didn't deserve forgiveness. I needed to apologize, but how could I?

Oh, hey, Jessica. My guard and best friend of the Dark— this supernatural community you know nothing about—threatened to use you against me, and I had to leave if I was going to have any freedom at all. My bad.

"I'm sorry I didn't show up Friday," I said, allowing the truth to take over again. "I honestly tried, but something came up."

"I didn't show anyway," she lied, and I had to hide my face. She was a horrible liar.

"Whatever you say, Jessica." I didn't want to discuss the truth any more than I had to. Plus, I'd have to mention Robb, and I definitely didn't want to discuss him. "When do you want to reschedule?" I asked. "It's due next week."

"Reschedule?"

I stared at her. "Unless you don't want to." *Wasn't this project a big deal or something?*

"No," she said, straightening up. Her fingers dug into her jeans. She was an anxiety attack waiting to happen. "I want to."

"Are you available tonight?" I asked, climbing to my feet. My entire body burned from the dream. I had to get out of here. "We can meet at my house."

Jessica didn't respond, and I heard her breathing cease. I turned to her, and her mouth hung open. I'd seen this reaction once or twice from Mindy—generally, when I took a moment to talk to her.

Suddenly, I was the tense one. *Was my house too intimate?* I didn't want her to think I was asking her out, because I wasn't. I definitely wasn't. I only wanted to avoid public.

I found the words. "Unless that's intrusive—"

"It's not," she said, and I reached into my bag for directions. "I know where you live," she added, and I got whiplash turning to her.

"Maybe you were staring at me." *And stalking me.*

"Robb showed me." Her face paled after she spoke.

Of course he did. "I see."

"So how about seven?" Jessica asked, finally standing. I relaxed, happy she wasn't sitting anymore. I felt strange looking down on her, but she was still shorter than I was—by a lot.

"Sounds good."

"Camille?" I sent out a telepathic message, hoping my guard was out of solitary, and I felt her Light energy bubble through my brain.

"What's wrong?" She had felt my dream.

"I'm at the willow," I responded, knowing that was all I had to say. She'd be here any minute. She was never far away—especially now that Luthicer caught us.

Crystal's high-pitch shout rumbled my eardrums, and I winced, glaring in her direction. Did these kids ever leave Jessica alone? "Looks like you have to go," I said, and Jessica frowned.

"Yeah." She bit her lip. "I guess I do."

I turned away from her before I was overcome by my thoughts. I actually wanted to ask her what was wrong. Apparently, I was acting strange too.

"Where are you going?" Jessica's voice trailed after me, and I forced myself to walk forward. "School's that way."

I barely looked at her. "I need to get stuff done, if I'm going to be able to help you tonight," I said. *Like training.* I had hours of it to complete, and I couldn't avoid it any longer. I had to go.

TWENTY

"YOU HAVE TO CONCENTRATE, SHOMAN," URTE BELLOWED OVER the explosion as I slammed into the white wall, gasping for breath.

My black T-shirt was shredded, and my skin was burning. I was already drenched in sweat, and it stung my eyes. The simulation room was kicking my ass.

I pushed off the wall and leapt to the side as a beam of light struck where I'd been standing. The wall shattered, dust flying over my arms, and I cursed, dodging another attack. My muscles strained against the abrupt movements.

Minutes before, I was acing my fight with Urte. I was quicker and stronger than he was, but his light replica was beating me every time. Her realness was eerie. She was tall, and her striking white hair blinded me. Her dark eyes were hollow, yet they followed me as she lurked from one corner of the room to another. Even for a light, she was impossibly flawless. She easily dodged anything I threw at her.

Urte warned me she would appear real, but I hadn't expected the illusion to be so—physical. When she touched me, I felt her. When she attacked, I heard her breath. When she moved, her hair followed. She reacted differently every time, and her shadow followed her wherever she went. Nothing about her seemed artificial.

A bright light filled the training room, and I rolled, attempting to avoid her attack, but my foot caught the tile. The blast smacked my body against the ground, and my teeth clenched as I wheezed, trying to breathe. This was ridiculous.

"Your endurance is too weak," Urte said, and I lifted my arms, blocking her endless assaults.

"You're not the one who's been fighting for two hours," I shouted back, knowing he was safely standing aside.

"No one knows how long your battle will be, Shoman," he said. "It could take seconds or years."

"Thanks for the reminder," I retorted, feeling her heat sizzle behind me.

I spun on my heel, grabbed her hand, and tossed her to the ground before she could blink. At least my reflexes were faster than hers were.

When she leapt up, I soared backward, twisting to the left and the right as she followed my tracks. We moved side to side, and, for once, my movements were ahead. Her eyes flashed, light vibrating off her tanned skin, and she growled when she repeatedly missed. Even a simulation could lose her concentration.

I used it to my advantage, and, within seconds, her face smacked against the ground. Her white hair sprawled around her, her arms straining to lift her body off the floor. I towered above her, unable to move.

This was my chance to end it all—to win the battle. I was tired and sweaty. All I wanted was to end the fighting, but I could only stand above her.

Urte sighed. "You need to be able to kill, Shoman," he said.

"I can," I said. She sat on her knees, but I only kicked her over, watching her squirm again. She could barely stand, let alone hurt me back. She wasn't even real, but I remained still.

"I don't think you can," Urte said, beginning to walk forward. He was going to end the simulation.

"I can—"

"Then prove it to me."

My jaw locked—the only part of my body that moved—and the light sprang to her feet. Light exploded into my chest, and I flew across the room, slamming into the furthest wall.

"See what happens when you hesitate?" Urte asked, and I blinked, watching the simulation walk toward me.

I spit blood out of my mouth and ignored my arm. It was bleeding. Overlooking the minor pain, I raised my hand and shot a blast of Dark energy her way. She fell backward, sprawling across the floor, and I wiped the blood from my mouth.

"What's the second descendant's name?" Urte asked, and I glared.

"I thought you wanted concentration."

"You also need to be able to think at the same time; you need to plan out strategies and understand what you're facing," he said, folding his arms. "What's the second descendant's name?"

I leapt to my feet, allowing shadows to curl around me. "Darthon," I said, focusing on the light as she stomped toward me. She shot near my legs, fast despite her injuries, and I mimicked her movements.

"Name three things the Light is capable of," Urte continued, and I growled.

"Illusion, poison, tracking." I fought the girl, avoiding her eyes. "And Darthon has my sword power." My words caused me to shudder. My dream consumed my concentration, and her nails dug into my arm. I tossed her away, forcing the images of Abby out.

"Name three ways you can fight back," Urte said, without scorning my mistake.

"Shadows, fly—sword." I lost my balance and tumbled to the ground, using the angle to slash at the girl's feet. She collapsed, and I pinned her, still thinking of Urte's question. "Unless it's before my birthday," I said. "Then I need to get help or escape."

Anger devoured my conscience. I had to run. I knew the rule, but the logic promised my futility. I was Shoman. I was supposed to be an undefeatable killing machine—someone whose existence fated a better future—but I couldn't until the designated time. If Darthon—a boy who hadn't asked to be born Darthon—was truly evil, I didn't understand why I couldn't end his life now.

Could I even do it? I doubted it. Evil or not, I was murdering another, and he'd be my age. He probably went to my school. Almost certainly, I knew him, and I would watch his short-lived life be mourned by his loved ones. Neither of us asked to be born descendants, yet I'd be rewarded with his death, and we couldn't prevent that. No one could.

"Shoman," Urte was quiet. "You need to control your anger."

I looked down at the girl I held on the floor. She was practically lifeless, but my vicious grip allowed her torture. I hadn't stopped beating her, yet I didn't notice.

I stretched my arm out, extending my hand, and my sword slashed through the air. I could kill. I wrapped my hand around the grip and slashed at the girl, but she disappeared. Around us, the broken walls and cracked floors glossed over, and I stared at the pristine training room. It showed no signs of my battle, and my sword dissipated.

"What the hell was that for?" I punched the ground. "I was going to do it."

Urte frowned. "That anger isn't healthy, Shoman."

My knuckles were white. "If anger will help me defeat Darthon, then I'll use it."

"And they will use it against you," he said, kneeling by my side.

I shook the hair from my eyes. "They can't use my emotions against me unless they poison me," I said, gripping my remedy. "And Camille stopped that."

"What happens when it runs out?"

"It won't." I stood up, avoiding Urte's green eyes. I stormed away, unable to argue with him, and grabbed the nearest water bottle. I chugged it, quenching my thirst, and panted. This was my third simulation of the day—each lasting longer than the one before—and I knew it was near dinnertime. Jessica would be at my house soon. I wanted to go, but I couldn't—not without completing my day's goal, killing.

"Why'd you stop me?" I asked Urte, knowing his answer. He didn't think I was ready.

"Shoman—"

"Do you ever think I'll be ready?" I asked, knowing he'd avoid the topic.

He sighed, grabbing his bristles. "With enough training."

I traced my finger along the side of the bottle, and condensation dripped down my skin like tears. I tore my eyes away. "I don't know if I can win—not in a year."

"You will be ready," Urte said, suddenly by my side. "Our community will prepare you."

"In time for December?" It was only nine months away. "It's not a lot of time."

"It isn't," he agreed. "But you have the entire summer. You won't be in school, and you can dedicate more time to training." He smiled. "It'll be fun."

"Fun isn't the word I'd use."

Urte chuckled. "I suppose you're right," he said. "But, as your strength grows, your abilities will, and training will get easier."

"I hope so," I said, walking toward the doorway. I picked up my bag and turned to my trainer. "Don't set up another one," I said, knowing we'd train through the night if I didn't leave. "I have homework tonight, and it can't be late."

His expression curled. "You act like these sessions are nothing."

My shoulders dropped. "If I don't do this, I'll fail this class, and then I'll be in summer school." *Maybe a lie.* "I can't train if I'm doing that."

Urte sighed. "Very well," he said. "Go."

"Thanks, Urte," I said, forcing my grin down as I began leaving, but Urte grabbed my arm.

"I'll take you home," he said. "I have to talk to your father anyway."

So much for a victory.

TWENTY-ONE

Jessica

I CLUTCHED MY MOTHER'S CAR KEYS AND HESITATED AT THE WALK-way. Welborn's house was blanketed with so much black-ness that it appeared to be a shadow even though I was several feet away from the front door. The weathered wood was black, and curving lamps twisted around the doorframe, creaking as the wind pushed against them. Even the curtained windows were dark, barely allowing the golden glow from in-side to escape.

Why did he have to live in a place like this?

I shook my head as I ran toward the front door, but some-thing brushed my shoulder, and I yelped. It was a branch. *Get ahold of yourself, Jess. It was nothing.*

"Hello, young lady—"

The man's voice split the air, and I jumped, nearly drop-ping my stuff. When I turned around, ready to defend myself, the older man blinked his pitch-black eyes. "Can I help you?" he asked.

I dropped my hands, my cheeks burning. "Is Welborn—er—Eric here?" I stuttered, failing to control my composure. My heart was still pounding. What had gotten into me?

The man raised his brow, and the golden light glided over his pale skin like water. "He's in his room," he said, pointing his thumb over his shoulder. "Come on in."

I nodded, grateful to be escaping the ghostly yard. You'd

think it was a cemetery. "Thanks," I said, removing my shoes in the entryway as I gaped at the inside of the home.

It was golden. The rich, dark-wooded furniture had golden designs traced over them, and a yellow kitchen extended over the first floor. Plants crawled up the wall like ivy, and, although the house was dim, the gold glittered vibrantly—like a hundred stars in the mist of fog.

"Who's here, George?" I heard the other man as he appeared at the top of the stairs. His shoulders rose as his brown eyes crawled over me, and I fought the urge to leave.

"Eric's science partner," George, the man who let me in, answered as he jingled his keys in the air. "I'm leaving for the night. I haven't fed the kids yet, and Jonathon should be getting home soon."

The other man barely lifted his hand as he waved. "We'll finish our discussion later."

George nodded, ducking outside. The wind creaked as the ancient foundation shifted beneath us, and I shivered, feeling the air dissipate from my skin. Everything about this house was cold.

Atop the stairs, the man cleared his throat. "I'm Eric's father," he said.

I managed a smile. "You have a lovely home."

His brow rose, and he shifted from foot to foot. "Thank you," he said, drumming his fingers against the banister. "—uh—" He didn't know my name.

"Jess," I said. "Jess Taylor."

"I haven't heard that name before," he said, tilting his face into the shadows. "Are you new to Hayworth?"

I nodded as a redheaded woman appeared behind him. Her brown eyes widened as they landed on me. I tore my eyes away from her. "I moved here at the beginning of the semester," I said, and his jaw locked as Eric's so often did.

"What are your parents' names?"

"Oh, stop pestering the poor girl," the woman said, smacking him on the arm. He grumbled, but she beamed in my direction. "I didn't know Eric was having a friend over," she said, waving me up the stairs. "Do you want a drink or some food? I could heat up some lasagna if you're hungry."

I relaxed. Why couldn't Eric be like her? "I'm fine, but thanks."

"I insist," she said. "My son, Noah, has refused anything but sweets all week; I'd love to feed someone real food."

Eric's father laid his hand on her shoulder. "Go heat it up, Mindy," he said, smiling for the first time since I walked in. Immediately, she beamed and bounced into the kitchen.

Mr. Welborn's eyes hovered over me. "Jess," he said, and his intensity startled me. "Please make yourself at home."

I nodded, but I had to force myself to walk upstairs. I passed Mr. Welborn quickly, and he leaned against the wall, watching me. "So—science partner, huh?"

Nodding again, I felt as if I had no words for the man. My gaze dropped, and I stared at my mismatched socks. "We're starting our project today," I managed.

"You don't do it in class?"

"No," I said, understanding Eric's attitude. "It's homework—for home."

"Does it take up a lot of time?" he asked, and I shrugged. "Why's Eric your science partner?" His interrogation continued. "I doubt you chose him."

My gut twisted, and I gaped at the older man. *He did not just say that about his own son.* But he did—and his expression was blank, emotionless about his callous words.

"The teacher assigned us together," I said, and he ran a hand through his thinning hair.

"Interesting."

"I guess."

Mindy, with perfect timing, entered the room, handing me a plate of lasagna. "Here you go, dear," she said, practically sparkling with happiness. "If you don't like it, don't feel like you have to eat it."

"Mindy, honey," Mr. Welborn spoke gently. "Jess should probably start working with Eric."

"Oh, of course." Mindy lightly slapped her forehead with

her manicured hand. "Silly me, nattering on like there's no tomorrow."

Mr. Welborn chuckled beneath his breath and pointed down a hallway. "Eric's room is the first one on the right."

"Thanks," I said, rushing past the couple before they could start talking again.

The first door was practically next to the kitchen. It was so close that I was surprised Eric hadn't come out to answer the door, or at least interceded on his father's interrogation. Then again, he was Eric Welborn. He probably didn't care. Or think it was strange.

I knocked, sighing heavily. *How could a parent be so cold?*

"Come in." Eric's voice broke through the door, and I opened it, stepping into his dim bedroom.

His floor was spotless, and his computer played soft rock music in the corner. A slideshow of pictures flickered across the screen, and there was Eric. Standing by his closet. His back turned to me. Shirtless.

I stumbled backward, hitting the wall. "I—I'm sorry," I sputtered, averting my gaze from Eric's half-naked body.

He turned around and tilted his head, staring at my alarmed self. I could see everything now. His stomach muscles, his broad shoulders, his toned structure.

"For what?" he asked, pulling a black T-shirt over his head.

"I—uh—" I stammered, forcing the images out of my mind. I hadn't even considered Eric's appeal until now. *Why was he so fit?* "Never mind."

He shrugged, but his green eyes landed on my plate of food. "You going to eat that?"

I shook my head, unable to speak, and he took the plate from my hands. He dug into the lasagna like he hadn't eaten in days, and I stared at his desk. There was a full plate of lasagna completely untouched.

He followed my gaze and paused. "I don't like Mindy thinking I enjoy her cooking," he said, shoveling more lasagna into his mouth. "And I don't," he clarified. "I'm just starving."

"Mhmm," I hummed, raising my brow as he finished off

the meal in minutes.

"If they ask, you ate this," he said, laying the plate down.

"As long as we finish this project, I'm fine with that."

He smiled and shook his brown hair away from his eyes. "I didn't ditch you again, now did I?" I froze. "We'll finish," he promised, stretching out on his bed. He leaned over and pulled out a stack of papers from beneath his bed, and then he stared up at me. "Are you going to stand there all night?"

I gulped. "We're working in here?" I asked. "In your bedroom?" My parents would never allow a boy in my room, let alone one they just met.

Eric's brow rose. "What do you think will happen, Jess?"

Blood rushed to my cheeks as my stomach twisted. "Nothing," I said, sitting down next to him. As if on purpose, he scooted closer, and I almost fell off the bed. He laughed, and I snatched the papers away, trying not to twitch.

"What's so funny?" I asked, biting my lip.

"Nothing," he sang back, still laughing. "Let's just get to work."

"Fine by me," I said, staring at the papers. Every page was filled with information and thoroughly organized. My jaw hung open. "What's this?"

"About half of the project," he said, shrugging as he rested on his elbows. "I figured we'd need it done sooner or later."

"You did all of this—by yourself?"

He cocked his head to the side. "You sound doubtful, Ms. Taylor."

"I thought you were busy outside of school," I retorted, crossing my arms, and he shifted.

"Who said I wasn't?" This time, he was the one who sounded bitter. "It isn't all done, you know. We should work."

Geez. This guy was emotional.

"Right," I agreed, falling into silence as he opened the chemistry book in front of me. He worked on the graphs, while I wrote our paper, trying not to look at him. It was hard to ignore his aggravation; it was practically pulsating from him. His face scrunched into concentration, and his knuckles were white as he clutched his pencil. Even worse, his hands were bruised.

Cuts covered his exposed skin, and some of them bled. A large bandage covered a slit, and a tan support wrapped around his left wrist. Another one supported his elbow. It looked like he had gotten into a fight—a bad fight—but I hadn't even noticed until I got close to him.

"Accident," he muttered, and I sucked in breath. "Sorry if blood bothers you."

"It doesn't," I said, and Eric pushed himself up.

"You wouldn't stare if it didn't," he said, getting up and stepping over me. Quickly and without another word, he picked up his trashcan. Beneath his computer table, a blue light spread across the floor, and he left.

I leaned over, looking for the source of light, and froze when I realized it was a nightlight. *Eric Welborn was afraid of the dark? What. The. Hell.*

"Who are you?"

My neck snapped as I turned to the little boy. He had a round face, and his brown hair framed his face like Mindy's did. He couldn't have been older than ten.

I smiled. "I'm Jess."

"Noah."

"Are you Eric's little brother?"

Noah's pudgy face scrunched up. "Are you Eric's girlfriend?"

"No—"

"Then we have the same answer," he said, folding his arms. "Eric doesn't want a brother."

"Noah!" Eric rushed into the room and pulled the boy's shirt collar. "Get out of my room."

Noah stumbled, reaching for the door. "You can't make me."

"Oh, believe me, I can," Eric said, shoving him forcefully.

"You're hurting me," Noah whined, opening his mouth to scream, and Eric spun the boy around, grabbing his shoulders.

"Don't," he said. "You're too old to act that way."

Noah's mouth shut, and his eyes widened. "I just want to hang out."

Eric leaned over, grabbing a bag of cookies from beneath his bed. "I'll give you these if you leave us alone."

Noah grinned. "And?"

"And nothing," Eric said. "Take it or go hungry."

Noah snatched the bag of cookies. "It was great meeting you, Jess," he said, winking. *Ew.*

"Out," Eric said, and Noah left as Eric shut the door, locking it. He sighed heavily, leaning against the door, and shook his head. "Stepsiblings, huh?"

"He seemed nice enough to me," I said, and Eric sat down.

"Or annoying," he said. "The cookies should shut him up for a while." Eric moved across the room and replaced his trashcan. The blue light dissipated, but I couldn't help myself.

"Aren't you a little old to be sleeping with nightlights?"

Eric's lips pulled into a small smile. "Yeah," he said. "But I've had it since I was a kid." His shoulders tensed, and he breathed, returning to the bed. He lay down, placing his hands behind his head and closed his eyes. "My father always kept the porch light on until my mom got home—except she didn't make it home one night." He paused, and I held my breath. "I keep the light on now."

I fiddled with my hands in silence. Robb and Crystal had explained how she committed suicide when he was young, but, for some reason, I was still filled with shock. "What happened?"

He opened one of his eyes, but he didn't say anything.

My fingernails dug into my thighs. "You told me to ask you instead of gossip," I defended. "So I'm asking you."

"I wasn't silent, because I was surprised," he said, barely moving. "I was silent, because I don't have the answer."

He didn't know why she killed herself? "I'm sorry."

"I didn't ask for pity."

I cleared my throat, blinking. "So, Welborn—"

"Eric," he said, and I stared as he smiled. "You might as well call me Eric."

"So, Eric," I managed, feeling his name slip off my tongue.

"Why'd you go by Welborn anyway?"

"Why do you go by Jess?"

I shrugged, writing two sentences on my paper. "Didn't have much of a choice."

"Crystal?" he guessed, and my eyes widened. It was as if he knew everything about my life, yet I hadn't told him anything.

"Don't look so surprised, Jess," he chuckled. "I've known her since kindergarten, and Robb was my best friend."

I pointed at him. "Best friends?" I asked. "I knew you guys were friends, but—"

He nodded, continuing to laugh. *How was this so funny to him?*

"I've changed," he said. "A lot."

"Since the accident?" The words fell out, and Eric's brow darkened.

"I thought they told you about that," he said, running a hand through his hair. "Hannah Blake." His eyes fogged over as he stared at the ceiling, and my entire body tensed. "She was friends with all of us—my girlfriend actually."

I bit my lip. *Why was he telling me this?*

"She died in a car wreck my freshman year; her parents did, too," he said, frowning. "I was the only one who walked away, and I didn't have a scratch on me."

Eric paused as he tapped his pencil against his forehead, his brown hair waving in front of his eyes. "I'm sorry," he said. "I shouldn't talk about this—"

"It's okay," I said, swallowing my confusion. "I'm glad you can talk about it."

His brow crumbled, and he tilted his head. "You're a good person, Jessica," he said, and I smiled.

"It's Jess, remember?"

He shook his head and cocked a grin. "I think Jessica is a beautiful name," he said, and his emerald eyes locked onto mine. "Would you mind if I called you that?"

"Do I have a choice?" I asked, and he laughed.

"Of course not."

"I'd rather be called Jess."

His eyes lit up at the challenge. "Jessica is better."

I sighed, my chest sinking. "Jessica it is then."

"You didn't have a choice, Jessica," he reminded me, and I dug my pencil into the notebook in front of me.

"Do you purposely try to piss me off?"

"I don't know," he sang. "Is it working?"

I glared. "What do you think?"

He smiled. "Yes."

"You'd be correct."

He laughed, hitting his knee, and I shook my head at him.

"You're one interesting kid, Eric."

He raised his brow and focused on me. "So I've heard."

I sighed at his confidence, wondering how he could go from hating me to confiding in me. He seemed completely comfortable with himself, yet I felt as if I was starting to lose my confidence. He was beginning to make me nervous.

"Can we—?"

"Yeah, yeah," he said, sitting up on his knees as he rested against my arm. "We can finish this project."

TWENTY-TWO

Eric

I ROLLED ONTO MY SIDE AND STARED AT THE WALL. IT'D BEEN TWO hours since Jessica left, yet I couldn't stop thinking about our conversation. I'd told her so much—too much—and I had no clue as to what had gotten into me. The only girl I told anything to was the nameless shade, and Jessica wasn't her—to my knowledge.

Anyone could be anybody. Even Mindy could've been a shade or a light, but we had no way of knowing. It was one of the main reasons I stopped being friends with Crystal and Robb. What if they ended up being someone I had to kill? I didn't want to think about that.

My door creaked open, and I listened to soft footsteps tiptoe across my carpet. I sighed. "Get out of my room, Noah."

He groaned. "How'd you hear me?"

Because I'm a shade. "You're loud," I said, flipping over to face him. The brunette boy blinked his brown eyes and clutched the half-empty bag of cookies against his chest. I sighed again. "What do you want?"

"I thought we could share the last few," he said, his cheeks ruddy.

"Not now, Noah."

His eyes squinted. "Jim said you had to." He referred to my father—his stepfather—by his nickname. His name was James.

I sat up, running a hand through my hair. Ever since I'd almost lost my friendship with the nameless shade, I'd been trying harder to sympathize with my stepfamily, but I wasn't in the mood. "I'm sleeping."

"No, you're not."

"Noah," I practically growled. "Please. Leave me alone."

"But I already did."

"Only when I gave you cookies," I pointed out, and he threw the remaining cookies on my bed.

"I don't want them anymore," he said, folding his pudgy arms.

"Fine," I said, refusing to touch them. "But that doesn't mean I'm hanging out with you."

"Then I'm not leaving you alone next time Jess comes over," he threatened, and I fought a laugh.

"She isn't coming back."

"Yes, she is," he said, raising his little brows. "You were practically drooling over her. I heard Mom and Jim talking about it."

"What did you just say?" I asked, sitting up, and his brown eyes widened.

"Mom and Jim—"

"Before that."

He tilted his head. "You were drooling over Jess."

"I wasn't drooling," I argued, only thinking of the girl I was training. She was my every other thought. I'd never felt so strange before—so vulnerable—yet I trusted her. I couldn't explain it, but it bothered me.

"There you go again," Noah said, smirking. "You haven't had that stupid look on your face since Hannah."

"Don't." I held up my hand and glared. "Don't talk about her." Hannah deserved to be remembered by her Dark name—Abby—not by humans who didn't even know her.

"Sorry." Noah's face paled. "I just thought—"

"You thought nothing," I growled. I hated my stepfamily.

Noah dug his foot into my carpet. "I wish I had a cool older brother like Johnny," he muttered. Johnny was his best friend. Just as annoying too.

"I'm not your brother," I said, waiting for him to leave, but he stood his ground.

"We have the same parents."

"No, we don't," I said, cringing. "Your mother married my jackass father; we're stepbrothers."

He frowned at my curse. "Still has the word 'brother' in it."

"That's it." I pointed to my door, and it sprang open, reacting to my powers. It slammed against the wall, and Noah leapt into the air. "Get out."

In a millisecond, he was gone, running past the door, screaming. I waved my hand, and my door slammed shut and locked. Then, I waited. My dim room illuminated, adjusting to my shade powers, and my vision burned. Using my powers had disadvantages. My clock shone, and I squinted my eyes as the secondhand ticked loudly. If my calculations were correct, my father would burst in at any moment.

"Eric."

Wow. He was earlier than usual.

"Eric." My father pounded on my door, and the wood shook against the hinges. "Don't ignore me; open this door."

I leaned my back against the wall and shook my head. "Come on in."

The doorknob shook. "Unlock this door now."

"You unlock it," I tested him, knowing he could use his powers at any moment.

Shadows shifted from my floor, and my father appeared in a mist. His black eyebrows furrowed together as he slowly melted back into his human form. His brow was gray.

I smirked. "Mindy must be downstairs," I said, knowing he wouldn't have used them if she was anywhere near him.

"Don't talk like that," he said, waving his hand, and I felt the silence barrier cloud my bedroom. He didn't want his human family to hear our discussion. "Why don't you give them a chance?" he asked, continuing to raise his voice. "I know Mindy isn't your mother."

Duh.

"And you're not used to having a kid brother."

I don't want to get used to that either.

"But they've been around for a long time—"

"Time isn't everything," I said, meeting his gaze as I used my last year of life against him. "Time is short."

My father's expression faltered and he hung his head, running a hand through his balding hair. "Not this again."

"If I have to live with it every day," I started, straightening my posture. "I think you should at least have to listen to it."

"Fine," he said, folding his arms across his chest. "How'd the project go?" he asked, changing the subject, and I fell back, rolling my eyes. *Of course.*

"We finished it."

He sat down on my computer chair. "What did you say that girl's name was again?"

My jaw locked, and I had to pry it open to speak. "I didn't."

"Jess, right?"

"Jessica," I corrected. "So what?"

He leaned his elbows on his knees and placed his chin on his hands. His brown eyes bore into me. "What's your relationship with her?"

I gaped at him. "You must be kidding me."

He blinked. "About what?" he asked, attempting to hide his thoughts, but he couldn't. Unlike me, he was a terrible liar.

"You think I like her," I accused.

He shrugged. "Noah said you wanted to be alone with her."

"To study."

"You could've studied in the kitchen," he pointed out, and I glared.

"With Mindy hovering over us? No, thank you."

He frowned, and wrinkles covered his cheeks. "I have the right to wonder, Eric," he said, dropping his tone. "I am your father, after all."

"And by being my father, you should know by now that I haven't been like that since Abby," I retorted, my lip curling. "Even if I wanted to, I'm not allowed, or have you forgotten that rule?"

His brow lowered, darkening his eyes. "That rule was placed for a reason."

"Why?" I asked, and he glared.

"You know why," he said, knowing I was forcing him to say it.

I raised my brow. "I've forgotten."

He growled. "Eric—"

"Your wedding killed her," I said, remembering how the Light attacked us on the way to his ceremony.

"No." His voice was a snarl. "Showing your sword to her killed her," he said, knowing what we all knew. I activated my powers. The Light traced me, and I was with her when they found me.

"But they didn't kill me," I said, shaking my head as I waved my hands in the air. The image of the blonde girl sent after us remained in my memory. She'd looked into the car, seen the death, met my eyes, and left me. She didn't care to murder me—only Abby. I still didn't have an explanation. Nobody did.

After a moment, my father sighed. "That was a blessing, Eric."

"Abby's death isn't a blessing."

"Your survival was."

"It shouldn't be," I growled, jumping to my feet and pointing at my chest. "They should know my identity. They should've already killed me, but they haven't," I said. "Explain that."

His shoulders rose, but he didn't speak. Something wasn't right.

"Is this why you don't like Mindy and Noah?" he asked quietly. "You blame them."

"This isn't about them."

"It is," he said. He was changing the subject. Again. "They barely knew Abby."

"You're right," I agreed sharply. "They knew Hannah."

He sighed, dropping his face. "Eric—"

"What?" I was too bitter to listen to his scorn. "You're the one who brought a human home."

"Mindy is a very nice lady."

"Very human," I said.

"There's nothing wrong with humans," he said, glaring. "You used to be friends with a whole group of them, both Abby and you."

"Exactly why I'm not friends with them anymore," I spat. "They could be shades—or lights—then what?"

My father didn't speak.

"What if Mindy was a light?" I asked, and he stood up, pointing at me with a shaky finger.

"Don't talk like that."

"Don't talk like what?" I asked. "Truthfully?"

His brown eyes twitched. "Maybe I should come back later," he said, dropping his gaze for the umpteenth time.

"Maybe you shouldn't."

He didn't seem to hear me as he grabbed the plates from my table and stared at the one I left full. He knew it was mine. "Why aren't you eating?" he asked, and I prepared myself to lie.

"Not hungry."

He sighed, breaking down our silence barrier, and moved toward my door. "I had a surprise for you," he said, reaching into his pocket. He pulled out keys and tossed them onto my bed. "It's in the garage; be safe with it." He didn't look at me. "Goodnight, son," he said, unlocking the door and leaving.

I shut it behind him, kicking my bed in a fit. I collapsed on it, gripping my scalp as my eyes flicked over the silver keys. *Dodge.* He'd gotten me a car.

I snatched them up, running my fingers over them, and my heart sank into my gut. As much as I appreciated it, the gift felt like a distraction. Between my mother's suicide and Abby's murder, it was obvious he wasn't telling me everything, and I wanted to know. I had to, and I was determined to figure it out, even if I had to learn the truth on my own.

Twenty-three

"**W**AS IT TOTALLY FREAKY?" CRYSTAL BOMBARDED ME WITH questions as she sat in Eric's chair, taking advantage of the few minutes before class. It was a half-day, caused from teacher-parent meetings, and our schedules were flipped, so our homeroom would be our last hour. Eric wouldn't walk in until the bell rang.

"No," I giggled, shaking my head. "It was nice."

"Nice?" Crystal raised her eyebrows and frowned. "That's so boring." She was looking for gossip.

"It was homework," I reminded her. "How exciting were you expecting it to be?"

"It is the Welborn house," she said, tapping my desk with her pen. "I was expecting a little bit of blood."

I cringed at her joke, remembering Eric's injuries. When he walked me out, his stride was stiff, and I knew he was sore from his so-called accident.

Crystal's dark eyes flickered over my expression, and she straightened up. "There was blood!"

"A little," I confessed.

"Oh?" She rocked Eric's chair back as she gaped at me. "What happened? Some freaky, satanic ritual before you were allowed to enter?"

I rolled my eyes. "Nothing like that," I said, aggravated by her exaggeration. "He must have gotten into a fight," I clarified.

"His knuckles were all shredded."

"Ew."

I nodded, reflecting on last night. Eric opened up to me, and I couldn't get his expression out of my mind. He was calm, even when he talked about something I thought was too personal for him to share with anyone, let alone me. I wanted to know where that Eric had been all semester. Between the instance at the willow tree and his house, I didn't know what to believe. Was he nice or mean? I couldn't decide. After meeting his family, I couldn't completely blame him. In fact, I sympathized with him. My family still hadn't relented on our agreement toward my biological family, and I was about to lose it.

I looked past Crystal and stared as Eric walked into the classroom. His face was down, and his brown hair waved in front of his green eyes. He switched off his headphones, meeting my gaze as the bell rang.

Lips curling into a smirk, he hovered away from the table, leaning against the teacher's desk and allowing Crystal to finish her conversation. As she continuously ranted, I wasn't even listening to her.

"At least you guys finished your project," Crystal said, oblivious to Eric's arrival.

"What?" I forced myself to turn away from Eric. "I thought Robb and you finished early."

"We did," she said, touching her short hair. "But Robb isn't coming to school today. He, apparently, had family business to take care of, so we're being deducted ten percent from our presentation."

"That sucks."

"You're telling me," she said, biting her nails. "I sent our teacher an email, and she didn't even care." She rolled her eyes but patted my leg. "Who knew Welborn could care more than Robb?"

"Hey."

We both jumped, our conversation halting as we turned around. Eric stood inches away, and the teacher hovered behind him, crossing her arms. I hadn't even seen them approach.

"Er—Eric," I managed, and Crystal stared.

"Hey, Jessica," he said, turning his gaze to my friend. "Crystal."

"Welborn." She returned the acknowledgement with a cold tone. "Hey."

His smirk faltered, and his lips thinned. "I hate to interrupt," he said, swinging his hand over his shoulder to point at our teacher. "But I probably need my seat."

Ms. Hinkel cleared her throat, and Crystal scrambled to gather her things. "Sorry, ma'am," she said, standing up. "I'll talk to you after class, Jess."

Crystal practically ran for her desk, while Eric calmly sat in his seat. He swung his backpack onto the ground, allowing his green eyes to linger on me. "Did you bring your half?" he asked, raising his brow.

I fought a blush as I placed my stack of papers on our desk. He didn't say anything. Instead, his eyes scanned the first page, and he smirked, laying a finger on the first sentence. "You have a spelling error."

"What?" I leaned forward, grasping the paperwork. He was right. My stomach sank. "Oh, no."

"Don't worry about it," he said, chuckling as he laid a thicker stack down. "I retyped the entire thing."

My jaw dropped. "You rewrote everything?"

"And added some," he said. "I had a lot of free time after you left."

That's it. This boy is crazy.

"But I'd suggest you put it in page protectors," he said, opening his bag before he pulled out a binder and materials. "Ms. Hinkel would love that."

"I'd really love it if you two stopped talking," Ms. Hinkel said, and I froze, feeling the entire classroom focus on my back.

"Sorry for interrupting," Eric said, barely looking at her as he leaned away from me.

She nodded, turning to the class. "I hope everyone remembered today's presentations," she said. "We'll start off with Annie and Justin."

The two students went to the front of the classroom and fidgeted with their paperwork. They began to talk, and I ran my hands over the slick page protectors. Slowly, as I listened, I put each paper in one, hoping Ms. Hinkel wouldn't lecture me on my lack of focus.

For thirty minutes, students flocked to the front, stumbling over themselves as they tried to explain miscellaneous sections from our book. It was painful to watch. Most kids were too embarrassed to be comfortable in front of the class, and I dreaded going myself. Would Eric even talk? I doubted it.

Through my peripherals, I glanced at my science partner as he fell asleep. He leaned his chair back on two prongs, but it didn't budge. Somehow, even in sleep, he kept the seat balanced. It was almost supernatural.

Ring.

Eric's green eyes shot open as the lunch bell pierced the air, and he sat forward, placing all four legs of the chair on the ground. He muttered to himself and stretched out his cramped arm. His knuckles cracked, and I cringed, realizing he removed his braces from the night before.

The class shuffled through the door, but the teacher blocked the doorway. "I'll finish the remaining presentations in private," she said. "But the rest of the class can go. Just behave. Don't make me regret it."

A few students cheered, and she moved aside, smiling as the students rushed to lunch. Eric's brow lowered, and I stood up and crossed the room to Ms. Hinkel. "Aren't we the only ones left?" I asked, knowing we were the last presentation.

She nodded. "Did you finish?" she asked, her gaze lingering on Eric.

Eric raised his chin. "The whole thing is right here, teach," he said, waving his hands in front of him.

Ms. Hinkel raised her brow, turning to me. "Did both of you work on this?"

My eyes slit into a glare, but I fought my anger and relaxed my face. "We finished it together," I said, and Ms. Hinkel's lips thinned.

"We could do it now," she said, and I wanted to scream at her power trip.

A hand landed on my shoulder, and I froze as Eric stood by my side. "We can do that," he said.

Crystal hovered in the doorway. "Want me to wait for you? I thought we could go prom dress shopping."

I opened my mouth, but Ms. Hinkel shook her head. "This is going to take a while," she said. "I presume you have your own way of getting home, Ms. Taylor?"

"No—"

"I'll take her home," Eric said, and everyone froze. He shrugged, waving a pair of sparkling car keys in the air. "I drove today; it really isn't a big deal."

"Very well," Ms. Hinkel blinked. "Ms. Hutchins, you may go."

Crystal's dark eyes widened as she stared at me. "You okay with that, Jess?"

I nodded before the thought occurred to me. "See you later," I said, and she dipped out of the room without another word.

Eric pulled the binder from my hands and laid it in front of the teacher. "I expect that you'll find this adequate," he said, and she straightened, taking the project from him.

She adjusted her glasses, turning to walk to her desk. Eric winked at me, and I spun away from him to hide my face. *Was he flirting?* I watched Ms. Hinkel as she hummed, circling a red pen over our paperwork. I shifted my weight from foot to foot, knowing I needed a perfect grade if I had any chance at finding my biological parents. My grade rested solely on Eric's work, and I was still in disbelief that he'd edited it.

In a matter of minutes, Ms. Hinkel closed the binder and sighed. She twiddled her fingers and removed her glasses, staring at Eric before looking at me. "Very good, you two," she said. "I'm quite impressed, especially considering how you had nothing done last week."

Eric ignored her comment. "What's the grade?"

"Excellent," she said.

"When will it be available for our parents to see?" he asked, and I stared at him. *He remembered?*

"A few days," she said, waving us toward the door. "You can leave now. I have to prepare for my meetings."

"Any way you can show this to Jessica's parents tonight?" he pressed, and my body tensed.

"They aren't going to make it," I said, and Eric's brow rose. The teacher nodded, and he grabbed his things. After that, he picked up mine and headed for the door.

In an instant, he was by my side, and his hand lingered on my back as he steered me out. "Come on, Jessica," he murmured, and I followed his touch as if I was hypnotized.

We walked through the emptied hallways, and Eric opened the door to the parking lot. "Where do you live?" he asked, and I gave him my address. He nodded, and I wondered how he knew the streets so well. *Right. Because Hayworth was tiny.*

He didn't speak as we neared one of the last cars in the parking lot, and I stopped, staring at his vehicle. It was an old black car, clearly refurbished, but I didn't know much more than that. It looked brand-new, although I knew it had to be generations old. It only had two doors, and the hood stuck out, but the slick paint was unscathed.

"This is yours?" I asked, and he unlocked the passenger door.

"It's a 1966 Charger," he said. "What do you think?" He opened my door before going around to his side to get in.

I stood outside of his car, and he leaned over, staring up at me. "Are you coming or not?" he asked, turning over the engine. Music blared from his speakers.

I nodded, unsure if he would hear me if I did speak, and sat next to him. I buckled my seatbelt and hugged my bag to my chest. *Why did I agree to this?*

I tensed as he leaned over and turned his music down, driving out of the parking lot. "You can relax, Jessica," he said, chuckling as his green eyes focused on the road. "I'm not going to crash."

"I don't know that," I said. "I didn't even know you drove." *Because you get picked up every day by Teresa—whoever she is.*

Eric's smirk dissipated. "You think I can't drive because I have a chauffeur," he said, pointing out my thoughts as if he could hear them.

"What else am I supposed to think?"

"I'd think the same thing." He shrugged. "And I didn't have this until last night."

"Present?" I asked.

He nodded, but his jaw locked. He wasn't going to tell me why.

"Is it your birthday?" I asked, pushing for information, and he turned away, surveying the road.

"No."

I dug my nails into my backpack. *Why'd he have to be upset all the time?* "It's a really nice car," I said, attempting to change the mood, and he smiled again. He looked better when he was happy, but it was so rare, I questioned if it was a mirage.

"I prefer manual transmissions and speed," he said. His father hadn't gotten him everything he wanted. "But don't worry," he continued. "I won't speed with you in the car."

I sighed. "Thanks," I said, gazing out the window. It was a nice day. People were outside, walking their dogs and jogging. Spring was arriving faster than I expected. The weather was so strange in the Midwest. One day, it was freezing; the next, it was hot and humid.

"She didn't look too happy," Eric spoke suddenly, breaking our silence.

I turned my eyes away from the road. "I think the teacher loved our project."

"I meant Crystal."

My brow furrowed, and I fought desperately to remain silent, but I couldn't. "She's not sure about you, Eric."

"I know," he said, completely unfazed. "I heard."

My stomach sank. "You eavesdropped?" *But how? He wasn't even in the room when we were talking about him.* Yet I believed him. His tone was too serious.

His lips twisted into a grin. "One of my many hobbies."

"Not many people would consider that a hobby."

"Fair enough." He laughed. "It's one of my many talents."

I glared at his sarcasm. "What are your other talents?"

His green eyes lit up, but they remained on the road. "That's not fair, Jessica," he said. "I've told you one of mine; you should tell me one of yours."

My stomach twisted. He wanted to know more about me. "Fine," I began hesitantly, wondering what he was thinking. "I'm good at telling if people are lying or not."

"Lying?"

I nodded. "You don't believe me?"

His shoulders dropped. "Care to test your talent?" he asked, barely speaking, and I tensed.

"Go for it," I dared, and he tapped his steering wheel.

"My favorite color is silver, I'm seventeen, and I wish I was still a kid."

I watched his face, but his expression never changed. His eyes never flickered, his throat never tensed, his hands hardly moved. He was impossible to read. His solid expression suggested one thing, all truth or all lies. And he couldn't be telling the truth. "They're all lies," I said.

He shook his head, and his brown hair shifted along his brow. "None of them are."

I swallowed. Hadn't his childhood been horrible? I didn't understand.

"It's not much of a talent if you're not good at it," he said, returning to his cynical self.

"I'm good at it," I argued, tightening my hold on my bag. "You're just intimidating." The words left me before I knew them.

He smiled. "Intimidating?" he asked. "I've never heard that one before."

My jaw dropped. "You must be joking."

"Lying actually," he said, barely glancing over. He illuminated. "Another one of my talents—which, by the way, you didn't catch. Again."

I grinded my teeth. "I can do it."

"I'm sure," he chuckled as he turned the steering wheel, missing the shortest route to my house. Did he do that on purpose? "I believe this means you owe me two of your talents."

I dug my nails into my palm, positive he was two steps ahead of me. Arguing with him was not only impossible, it was a trap. I turned away and glared out the window, wishing he hadn't missed the side street.

"You look mad," he said, quieter this time.

I wouldn't look at him. "I am."

"Why?"

"Because I don't get you," I admitted. "I have no idea why you're acting this way, and it makes me feel like I don't know you."

"I didn't realize you wanted to know me," he said, and I turned around, momentarily meeting his eyes. They were dark, shadowed by an expression I hadn't seen before.

"Why wouldn't I?" I asked, feeling heat crawl over my neck. "We've already spent a lot of time together."

"For a project that's completed, Jessica," he said, and he shook his head, driving silently through my neighborhood. I waited for him to speak, but he didn't. Soon, we were at the end of my driveway. Eric shoved the gears into park, and I reached for the door, but he locked it.

"Why are you so interested in my life?" he asked, and my heart pounded. I didn't say anything. His eyes met mine, filled with an intensity that made me shudder. "It's not that great."

"I know," I managed. My voice was shaking.

His face reddened. "But you ask questions."

"And you answer them."

His mouth opened, but then it snapped shut. He sighed, turned away, and grabbed the steering wheel as if he were driving again. We remained parked. "I'm Eric James Welborn," he stated, his voice wavering into an awkwardness I'd never heard with his normally confident and cocky attitude.

James? His middle name felt personal—like he had opened up a side of himself he'd forgotten about. But I didn't feel intrusive. I felt comforted, like I already knew the answer before he'd spoken it. But I hadn't.

"Your name doesn't tell me who you are," I said, surprised by my fluidity.

He barely smiled. "Maybe I like it that way."

"I don't."

His head dropped. "You don't always get what you want, Jessica."

"Most of the time, you do," I debated stubbornly, knowing my desperation was evident. I didn't even believe my words.

His face scrunched, and he peered at me through his hair. "I don't know what world you come from, but I can't relate."

"What do you mean?" *What did he want that he couldn't have?* I wanted to know.

His lips thinned. "That's a different story for another time."

"A different story or a different lie?"

"I don't know." He smirked. "Use your talent and tell me." His eyes darted behind me, and he straightened up. "I think your mother wants you inside," he said, and I spun my torso.

My mother was leaning out an upstairs window, waving her hands wildly. "Jessie!" Her shout broke the barriers of the car, and my entire body tensed.

Eric chuckled beneath his breath. "Jessie?" he asked.

"Don't," I said, raising my hand to him as I grabbed the handle with my free one. He unlocked it before I even remembered to check, and I opened it, stepping out. "Thanks for the ride."

"Thanks for the conversation," he said. "See you later, Jessica."

"Bye," I said, shutting the door to our conversation and my embarrassment. He drove away, and I watched his black car zip through the street. What had gotten into me? I didn't know, but I hated to admit the truth. I liked it, and I hoped he meant his words.

I wanted to see him again.

TWENTY-FOUR

THE LIGHT'S HANDS SPACED APART AS SHE QUAVERED, STEPPING backward. Her shadowed eyes widened, and her coarse breathing raged against my eardrums. She was going to die, and both of us knew the moment was coming. It took seconds.

I locked my feet with the ground as a bead of sweat trickled down the side of my face. In a moment of concentration, my descendant sword spun out from my fingertips, and I grasped the handle. I lunged forward, every muscle in my body bracing for a counterattack, as I sliced her body. The sword went through her too easily, as if she were air, and my eyes closed involuntarily at her death. I didn't want to watch, even if she was a replica—another simulation created by Urte.

Good thing Urte wasn't here. I breathed, knowing her body would disappear with the training session. He'd make me look.

Body heat from another individual thundered against my back, and I tensed, spinning around with my sword to strike. But I froze.

"Whoa." Pierce raised his hands into the air, and his green eyes flickered over my blade, inches from his neck.

My blood singed against my veins as my sword dissipated, returning to my body. "Sorry, Pierce," I said, stretching my arm over my head. "I wasn't expecting anyone to join me."

"I can see why," Pierce said, running his hand over his neck. I wondered if he had felt the blade's heat. "Was that—?"

I nodded. "Urte wants me to be comfortable with the sword again."

Pierce grimaced. "My dad says you're doing really well."

"That's not what he says to me." I chuckled, knowing Urte was pushing me to do better with harsh words. He hadn't complimented my growth once. "How'd you know I was here?"

Pierce's eyes lit up. "Your car."

I wanted to frown, but I couldn't. It was my dream car—a classic black, two-door coupe—and my father had gotten it for me, no questions asked. But I knew why. It was possible that I only had one year to live, and his gift felt more like a departure gift than an encouragement for the future. I wasn't sure how to be completely grateful when it was partially meant to comfort my dad's conscience.

"It's really nice," I admitted, but thoughts of Jessica flickered through me. She was the only person I'd driven in it so far, and, honestly, I wanted to keep it that way.

"I'm happy for you," Pierce said, rocking back on his feet. "Even if it is a strange time to be happy."

I smiled, "Thanks."

He shrugged, and that was the end of our conversation. The training room door burst open, and Brenthan, Pierce's little brother, rushed in. "Shoman!"

"Hey, kid."

"Brenthan." Pierce grabbed the back of the boy's shirt. "What are you doing here? Did you follow me?"

He blinked. "I want to hang out with the first descendant, too."

Pierce released his brother, knelt down, and sighed. "Shoman is still Shoman, Brenthan," he said. "Learning about the prophecy shouldn't change that."

Brenthan ignored his brother and gazed up at me. "But you're important."

"Everyone is," I said.

"But they talk about you, and they always will," he countered, straightening up. "I wish I had powers like you."

"You will one day," I said, trying not to grimace.

Brenthan shook his head. "I'll never have a sword."

"Brenthan," Pierce smacked his brother on the backside of his head. "You're being an idiot," he said, knowing the repercussions of expectations being the first descendant held.

"What?" Brenthan rubbed his head. "It's so awesome."

"I'm glad you look at it that way," I said, forcing an uncomfortable laugh.

"Can you teach me something?" he asked, and I finally grimaced.

"He's busy, Brenthan," Pierce said, attempting to steer him to the doorway, but his little brother dodged him.

"Are you training?" he asked me. "Can I watch?"

Pierce crossed him arms. "No."

"I asked Shoman," he said, and I stepped between the brothers, trying not to laugh at their obvious brother connection.

"Your older brother is right, Brenthan," I said. "You're not even allowed in the training rooms yet; it's too dangerous."

As the words left my mouth, the room shook, and the lights flickered like fires suddenly ablaze. The protective glass exploded from the ceiling, and I grabbed Brenthan, blocking my eyes as I hovered over him. Pierce hissed, and we fell into darkness, our heartbeats echoing in the empty room.

"What was that?" Brenthan nearly shouted, and I clasped my hand over his mouth. I could feel it, the raging energy of sizzling electricity. It was as if Luthicer was digging his nails into my arm all over again, except I wasn't in pain. It was a memory recognizing what I was sensing in the shelter.

"*The Light is here,*" I telepathically talked to Pierce. Brenthan wouldn't be able to hear us.

"*What?*" Pierce's voice was a migraine of panic. "*Are you sure?*"

The training room shook again, and I knelt down, holding Brenthan in front of me. I no longer blocked his lips, but he didn't speak. Even he knew something was wrong.

"Get Brenthan to the back of the room," I said. *"And be pre-pared to fight."*

"Wha—?"

Smoke bellowed beneath the door, and the tile floor splin-tered throughout the room. "Now," I shouted, pushing Bren-than toward his brother. Pierce grabbed the boy, nearly tossing him to the other side of the room, and positioned himself in front.

"What's happening?" Brenthan whined, but Pierce ig-nored him.

I zoned my senses, bringing them in before throwing out, reading the shelter as far as I could in the mist of suffocating smoke. I couldn't see what was down the hallway, but I could hear the tapping.

Footsteps.

Whoever was coming was close. My fingers spread out, crackling with the desire to activate my sword. But it was prac-tical suicide. If this person was a light—and I was almost posi-tive they were—they'd sense me, and they'd attempt to kill me. I couldn't risk an attack when I had Pierce and Brenthan by my side.

I locked my jaw, preparing to kill the intruder with my bare hands if that meant protecting a child. The footsteps got closer and closer, and the shadow of a body curled beneath the doorframe. I held my breath and waited for any sign of movement, listening to Brenthan's panicked gasps and Pierce's grinding teeth. *This was it. This was the moment of my life I would have to adapt to killing others in order to save the Dark.* I had no choice. It was my destiny.

I activated my powers, and my sword tore through the door, ripping the wood into pieces.

"Shoman," Camille's scream vibrated my skull. *"Deactivate, now!"*

My sword disappeared before I even made the mental de-cision. No light could imitate my guard. I knew her better than I knew myself. Her energy was unrepeatable.

Through the smoky debris, Camille's white hair spiraled

down her arms, and her face was coated with dirt. Urte was next to her. His eyes were wide. "Are my boys with you?"

"Dad!" Brenthan pushed past me, wrapping his arms around his father's wide torso.

Urte's chest sunk as he exhaled, acknowledging Pierce. "Good to see you guys," he said, barely looking at me. "You missed Camille by an inch."

Camille raised her brow. "Way to almost kill me," she said, but her lip pulled into a smirk. She was proud.

"What happened?" I asked, ignoring the small talk. The entire hallway smelled like fire, and I could smell blood, jarring and fresh. The shelter radiated with Light energy, and I knew it wasn't Camille's or any other half-breed we'd taken in. It was too asphyxiating.

"We'll explain in the office," Urte said, herding us down the corridor as the ground rumbled, signaling the continuation of the attack.

TWENTY-FIVE

"YOU OKAY?" CAMILLE WAS SITTING ON MY COMPUTER DESK, HER feet kicked up on my computer chair, and I leaned back in it, kicking my feet against the desk.

"I'm fine," I said, practically upside down as I stared at Pierce. Brenthan slept next to him. None of us had returned to our human forms. Too much adrenaline ran through us, and Mindy was guaranteed to leave us alone. My father managed to distract her with excuses upon excuses, and she left the house with Noah, but I couldn't concentrate long enough to even eavesdrop.

"The light was close to your room," Camille said, widening her blue eyes. "Too close if you ask me."

Pierce's white skin somehow paled, and I sighed heavily. "I was prepared to fight," I said.

"I could tell." Camille beamed, her teeth bright against her dirt-covered face. "I'm proud of you, Shoman. You're doing so well."

"Thanks."

Camille opened her mouth to speak again, but she stopped, cocking her head to the side. Her face scrunched up, and her nose twitched. "Your father needs to speak to us, Shoman," she said, jumping off my desk.

"I'll be there in a minute," I said before switching to telepathy. *I have to check on Pierce first.*

She left my room, and I shook my head, concentrating on my best friend. "What's up with you, Pierce? Are you okay?"

He nodded.

"Are you sure?" I asked, prying as I spun my chair around to face him. "You don't look so good."

He rubbed his forehead. "Physically? I'm fine," he began, his eyes hovering over his sleeping brother. "As much as Brenthan's a brat, he's my brother. I love him. And if that light attacked when you weren't there—" A frown twisted onto his lips. "I couldn't stand up to something like that. I would have no chance against a light."

"But it didn't happen," I said, and Pierce shook his head.

"It will." *"The Marking of Change,"* he finished telepathically as if he couldn't hear the words spoken.

My fingers dug into my kneecaps. "That battle is between Darthon and me, not anyone else."

Pierce raised his brow. "Do you really believe that?" he asked, and I turned my face, unable to meet his eyes. I didn't know what to believe. He sighed heavily, and his foot tapped the edge of the bedframe. "This isn't your fault, Shoman. If it wasn't for you, we could be dead."

"If it wasn't for me, you wouldn't have been in that corridor," I said, standing up to follow Camille. "I'll be back."

Pierce was still as I passed him, openly walking down my hallway as a shade. It would've felt freeing if it hadn't been under the circumstances of an attack. I only knew two things. The Light did it, and we captured one of them. Nothing more.

"How much damage was done?" Camille's voice echoed into the hall, and I leaned against the wall outside.

"Quite a lot," Urte said. "I'm afraid training might be out of the question for a while."

"Perhaps that's why she attacked," my father said as I entered the room and met his eyes for the first time since he handed me the car keys. Unlike Urte, he didn't rush across the room to hug me. Instead, he nodded, and I turned away.

"The light was a girl?" I asked, and my trainer confirmed the news.

"She was after you no doubt."

My father sat at his desk, drumming the wood with his fingers. "Then why would she bother killing three innocent shades that are obviously not him?"

My gut twisted. "Three people were killed?"

Urte ignored me. "She was making a statement."

Camille agreed. "There's more to this light than we think."

"That's why we should interrogate her," Urte said.

I saw myself in my father as his jaw locked, popping his upper cheek out. His blue eyes fogged over, and he rubbed them. "Do we know anything about her?"

"Her name's Fudicia," Camille said. "And she's too powerful for her age; she must be ranked very high."

My father nodded. "Capturing her had to be difficult."

"Luthicer helped, Bracke," Camille said, squaring her shoulders. "The only strange part was her surrender. She could've escaped."

"Was it a suicide mission?" I asked, and Camille shook her head.

"That's outside of Light culture," she said. "They are destined die, but they'll fight it until the end."

My throat tightened, and my father stood, leaning against his desk. "This attack doesn't have value," he said. "I cannot find a purpose for this."

"That's why we ask her."

"What makes you think she'll answer?" he asked, and Camille sucked in a breath.

"Knowing the Light, this is part of a bigger plan," she said. "They sent Fudicia with a message; we might as well hear it."

"I want to go with," I interceded, and everyone acknowledged my existence for what seemed to be the first time since I walked in.

My father groaned. "Shoman—"

"I'm the first descendant." I held my ground. "I need more experience with the Light if I'm going to defeat it."

My father's eyes burned a brilliant cerulean, and he touched his chin. "You have proved yourself," he said beneath his breath. "But I'm not sure you want to handle this tonight."

"I don't want to," I said, refusing to drop eye contact. "I have to."

Urte smiled, and my father's eyes flickered over my face, scanning my expression as if he were searching for something he'd never find. "Okay," he said, stepping away as shadows crawled across his chest, legs, and arms. "Let's go."

———— ✦ ————

She was chained to the wall, and, as much as I hated to admit it, Fudicia was surprisingly beautiful. Her thin eyebrows arched high on her brow, lining up with her pale hairline. The blonde hair fell in front of her boney cheekbones, and her pitch black eyes studied us with a lingering lust. She licked her broken red lips at the sight of us entering her cell, and her face lit with excitement, not fear. I had never sensed such dominance, yet I was more focused on her age. She couldn't have been older than I was.

"I wasn't expecting to meet the first descendant so quickly," she said, and I stepped forward, studying her facial structure, hoping to recognize her for who she was as a human. She flashed her teeth. "Even you should know our bone structure is different when we transform."

I met her eyes, controlling my movements as if I was preparing a lie. "What do you want?" I asked, knowing Bracke, Urte, and Camille stood behind me.

Fudicia's pupils fluttered beneath her warrior-like eye shadow. "To gather information on you actually," she said. "You're a lot weaker than I was expecting."

"Darthon must be in a worse position if he had to sacrifice someone just for me." My expression never faltered. I kept my muscles in place.

Her lips twitched, briefly but noticeably. "That's where you're wrong," she said, leaning against her chains. I could smell her sweet breath and the dried sweat on her skin. "This is far from a sacrifice."

I didn't move. "You won't be released for a very long time."

"I'm already gone," she said, and I stepped back as her body turned as transparent as glass. Urte shot forward, grasping at the air, but it spilled through his fingers like water, melting over the ground.

"I'll be back for you," she said. "Might want to learn the truth before then."

Her body, as solid as it had been, was gone, and fog replaced her. *The truth?*

"Go on alert," My father bellowed down the corridor. "Fudicia escaped."

Sirens screeched through the rocky shelter, and I covered my ears, wincing at the deafening noise. She'd be back. I closed my eyes, listening to her words over and over again, blocking out the chaotic world surrounding me. And she'd confirmed what I already thought. I didn't know everything. But she did, and she was gone.

"What time is it?" I asked over the noise, and Urte waved his hands, ordering shades from the halls to search the forest.

"Late, why?"

The nameless shade I was training. She'd be by the river. Someone would find her.

"I have to go," I said, rushing away, and my father latched onto my black jacket.

"You can't go out there," he said, his face burning.

I pulled away, splitting into the shadows before he could stop me. My skin and muscles tore as if I was being unwrapped, and I grasped my chest as I solidified outside the forest. Shadows of fog and mist pushed out around my body, and I wavered on my knees. I had transported too quickly.

"Shoman." The girl rushed to my side, and her black hair waved in front of her face. "Is everything okay?"

"No." I laid my hand on her arm before dragging her toward the road. Shades wouldn't risk being seen by cars. "You need to go home," I said. "It's too dangerous right now."

"What?" She attempted to stop, but I led her closer to the street. I wasn't going to let her linger any longer than she already had. "What is going on?"

"I'll explain everything later," I said, lampposts spreading golden light across our white skin. It didn't even color us.

She clutched my arm when I dropped hers. "Are you okay?" she asked.

"I'm fine."

"Promise?"

"I promise," I lied.

"And I'll see you again?"

"Of course." I didn't lie. I wanted to see her as soon as I could. I didn't want her to be targeted by Fudicia or anyone else for that matter. "Be here in two days at our usual time. I'll be here."

She beamed. "See you then," she said, vanishing with ease.

I stepped back, struck with the two powers I'd seen. Fudicia was young—too powerful for her own kind—and so was my trainee. *Might want to learn the truth before then.* Fudicia's words struck against the reality of their abnormal powers. I'd always known something wasn't right, but I didn't know Fudicia was aware of whatever that was.

TWENTY-SIX

THE MAIN HALL WAS DECORATED WITH ROWS OF WHITE CANDLES. They'd been burning for such a long time that the wax was dripping onto the red silk beneath them, spreading out like liquid pearl rivers. The flames barely flickered, but the golden light managed to radiate the large meeting hall.

Shades, with their black clothes and dark hair, filled the room like a giant shadow. Tears came from many, but most of the guests attended out of respect, rather than loss. Everyone knew the three murdered shades, two elders and their daughter, but now we knew their human names too, Lewinsky. Whenever shades were killed or unconscious, they returned to their human form. It was uncontrollable.

My father reported their deaths to the police through the council. We didn't know which officers were Dark members, but we knew there was a connection. In this case, the Lewinsky family died from carbon monoxide poisoning. The mother had neglected to open the garage door when she was heating up the car. No one questioned it beyond that, and one day later, we were throwing a memorial service.

I felt as if every shade was watching me or trying to avoid watching me. Everyone knew the truth, after all. The Light attacked to get to me, and the Lewinskys were the first in a list of many who would probably die.

"I hate funerals," I said, fighting the memories of Abby's. It was the last one I'd attended.

"I don't think anyone likes them," Pierce mumbled, chewing on a bite-sized sandwich from the refreshments table.

Camille cringed. "I cannot believe you can eat right now."

Pierce stopped chewing. "Why?"

"Forget it." She rolled her dark eyes and fidgeted with the sleeves of her dress.

Pierce met my gaze. *What's her problem? PMS?*

I fought a grin, knowing Camille could sense our telepathy. She had a connection to my mind at all times. *Probably.*

"What are you guys talking about?" Camille asked, glaring at Pierce. He was always the cause of mischief.

"Nothing."

"Whatever," she said, reaching into her purse for a hat. It was black, and she rolled up her white hair, pushing it beneath the cap. She despised looking like a light, especially during such a time where the reminder could hurt someone.

Pierce gulped down his food and frowned. "Does anyone see our parents?"

Camille paused, and a piece of her white hair waved in front of her face. I looked around, searching the crowd, and stopped. "No."

"Me neither," Camille said, straightening up. She was supposed to know where everyone went; it was her job. "They must be having another meeting."

I raised my brow. "Right now?" I asked. "Couldn't it wait?"

Pierce stretched his arms out and cracked his knuckles. "Sounds like it's a conversation not meant to be heard."

I smirked. "Sounds like something we need to hear."

"What are you boys thinking?" Camille asked, scrunching her brow. "If they don't want us to know, we shouldn't go."

"We aren't going to it," Pierce said, unable to fight his grin. "We're just dropping by."

With another glance at me, Camille relented. "Fine, I'll take you," she said, beginning to walk toward the meeting, but I grabbed her.

"We know a better way," I said, steering her toward Pierce.

"Follow him."

———————◆———————

"Ouch." Camille stumbled in the thin, dark hallway, and her black cap tumbled off her head. She cursed the secret pathway Pierce and I had found as children while exploring the shelter's grounds. Abby was the only other person who knew about it, and she showed us how it led to the library—where the elders held most of their discussions.

"This is ridiculous," Camille ranted as she tripped again. Being half-light, she couldn't see as well in the dark as shades could.

I shushed her. "We're getting too close for you to slip up."

"Yeah," Pierce said, blinking his glowing green eyes as he turned around from atop the creaking stairs. "If we get caught, we're blaming you."

"Doesn't matter," Camille said. "We'll all get in trouble."

"Calm down," I said. "And stop talking." Even if we were silent, it was very likely we'd get caught. Elders, especially my father, had heightened senses. He could tell if shades were talking telepathically, let alone in the same room as him.

We fell into silence as we walked through the thin space between the walls, glancing out the cracks to see where we were. In moments, we were right on top of them. Pierce froze, and I grabbed Camille's hand to stop her from tripping into us. She held her breath and peered out a vent dug into the wall. The highest four elders sat at the round table with the exception of Luthicer. As usual, he paced.

"She threatened your son, Bracke," Urte spoke as Pierce curled his fingers around the wood to watch.

My father leaned on his elbows. "I know."

"But what could it mean?" Eu asked, digging his nails into the thick mangled threads he called his hair. "Her threats. Her words. She said—"

"We all know what she said, Eu," my father spat. "The question is what we do about it."

Luthicer tapped his long fingers along his black suit. "This Fudicia girl had more power than we thought," he said, walking in two tight circles. "More knowledge too."

Eu's pudgy fingers curled into fists. "Do you think she knows about the third—?"

My father hit the table, jumping to his feet. "We will not talk about her in this council," he said, pointing a shaky finger at the short man. "Not today. That is an order."

"But, Bracke—" Luthicer began to argue.

"An order, Luthicer," my father said, glaring at the half-breed elder.

Luthicer, instead of his usual fighting, nodded. Camille's grip tightened around my hand, squeezing my bones together in what was supposed to be a comforting gesture.

"What do you suggest we discuss, Bracke?" Luthicer asked, sitting down only to stand back up. "It's a possibility she came here to trick Shoman."

Urte leaned on the wobbling table. "Trick him into what?"

Luthicer's black eyes shifted. "Leading the Light to the third—" he paused when my father's glare met his gaze. "With all due respect, sir, you need to consider this possibility."

My father's lips pressed together in a thin white line. "The Light wouldn't inform all of their soldiers of the whole prophecy."

"Bracke is right," Urte said. "The Light wouldn't risk giving that kind of information to their people. It'd be too risky; they'd ruin their only chance of survival."

My body chilled. The Light had a survival plan? And the prophecy allowed it?

"I didn't say they'd risk that information for just anyone," Luthicer clarified.

My father's brow fell, sending a shadow across his glowing eyes. "Then what are you saying?"

Luthicer cleared his throat, but Eu spoke first, "Fudicia is of high power."

"That's ludicrous," Urte said. "She couldn't be twenty."

"And you suggest Camille is much older?" Luthicer asked,

allowing his words to linger. Urte's shoulders rose, and my father sucked in a breath, his face turning red.

"Fudicia is Darthon's guard?" he asked, and Luthicer lowered his chin.

"It's a high possibility."

My father rubbed his temples, and his hair stood up toward the ceiling. "There has to be other explanations," he said, so quietly that I barely heard him.

"Think about it, sir," Luthicer said, sitting next to my father. "Fudicia attacked the community as if she were an inexperienced light and escaped because she knew we'd treat her as such."

My father paled. "And I brought Shoman to deal with her."

Eu kicked the table as he stood. "She could be tracking him."

My father cursed. "Their plan worked better than they even planned."

"We shouldn't worry," Luthicer said, laying his hand on my father's shoulders. "Even with the reading, she can't track him unless he uses his sword outside of the shelter."

Eu huffed. "And we all know he's done that before."

Abby. Camille's and Pierce's eyes flickered over my face, but I refused to look at them. I needed to hear everything the elders said. It'd only been minutes, and I was already hearing more than I ever imagined. The prophecy was changing, and so was my guarantee of success. Even Luthicer had changed; he was defending me.

"Shoman is very powerful," Luthicer said, seemingly a different man. "Sometimes I wonder if he'll be too powerful for his own good."

"His training is going well," Urte said.

"But what will that do if the Light is aware of his weakness?" my father asked, and the room silenced.

My weakness?

"He could die," Eu said, managing to speak before the others. "But so could Darthon. They share the same weakness."

"And training will be useless if they find the third—" My

father's voice drifted away, and the room erupted into noise. Urte and Luthicer were the loudest, bickering inches away from one another, while Eu attempted to speak every few seconds.

My father remained silent. He was pale and his frown curled deeper into his skin. His mangled hair was as dark as his expression, yet he looked as if he were barely present. His eyes were fogged over, and he stared at the wall. His mind was elsewhere. But, soon, his blue gaze refocused, and his arm disappeared and reappeared out of the shadows as he hit the table.

"Silence," he bellowed, his voice ripping through the library. His eyes landed on his red hand, and he rubbed it against his arm, sighing heavily. "We've discussed everything there is to discuss," he said. "Find this Fudicia girl, and protect Shoman. That's all."

The men nodded. "The funeral should be ending soon," Eu said, looking at the clock as he stood.

Luthicer moved to his side. "How is Shoman taking all of this?"

"Indifferent, I suppose," my father said, his face scrunching up. "He's completely emotionless. I can't tell what he's thinking."

"Maybe that's for the best," Luthicer said, and my father shrugged.

"I'm sure there's nothing to worry about," Eu agreed.

My father shook his head. "It isn't Shoman who I am worried about."

The grandfather clock chimed, and I took advantage of the noise. I pushed past Camille and walked away from my friends, fleeing from our hidden pathway. I dreaded the sweat dripping down my face, fearing that one of the elders would hear it slide against my rough skin. It took all my willpower not to cough or scrape against the wall, and I knew Pierce and Camille were doing the same. Behind me, their coarse breathing was rigid on my chilled neck.

"Come on," Pierce slid between Camille and I, sprinted ahead, and cracked the wall open. For the first time in my life, the light was comforting. "It's safe," he said, shoving it open, and we followed him out.

Camille slammed it behind her, and I pressed my back against the wall, breathing hard. Funeral goers rushed past us, and Pierce wiped the stifling sweat from his brow, shaking his head. "What the hell happened in there?" he asked, and Camille hugged herself.

"They lied to us," she whispered, her black eyes widening. "Can you believe that?"

"I kind of knew," I admitted, shoving my hands in my pockets. My friends gaped at me. "But I didn't know the details."

"We still don't," Pierce exclaimed, dropping his tone as others looked our way. "Did you even hear what they said? Fudicia could track you—"

"I'm not concerned about that," I said, waving the thought away.

Camille raised her brow. "What else could possibly be important?"

"The Light wouldn't have informed all their soldiers of the whole prophecy," I repeated. "The whole prophecy...what did they mean by that?"

Camille fidgeted with her dress. "We know the prophecy."

"Do we?"

She sighed. "The elders wouldn't hide anything important from us, especially you, Shoman."

I shook my head. "They talked about a weakness. I've never heard about it before."

Pierce blanched, and he looked between us. "I was hoping you guys knew what it was, but didn't want to tell me."

Camille shook her head, and I mirrored her. "I have no clue what they're talking about."

"But it's Darthon's weakness too," Camille said, and a group of preteens walked past us. She lowered her face and pulled Pierce and I close. "We shouldn't talk about this."

"Not now," Pierce agreed.

I agreed, stepping backward. "Tell my father I went home,"

I said, readying to transport. Camille grabbed my arm, shaking her head.

"You can't just leave."

"Tell him it reminded me of Abby too much." I gave the excuse, feeling guilt for using my friend's death to my advantage. "I have to go."

"You better stay home," she said, glaring.

"I will," I promised. "I have to go think this through."

TWENTY-SEVEN

"**A**RE WE GOING TO HANG OUT SOMETIME?" ROBB ASKED, RUNning his hand through his dark hair.

"Of course," I said, walking with him to our lockers. School was over. "I've been busy."

"Me too," he said, and I laughed.

"With what? Chasing girls?"

"Chasing you," he said, and I rolled my eyes. Crystal was right. It was a matter of time before Robb attempted to hit on me. I only expected it to be less cheesy.

"Chasing me won't be much fun," I said, attempting to write off the flirtation.

"Not through your eyes."

I forced a laugh and turned on my heel. "See you around, Robb," I said, waving as I left him in the hallway. I didn't have the patience to deal with his hormones. Robb was my friend, strictly platonic, and I already had my eyes on someone else.

I twisted my combination into my locker and opened the small box designed to hold all my textbooks. *Yeah, right.*

I emptied my bag into the crammed space and glanced in the mirror Crystal installed, but I didn't look at myself. My eyes gazed past my face and hair, and I refocused behind me, staring at the boy down the hall, Eric Welborn.

He hadn't been in class today, but there he was, standing at his locker arguing with a girl. She was wearing a black dress and a black cap that blended in with her black hair. I barely recognized Teresa, but I noted how they matched. Eric was in dark slacks, a pressed white shirt, and a black jacket was thrown over his shoulder. He looked good. Really good.

"They're going to the Lewinskys' funeral," Crystal whispered as she leaned against the locker next to me. "I think it has been going on all day. I'm surprised they came back to get homework."

"Funeral?" I asked, trying to look away from him. "Who died?"

"The Lewinsky family," she repeated, rolling her eyes.

"Who are they?"

Crystal shrugged. "This sweet, old couple that lived with their daughter," she said, divulging in the opportunity to spread news. "They left their car running in the garage, and the carbon monoxide did them in," she said, leaning even closer. "Mr. Welborn was the one who found them. Figures, right?"

My knees locked. "Did Eric know them?"

"I guess." Crystal bit her pierced lip. "The funeral is private," she said. "Nobody even knows where it is, so I suppose it's only closest family members and friends."

"That's horrible."

"I'm pretty sure the Welborns are used to it," Crystal said, and as the words left her mouth, Eric spun around.

His green eyes locked on Crystal, and she leapt behind me. "That's so creepy," she muttered, grasping her necklace. "He couldn't hear me, right?"

I looked back at him, but he was walking away, Teresa leading. I sighed. "I'm pretty sure he did," I said, logically knowing it'd be practically impossible. "I feel bad for him, you know."

Crystal cringed. "Why? It's his fault he's so secluded."

"Is it?"

Crystal groaned. "Who cares?" she asked. "Your project is over, and I need a prom dress. It's next month."

I shut my locker and threw my bag over my shoulder. "I can't tonight."

She pushed her lips together and whined. "But Robb and I were going to the bars tonight; we wanted you to go."

I shook my head. "Not tonight." *And not when Robb is trying to date me.* "You guys can have fun without me."

"We do that all the time," she said, unwrapping gum and laying it on her tongue. "We'd like company for once. Robb's other friends hardly make it."

"I didn't even know he had other friends," I said, and Crystal laughed.

"He has a girlfriend," she said, and I tensed, wondering if I should tell Crystal what he'd said earlier that day. "Her name's Linda, and her half-brother, Zac, hangs out with us sometimes."

"You guys haven't really mentioned them before," I said, moving toward the front door.

Crystal shrugged. "If you were coming to the bar, you'd meet them." She winked.

"I can't," I repeated, opening the door. "But can you give me a ride home?"

She smirked, allowing her lips to curl onto her cheek. "What? Is Welborn's Charger not good enough for you anymore?"

My mouth opened. "How do you know what he drives?"

"Really?" She stopped walking just to cock her hip. "It's impossible to miss in the parking lot. The entire school is talking about it," she said. "Not to mention that he took you home in it."

I grabbed her arm. "You were the only one who knew about that."

She smiled. "Not anymore."

"Crystal!"

"Oh, relax," she said, waving me away. "It's not like he's your boyfriend."

I sighed, shaking my head side to side. "What kind of dress do you want?" I asked, changing the subject, and she babbled from that point on the entire way home.

———◆———

"Jessie?" My mother stepped into the hallway and tied her blonde hair up. "Can we talk to you for a minute?"

I dropped my bag on the floor and sighed. I was too tired to talk. "I guess."

She gestured to the kitchen, and I sulked across the floor toward the table. My dad was seated, but my mom remained standing. I hovered in the doorway. "What's going on?" I asked. "Did I do something wrong?"

"No, Jessie." My mom smiled. "We just need to talk to you."

"About?"

"About your parents," she said. "While you were working on your project…" My mother stopped, and my father forced a smile. "We were working on finding information for you."

Heat crept up my neck. "Really?" I asked. "Did you find anything?"

My mom nodded, but frowned. "Are you sure you want this, Jessie? It's going to be very difficult."

"I am."

My dad stood up, pulled a manila envelope from his coat, and handed it to me. "This might help," he said, and I grasped it. He smiled. "Open it."

I unfolded the envelope and studied the paper. The newspaper crinkled beneath my fingertips, and my gaze traced over the old words and four pictures. "An article?"

The title, *Two Die in Horrific Crash*, hovered over a photograph of a mangled car. The victims, Joseph, Lynne, and their baby daughter, were placed below.

My mom leaned over and pointed to the adults. "Those are your parents, Jessie." She moved her finger to the baby. "That's you."

"I got a copy from the library," my dad said, and my hands began to shake.

"How do you know this is them?" I didn't want to be disappointed.

"That was the only fatal crash in Hayworth the year we adopted you," he said, and I stared at the couple.

They were beautiful, and they were my parents. My mother had thick, gorgeous brown hair and deep brown eyes, while my father had my blue eyes and short brown hair. They looked so happy, their smiles as wide as the camera lens. I hadn't imagined they'd look so perfect—but I still didn't feel anything for them. They didn't seem real. What was wrong with me?

"Thank you so much," I said. "But I need to figure out more."

My father chuckled. "That's why I got you that article," he said. "Who wrote the article, Jessie?"

My eyes shot down to the bottom, and I wondered how I hadn't noticed before. There was only one name in bold, and it was beneath my baby picture. Lola Hutchins. Crystal's mom.

TWENTY-EIGHT

THE SMALL STONE SKIPPED ACROSS THE MOONLIT WATER, RIPPLING the river into tiny waves, and it reminded me of what it was like to fly. The slick, black surface illuminated with the reflection of the stars and moved against the wind. The full moon shone against both.

A stone collided with mine, and they sunk to the riverbed. I smiled, tossing another, and the nameless shade followed my game, hitting mine until they sank or skipped past. We'd been sitting together for over an hour, but I still hadn't told her why I ordered her to leave for two days. She hadn't bothered asking either.

"You're quiet," she said, breaking our eerie silence as if we'd never had one before. I tried to remember a moment we hadn't spoken, and I couldn't recall. We were always talking about something.

I tossed a pebble as her purple eyes grazed across my peripherals. She sighed, and she pulled her knees up to her chest. I barely glanced at her, but her porcelain face was filled with worry, and my stomach churned. I was tired of making everyone around me feel negatively. It seemed like it was all I was good for.

"I killed someone the other night," I said, knowing it was a partial truth. The simulation wasn't a real person, but it felt like a real person, and killing her wasn't what was bothering me. Fudicia was.

Her purple eyes met mine, but they didn't widen. "Really?"

"She was a light," I said, feeling guilty for the lie. "She wasn't real; just a simulation my trainer created." I shook my head, more bothered by the fact that I almost struck Pierce. "But she seemed real, and I can't get her face out of my head. It's like I'm having nightmares, but I'm awake." I exhaled and realized I'd forgotten to breathe. My chest was tight.

The mysterious girl listened, seemingly unfazed. "Why'd you kill her?" she asked, laying her cheek on her knees. Her eyes never left mine.

"I had no choice."

She smiled. "You always have a choice, Shoman."

"I won't in battle," I said, grabbing a stone and chucking it at the water. It didn't even skip.

She tensed up. "What kind of battle is this? It's nine months away, and you're stressing out about it—"

"Because people are going to die," I said, collecting a handful of stones.

"Like the Lewinskys?"

I dropped the stones, and her eyes widened when I went rigid. "How do you know about that?"

"It was a guess," she whispered.

My chest pressed against my ribs. I'd just revealed another part of my life. The Lewinskys were shades. They'd died in the Dark, not in their home, and now this girl knew.

"Don't worry," she said, leaning over to push my leg. "I figured no one knew. The death just sounded strange to me."

I raised my brow. "Who'd you hear it from?"

She shook her finger. "You told me I shouldn't talk about my human identity. I can't tell you that."

So she wasn't going to slip up, even though I did. For once, I wished our facial structures, along with our bodies and clothes, didn't morph when we did. I'd know who she was then, and I could assess whether or not her knowledge was a threat.

She picked up a rock from between us and tossed it between her hands. "What's it like—killing someone?" she asked, avoiding eye contact.

"Wonderful."

This time, her purple eyes widened, and she nearly snapped her neck to meet my eyes. I chuckled, shaking my head back and forth. "Don't get me wrong," I said. "I never explained how Urte got me to do it."

"Urte?"

"My father's guard."

"And your guard?" she began. "Was it that girl with the white hair?"

I froze. "When did you see her?"

"The first night we met," she said, blinking. "She came out of the forest looking for you."

I stretched my arms, forcing my shoulders to relax. This girl knew too much, especially since I thought she'd left before Camille exposed herself, but she hadn't. "That was my guard," I said, wanting to know exactly how much my trainee had picked up. Had I really been that careless?

"But how did Urte get you to kill the light?" she asked, returning to our original conversation, and my jaw hurt.

"I couldn't at first," I said. "I don't want to believe I'll have to one day."

She sucked in breath. "This is real, isn't it?"

I nodded, and she scooted closer. Her black hair whipped in the wind and brushed against my exposed arm. I watched it flutter over my chest. "Urte told me to concentrate on the person I cared for the most," I began, whispering. "And I could let the light live if I wanted my loved one to die."

She reached over and laid her hand on my leg. I grabbed it, and her fingertips moved across my palm.

"I didn't hesitate after that."

"That must have been difficult," she said, and I shook my head.

"Not when I was choosing between the light and you."

She tensed, and her fingernails dug into my wrist. Heat rose from her palm, and I felt her hand shake as her shoulders rose. "Shoman—"

"Don't think of me differently," I said, interrupting her before she could clarify our friendship. But she was holding my hand. "I used you, because you are the closest person I have. You've helped me more than you know. Honest. I don't want you to think it's anything more than that." I added the rest telepathically, *"The only reason I'm sane is you."*

Her pupils grew. "Did you—?"

"You can talk telepathically, too," I said, hoping the exposure of powers would relax her. "It takes time to tune your energy and match it to others, but I'm sure you'll figure it out."

She beamed, letting go of my hand to plop backward onto the grass. She lay on her back, giggling, and grabbed my sleeve. "Come here," she said, tugging me toward the moist dirt.

"What?" I felt the water seep through my T-shirt, but I didn't shiver. I rolled over to stare at her. "Why are we doing this?"

"Just lay with me for a second," she said, lying by my side. "It's not that hard."

I tried to look at the stars, desperately trying to see the beauty she obsessed over, but it looked like a sky to me. Nothing more. Just little balls of fire and light against the blackness of night. Nothing special.

"I still don't see the point of this," I said.

"You'll see in a minute," she said, and I heard the grass shift as she rolled over, laying her head on my chest. I stiffened, but she grabbed my arm and wrapped it around her torso. "Your heart is racing," she said, relaxing against me.

"Mhmm," I hummed. Why was she doing this? Slowly, I placed my hand on her arm, and the coldness of her skin tickled my fingers. She was colder than me, but the closeness of another body was so warm. I'd forgotten what it felt like.

"Why are we doing this?" I whispered into her black hair, my eyes locked on the night sky.

"Because," she whispered back. "It's calming."

"You're strange."

"And you're stressed," she said.

I laughed, and her head followed my chest as it rose and

fell. "You're trying to help me?"

She tilted her head back and met my eyes with a smile. "I don't think killing that light girl is what's really bothering you."

"Why do you say that?"

She returned her ear to my sternum. "Urte found a way to make you comfortable with killing. Your silence is too strong for something resolved," she said. "And I haven't forgotten about what you said two days ago." She laid her hand on my stomach. "What happened?"

I held my breath. "I'd rather not talk about it."

"You'd rather not talk about it or you're not allowed to talk about it?" she asked, and I smiled. She knew I wasn't allowed to talk about everything in the Dark. "That's what I thought," she said, taking my silence for an answer.

I sighed, running my hand over her thick, black hair. "I think my father is hiding something from me." I waited for her to speak, but she remained silent, listening. "I heard him speaking to the other elders—about my weakness," I said. "But I don't know my weakness. They're keeping a part of the prophecy away from me."

"I don't know the prophecy," she said, and I patted her shoulder.

"I know," I said. "But I still can't tell you."

She breathed and her shoulders rocked as she adjusted. "I know."

"But I think the weakness has something to do with the prophecy," I continued, unable to stop myself. "My guard disagreed. She didn't want to hear it at all."

"The white-headed girl?"

I nodded, my head pushing against the grass. "Her name is Camille."

"Why does she look different from you and me?"

"What do you mean?" I asked.

The girl tapped her nails against my stomach. "She has white hair and dark eyes," she said. "You and I have dark hair and light eyes."

I was calm, but surprised she'd observed something so

definite when comparing the three of us. She saw the pattern from the beginning. "So you noticed?" I asked, unsure how to explain.

The girl nodded, but she managed to keep her head on my chest. She didn't want to move. She was too comfortable. And I was, too. I didn't want her to leave.

"Camille's a half-breed," I said, allowing the heavy words to fall from my lips. "She looks like a light, but she's both."

"Why doesn't she look like a shade instead?"

"Genetics." I shrugged. "She looks like a Dark member during the day and a Light member at night." I spoke before realizing the amount of personal information I'd revealed. I cursed and sat up, nearly pushing the girl off me.

She grabbed my arm. "What?" she asked. "What's wrong?"

"Nothing," I muttered, rubbing my temple. How could I be so stupid? Camille's life as Teresa Young could've been jeopardized.

The girl's face fell, and she moved away. "You told me something you aren't supposed to," she said, and I shook my head.

"No, I didn't," I lied.

"I know what Camille looks like during the day," she spoke without hesitation, and I stared at the purple-eyed girl. I couldn't even be mad at her; it was my fault.

"I shouldn't have said that."

"But it's okay," she said, trying to touch me again, but I moved away. She placed her hand in her lap. "I'm not a light."

That I know of. "I know."

"No, you don't," she said, shaking her head. "If I've learned anything from you, it's to remain private. I understand your frustration, even if you don't believe I do."

She returned to lying on the grass, and her purple gaze traced the sky. "It must be hard for Camille to look like something she hates," she said, never reaching for me. "I never look like a light."

I frowned, knowing she'd just exchanged personal information for trust. "You shouldn't tell me anything about yourself," I said. "Don't trust anybody else—no matter how close you are to them."

Her purple eyes squeezed together, and her brow furrowed. "Can I trust you?" she asked, and I plopped down next to her, lying on my stomach.

"That's your decision."

She turned her face, inches from mine, and stared at me. "I trust you, Shoman," she said. "More than anybody."

I froze from her words. How could she recognize her emotions, let alone express them so easily? I could barely stand my own conscience. Sharing it with someone seemed impossible, yet I had with a girl I barely knew. I didn't even have a name for her, shade or human, but I didn't need one to know her.

"I trust you, too," I said, returning to our conversation, my mind racing with possibilities. I didn't want it to end, and I definitely didn't want it to end because of the Marking of the Change. If anything, I wanted to survive—not for my kind, but for trust, for friendship, for another being.

I'd found something to live for, and I wasn't going to die, even if I didn't know the entire truth before I made the promise.

TWENTY-NINE

Jessica

L
ONG NIGHT?" ERIC ASKED AS HE LAID HIS HEAD ON THE DESK and peered at me with his green eyes.

I nodded groggily. Ms. Hinkel was allowing a study hall in our homeroom today, but I couldn't concentrate. I hadn't slept. "How about you?" I asked, and he shrugged.

"Same, but it was worth it," he admitted with a stifled laugh. "Unlike you, I'm not tired."

"I'm not that tired."

"Mhmm," he hummed, and I pressed my forehead against the cool table, ignoring his ability to irritate.

"What were you doing last night?" I asked.

"Getting some stresses out I suppose."

I peeked through my curls. "I heard about the funeral." The confession rolled off my lips. "I'm sorry to hear that."

His jaw popped. "But I'm used to it, right?"

I whistled low, knowing he was referring to the day before. "So you did hear Crystal."

He shrugged and lifted his head, pressing his back against the chair. I mirrored his movements and opened my mouth to speak, but was interrupted.

"Ms. Taylor, can I see you at my desk?" Ms. Hinkel asked, and I straightened up. Eric, on the other hand, didn't move.

I pushed my chair back and hurried to her desk. "Yes, ma'am?" I asked, fiddling with the ends of my hair.

She moved a photograph around on her desk. "I hope I'm not out of line, Ms. Taylor, but your mother told me about your parents."

My heart lodged into my throat. "They did?"

She nodded. "They thought I might know them, because I've lived here my entire life." Like everyone else in Hayworth. "But I didn't know them personally, but if you need help looking up anyone else, I'd love to help."

"Er, thanks," I said, stepping backward. I'd rather not discuss my personal life. "Can I go back to my desk now?"

Ms. Hinkel nodded, and I spun on my heel, practically running back to my desk. I slid into my seat, clutched my bag, and threw books on the table, desperately trying to distract myself. Did she seriously have to say something in the middle of class? The entire class had to hear. My face was burning with embarrassment. My fingers shook, and my pencil rolled across the table, toppling off.

I sprung forward to grab it, but Eric caught it, inches from me. His eyes met mine, and I noticed the electric streaks in his emerald-colored gaze.

We scooted backward, and he laid my pencil in front of me. "No one paid any attention," he said, running a hand through his hair. His bangs stood up with static.

"Except you," I guessed.

He laid his hands on his knees. "I didn't know you were looking for your family," he said.

"I wasn't," I sighed. "I needed good grades before I could."

His jaw rocked. "And that's why you were so pushy about the project."

I nodded.

"I expected something more normal, like being able to hang out on the weekends—or prom," he said, and I tapped my nails along my thigh. I kept forgetting about prom. I had more important things on my mind.

"I'm not as normal as you'd think, Eric," I said, and his gaze darkened.

"Neither am I."

159

I giggled at his darkness; his personality was beyond bizarre. "I never said I thought you were normal," I said, and he managed a smile.

"And you think that's funny?"

"How couldn't I?"

His smile stretched into a grin. "You're one interesting girl, Jessica."

My blood tingled through my veins, and I shifted in my seat. "You're pretty interesting too."

He frowned. "Interesting isn't what I'd call it."

"What would you call it then?" I asked, and he dropped his eyes, looking at the blank papers in front of him.

"I can't say."

"I don't believe that," I said, and he raised his brow beneath his shaggy hair.

"I never asked you to."

The bell rang, but we didn't move. Our bags remained at our feet, and our chairs stayed in place. He stared, widening his green eyes, and I bit my lip, unable to move. "Did I say something wrong?" I asked, and he shook his head.

"No," he whispered before his mouth snapped shut. He scooted back, and I felt a hand on my shoulder.

I turned around as Robb leaned over to pick up my bag. Crystal smacked her gum and grinned. "Are you coming or not?" she asked, and I stood up, turning my back to Eric.

"Yeah," I said, even though I didn't want to.

THIRTY

S HE WAS LATE.
I'd been waiting by the river for an hour, and I hadn't even heard from her. I sat for fifteen minutes, and then I paced like Luthicer, unable to remain still. Had she been caught? I didn't know, and I didn't want to consider the possibility until it was too late not to.

"Shoman." She appeared out of the shadows, misty and dark. Her pale face was reddened, and her hair withered like black snakes trying to return to the shadows.

I rushed to her side, laying my hands on her boney shoulders. "What's wrong?" I asked, and she reached up, folding her fingers around my wrist.

"I shouldn't stay; I—I can't do this anymore; I have to go—"

"What?" I searched her face, but she refused to meet my gaze. "What's going on? Talk to me." She shook her head from side to side. "Please."

"You wouldn't judge me?" she asked, biting her lip.

"Never."

Her nails dug into my skin, and she stepped back, letting go. "I'm not like you, Shoman," she said, voice shaking. "I can see it in your face; I can feel it."

My shoulders stiffened. She hadn't acted this scared since I first saw her by the river. "Feel what?" I asked, and she threw her hands into the air.

"I'm stronger than I'm supposed to be, aren't I?"

I avoided her purple eyes, unable to confirm her worries. I knew the truth—she was—but I couldn't tell her that. I had no explanation as to why, and her power, to be quite honest, was terrifying.

The shadows consumed her, and then she was in front of me, solidified. She grabbed my hands and held them up. "I am, aren't I?"

"No," I lied. "You're not." I just wanted her to breathe.

"I know more than you think," she said, dropping her face. "I know how to use powers you've never taught me."

Impossible. "Like what?"

"I don't know." She hesitated. "I can't explain it all."

"Then show me."

Her brow scrunched above her nose. "I don't know about this."

"Because you don't have an explanation," I said. "If you show me, I can tell you what it is." *And if it's anything like your previous powers, it'll probably be sparkles.*

She searched my face, and her purple eyes glowed. "Okay," she breathed and took a step back. She locked her feet and spread her fingers apart. A severe wind whipped between us, and her black hair burst around her face. A bright cyclone spun in front of her, and then it condensed, forming into violet metal. A sword sat in her hands.

I leapt back. Only descendants could do that—and I was one of them. My palm shot out instinctually, and my sword split through the air, resting in front of me.

"Who are you?" My voice ripped against my throat, and she stumbled backward, barely steadying her weapon.

"Shoman?" Her back was against the nearest tree as she stared at my mirrored sword. I'd told her it was impossible. "What are you doing?"

"Who are you?" I asked, considering my only possibility, Darthon. But I knew he was a male, and she wasn't. She had to be an illusion, a mask he wore to test my abilities. My grip tightened. "Tell me who you are."

"I'm—I'm—" She shook her head, and the tip of her sword dipped. "I can't, but it's me. I'm your student—"

"I don't believe you."

"Please." Her eyes began to water, and the purple sword flickered, disappearing into the shadows. She'd lost her concentration, and she held her hands up. "Put that away. I haven't changed."

This was my chance to kill her—or him. She was disarmed, but her powers vibrated off her, and they were vibrant. I hesitated, studying her expression. Her purple eyes were wide, and her black hair stuck to her cold face, blotchy with tears. She was petrified. Her fear was tearing my concentration apart.

"What did I do wrong?" she asked, and I stepped closer. She stomped her foot, screaming. "Please, Shoman. Put that away."

Blue streaks of power swirled around my blade, and I knew how it represented my adrenaline. My heart was pounding, and I was ready to strike. I could kill her for her power, let alone exposing mine. The Light was surely tracking it, and Fudicia already had my signal.

"Shoman!" Her voice barely penetrated my ears. "I'm telling the truth, please."

I didn't budge, and tears spilled over her long eyelashes. Her lip quavered, and she grabbed the bark, twisting her torso around the trunk. "Wait!" I shouted, but it was too late. She bolted, not even bothering to use the shadows, and ran across the ground like a human.

I absorbed my sword and ran after her. I swung through the thick brush, scraping against the bare branches and tickling leaves. I kept my eyes locked on her black hair, but she dodged every tree, branch, and stone. I didn't have time to look for them. I hit every one.

"Wait," I tried again, but her body burst into smoke, and I hit the ground, cursing.

What the hell was happening?

I leapt to my feet, shook off the dirt, and threw my senses

out. She was out of my radar, but I knew where she was headed. I compressed my molecules, squeezing my organs and skin together, and ripped them open again, landing on the street feet away from the river. She always left that way, and just as I planned, she ran right past me.

With one arm, I stopped her, and she screamed, pushing off me as I held her. Her nails dug into my skin, and I winced, stepping on her foot before she could kick my shin. "Screaming will only get us both caught," I said as she continued to fight. "Be quiet."

"Let me go." She squirmed against my chest. "Someone, help!"

"I'm sorry I have to do this," I said, laying a hand on her cheek before she pulled us to the ground. Her entire body stiffened, and I knew she was paralyzed. I had the power—as did most elders—but I'd never used it on a real person before, and I didn't like the feeling.

Her skin was cold, and her heartbeat slowed beneath my fingertips. I could feel her blood freeze in her veins, and her eyes widened as I lifted her face to look at her. They were blue. Her emotions almost turned her back into a human.

I looked away and sat her on the curb. "You have to listen to me," I said, knowing how the power would affect her. It generally made shades sick. "I'm not going to hurt you, understand?"

She didn't nod, and I had to remind myself that I'd taken her motor movements away. As long as I touched her, she couldn't move, and I kept my hand on her arm. "That prophecy I couldn't tell you about—there are two descendants; the first is from the Dark, the second, Darthon, is from the Light," I explained. "And you just used a power unique to them."

I swallowed, understanding my exposure. She knew who I was now. "But you're not Darthon, and that means there's more to the prophecy than I knew, and you're that part," I spoke as the realization came to me. "But the Light might know, and they could be after us right now. They can trace a descendant's power, and we just used it."

I let her go, knowing she'd have a moment before my energy fully left her bloodstream. "I'm trying to help you, but you have to let me," I said. "You'll probably feel really sick."

She leaned forward and gasped, pushing her head between her knees. She heaved, and I fought the temptation to touch her. I'd probably paralyze her again. It took a minute to tune the power down.

"Are you okay?" I asked, and she gripped the curb with shaky hands.

"What you said," she breathed, keeping her head down. "Is it true?"

"Every word."

She laid her cheek on her knee and looked up. Her blue eyes were purple again, but I shivered. They had looked so familiar before. "But that means," she began, sucking in breath. "You're the first descendant?"

"I told you I couldn't be a guard," I joked, but she didn't smile.

"What am I then?" she asked. "Am I Darthon? Do I have to fight you?"

I shook my head. "You can't be," I said. "For one, you're a girl, and you are too frightened to be." I ran a hand through my black hair and shook out the dirt it collected. "And I trust you." *Because I can't help it.*

"But—" Her fingers shook as she spread them out to stare at her palms. "How do you explain my power then?"

I frowned. "There must be a third," I said, and she tensed. I grabbed her hand, holding her shaking fingers. "Don't run. I'll figure this out."

She stood up, and I followed her. "I—I don't know what to say, Shoman," she said, on the verge of tears. I searched for her blue eyes, ready to study them again, but they remained violet. "I can't fight you. I can't be in a war."

"You don't have to be," I said, unsure if my words were truth. "The fight is between Darthon and me."

"But I have your power."

"I know," I managed to speak through the pain of my sinking chest. "How long have you been using that sword?"

"Just tonight." Her lips twisted. "But I've known about it all along."

The blood drained from my face. Her words described the very instance I showed my sword to Abby—a time that initiated her death. I'd felt the power in my veins for days, and I couldn't hold back any longer. Now my student was doing the same thing, and I was in Abby's place.

"You have to go home," I said, dragging her toward the forest. Energy was easier to muster in the dark. "Don't activate any powers for two days, okay? I'll find you then."

Her footsteps echoed behind me. "I'm scared, Shoman," she said, and I stopped her at the edge.

"It's okay," I said, laying my hands on her shoulders. Strands of her black hair twisted around my fingers, and I lifted them, watching purple sparkles drift to the ground.

"What if it isn't okay?" she asked. "What if nothing is?"

I wrapped my arms around her and pulled her against my chest. Aside from the first time, I'd never touched her first, but I couldn't stop myself. I wanted to protect her, and, if I couldn't do that, I'd at least be there for her. I wanted to stay with her, guarantee her safety, but I couldn't. I never could.

"Shoman?" she whispered against my neck, but didn't ask any questions.

It felt too right to be next to her, to feel her heartbeat against mine, to smell her shampoo or see the marks of her past in her eyes. It felt too right to see her and know she saw me back. It felt unnatural to leave her in the darkness with nothing.

I gave in.

I leaned back, lifted her face, and kissed her. She gasped, breathing against my lips before kissing me back. Her hand pressed against my neck, her fingers twisted into my hair, and I pulled her hips against mine. She didn't stop, and I didn't want her to.

I was Shoman—Eric Welborn—and I didn't like anybody. I didn't want anybody. But, apparently, I did. I wanted her, and

I had her all at the same time. Finally. I'd wanted it for longer than I even knew. I understand that now. But I had to let go. If she was going to be safe.

My hands wrapped around her hips and I pushed myself backward, stepping away. Her breath fogged out, drifting between us, and her eyes fluttered open. Her cheeks were rosy.

"You have to go," I said, letting go of her. "Now."

Her chest rose as she sucked in breath. "You'll see me again, right?"

I nodded. "I promised that days go, and I intend to keep it."

She smiled, stepped forward, and leaned up to kiss my cheek. Her warmth drifted over my skin, and goose bumps trailed down my neck as she moved away. "Good night, Shoman," she said, and I bit my tongue to prevent from shouting after her as she dissipated.

I wanted to stay with her, but I needed to get home. I had questions, and my father would have the answers.

THIRTY-ONE

I BURST INTO MY FATHER'S OFFICE, SHADOWS TRAILING AFTER MY HU-
man form. My rage controlled my body, and the double
doors leading into his office nearly split off the hinges.

His glasses fell off his nose as he shot up from his desk.
"Eric?"

"What have you been keeping from me?" I shouted, slamming my hands on his desk.

He straightened, whisking his hand through the air. The
air condensed with a silence spell. "Keep the ruckus down;
Mindy could hear you."

"I don't goddamn care about Mindy." The dangling ceiling
lights swung against my raising aura. "Since when has there
been a third descendant?"

My father's knees gave out, and he collapsed in his chair.
His face paled, and he hunched over as if he were about to
vomit. "Who told you?" he whispered.

My gut churned. So it was true; she wasn't Darthon.

"I found out myself," I said, curling my fingers into a fist.
My heated fingers, like sparks of fire, pressed against my palm.
"I met her."

He lifted his face, his brown eyes blank. "Eric, you must
understand—"

"Understand what?" I spat. "That you lied to me? That the
elders lied to everybody?" Even I'd been told there were two

descendants, not three, at the Naming.

"I was protecting you," he said. "They were protecting you."

"From what?" I asked, waving my hands out. "She isn't dangerous, even if she's more powerful than I am. If anything, she's teaching me more than Urte. She's protecting me."

My father jumped up. "She knows about our world?" he asked, and my brow scrunched.

"I taught her."

My father's shoulders rose, and his brown hair spiked black. "What have you done?" he asked, his transforming eyes glaring into mine. The blue color burned, and he slammed his palm on the table. A shadow opened up on his carpet, and the elders sprung through as if waiting for the unlikely moment.

"What's wrong?" Luthicer asked, grasping at the air. Urte and Eu blinked, stretching out, and I knew what'd happened. My father had forced their transportation.

"The third descendant knows," my father said, and Luthicer's dark eyes flashed white.

"What?" His bellow echoed. "Since when?"

"How is that possible?" Urte asked, clutching his bristled chin like a safety blanket. "She left Hayworth years ago."

"Well, she's back," my father said, and I stepped between the ranting men.

"What the hell is going on?" I asked. "What aren't you telling me?"

My father raised his hand to my face, keeping his focus on the elders. "Collect a force. Find her, and bring her back here," he said. "And don't come back until you have her with you."

"Yes, sir," Eu said, disappearing with Luthicer by his side.

I grasped for their air, but they were gone. "Wait, what?"

My father ignored me again, but Urte met my eyes.

"What are they doing?" I asked. "If they touch her—"

Urte's hand shot up and touched my face, and I fell to the ground, completely paralyzed. He'd used the power I'd used only minutes before. I couldn't move, and my heart clenched against my ribs.

"You need to calm down, Eric," Urte said, kneeling in front

169

of me. His green eyes were slits. "Calm down, and we'll explain." He turned his face to look at my father. "Bracke, you need to show him the rest of the prophecy."

"That's against our code—"

"It could also save our lives," Urte said, and blood began coursing through my veins. He'd barely touched me, but the paralysis aftermath twisted my mind.

I blinked, grabbing my temples. I preferred nausea. "The rest of the prophecy?" I croaked, attempting to stand.

My father moved across the room and grabbed my arm. "Relax," he said, closing his eyes. "I have to take you somewhere." And we disappeared in a cloud of smoke.

———◆———

I recognized the room immediately. The roof was decorated with the stars. It looked infinite, but I knew it wasn't. It was an illusion, created by Luthicer, and I'd figured it out shortly after I learned how to fly. The room used for the Naming was occupied once a year, so I used it as a training room until I was old enough for my own. If I'd only known it was lies, I wouldn't have bothered.

"Why here?" I asked, rubbing the chills off my arm. I'd transported too much for one day. It was meant for emergencies, not fun. It took too much energy to do.

My father sighed. "Because they can explain."

He pointed to the four shadows—two men, two women—silhouetted against the blue wall. They were never solid, and I'd never asked why.

"Bracke," I couldn't tell which one spoke. "We weren't expecting you for another year."

"It's time he knows of the third descendant," my father said, and the last woman moved.

"But the Marking of Change—"

"Is jeopardized."

Another silhouette turned, revealing a protruding chest. "We have no other choice?"

"None."

"Very well," she said, and the group clapped their hands together.

The dark room spiraled, stars and mist, as reflections of my past blurred with images of the prophecy—the history of the Dark. I saw myself at thirteen, seated cross-legged on the floor, laughing as Abby joked about the Naming. Our instructor scorned us, and I recognized the look in his eyes, sympathy. He knew what I'd learn about myself only minutes later. Then he was gone, and I saw Camille, my father, and even my mother for a moment. Time flew past us, and the ancient world sprung from the ground—pillars and all.

One man, dressed in black silk, laid a sword on a scroll of paper, and it sunk into the words. Now it was in my blood. I'd seen the images before.

"I'd prefer if we skipped this part," I said. "I know it already."

"As you wish," the chorus responded, and the image flipped. Two crowds of people, now the Light and the Dark, faced one another in a field of crumbling flowers. Fire raged behind them, and the sky blackened with smoke. I wasn't there, but I couldn't breathe.

"As you know," a woman narrated. "We were one clan until the Light split us in two."

"What does this have to do with the third descendant?" I asked, waiting for the picture to move, but it didn't. The people remained frozen.

"The Light believed they could separate without repercussions," she explained. "But energy doesn't work that way. It must remain equal."

"There was a bind, Shoman," my father said. "It kept the Light and the Dark together."

"Where'd the bind go?" I asked, and he laid a hand on my shoulder.

"It became its own," my father said, and my eyes flicked over the picture. More people appeared, torn between the families. "And the Light wanted it for themselves." One group began to claw at the people, while the others remained still.

"They wanted extra power."

"And the balance was lost," a woman added. "The Light wanted the third clan to be so powerful that even you, Shoman, couldn't destroy them."

"But they resisted?"

My father nodded. "And the bloodline for the third descendant was born."

I shook my head. "For what purpose?" I asked, staring at the war as it twisted into bloody chaos. I knew the story. No one won, and the powers were stripped and sealed with a treaty—the prophecy. The powers would only return generations before the descendants, and the descendants would determine which clan would dictate the power. Over time, the Dark became the destined winners, but I had yet to get an explanation.

"Because of the Light's greed, the third clan, being one of purity, rebelled from the treaty," a man spoke, and his silhouette soared across the wall. "They joined the innocent clan, the Dark."

"That's why she's a shade," I guessed, and wind pushed against me.

"Her clan's decision wasn't made without sacrifice," a voice said, and I turned around. "In order to keep the balance, she couldn't just join the Dark. She had to weaken it."

I froze. "That doesn't make any sense."

"It does," they said. "When she only weakens you."

The floor flipped, and I shivered as my vision blurred. The walls weren't black—they were gold, and the room filled with furniture and light. We were back in my father's office, and my molecules were spinning.

Urte sprung up from the desk, and my father walked past him. "They weren't done," I said, and my father stopped, hand on the door.

"I know."

"Bracke," Urte said. "He needs to know."

I agreed. "What did they mean by she weakens me? I've never felt stronger." She was the weakness they'd talked about during the funeral. I knew that now. "I need to know."

"Shoman," he sighed and turned around. "I can't—"

"Dad." My voice was harsh but desperate. "If you don't tell me," I paused. "I don't even know what will happen, but you do. And I need to know."

"Eric," Urte began, ready to divulge the information, but my father raised his hand.

"He's my son," he said. "I'll tell him."

"Then do it," Urte said, and my father met my eyes.

"You'll fall in love with her."

The words burned like her fear and tears when I pulled my sword on her. My stomach dropped to the floor, my heart skipped every other beat, and my nausea spun my gut into pieces. I was supposed to love her. I was supposed to feel for her. Even my emotions didn't belong to me. It was fated by something I never asked for.

"But I don't," I said. "Love her, I mean." I'd only kissed her once. How could the prophecy base love off a promised future before the children even existed? I wanted to hit something.

My father sighed, knocking the back of his head against the wall as he leaned backward. "I said, 'you will,' not 'you are.'"

I shook my hands in front of me. "That's ridiculous."

"Yet you betrayed your kind to meet her," he said, raising his brow. "That isn't the son I've raised."

My esophagus burned. "You raised me to hate for a reason," I realized, speaking out loud, and he nodded stiffly.

"The Light tracks you to find her," he said. "They can absorb her and use her against you."

"Absorb?" The words were unnaturally heavy. "What does that mean?"

"We don't even know, but the Light could win if they got her." He slowly melted into a human, but his gaze never faltered. "They will kill her, Eric; they'll kill anyone you love."

My knees locked to prevent my fall. "Abby."

Urte sucked in a breath. "When you showed her your sword, the energy lingered," he said. "That car wreck wasn't an accident."

I remembered the blonde girl peeking in, the light. I

thought she would kill me. "But they left me alive."

"They didn't know the first descendant was in that car," my father said. "Just that Abby had been near him, and that was reason enough to attack."

I swallowed despite my dry mouth and shivered. "I can't believe this." Even though it was beginning to make sense. "I killed her."

"The Light killed Abby," my father said. "Not you."

"But they thought she was the third descendant because of me."

"They shouldn't have," Urte said. "They knew the third descendant was gone."

"Gone?" I raised my brow, and remembered what she'd told me. She was adopted. "You put her in an orphanage?"

"Not exactly," Urte said. "Her family fled when she was born."

I shook my head. "How'd they know who she was?" I asked. "We aren't Named until we're thirteen."

Urte's eyes flickered over to my father, and his face fell. "The mothers seem to know upon birth."

My mom? I looked at my dad and opened my mouth, but closed it. I couldn't ask. Not now. "So they fled because of me?"

My father shook his head. "They fled because the Light would find her too easily," he said. "And they didn't want you to sacrifice yourself for her."

My chest knotted. "They knew me?"

He didn't confirm it, but he spoke anyway. "If you respected their memory at all, you'd stay away from their daughter," he said, freezing me. "Our victory resides on both of your lives, and running around with her risks that."

"But—" I promised to see her in two days. I can't leave her. Not without an explanation.

"No 'buts,' Eric." My father's voice rattled against the lights.

"I can't leave her oblivious to this," I said, trying to justify myself. "She won't turn her back on what she is, and if I leave her out there alone, she's just as likely to be caught."

Urte stepped forward. "How much does she know?"

I glanced over. "Everything but this."

My father's palm slapped the wall. "How long have you been talking to her?"

"Months."

He ran his fingers across his face. "And no one caught you?"

"No," I said. "I made sure of that." Except tonight. The Light must have felt our power.

"I told you not to go out by yourself, Eric," my father said, and I shook my transformation off my human skin.

"Now I know why," I said, glaring.

His brow lowered. "How could you do this to us?"

"She was frightened." I threw my hands up. "She had no idea what was happening to her, let alone what she was. I had to help her—"

"Then you felt the need to love her, too, right?"

I pointed at him. "You can't blame me for that." The words left without denial, and my fingers spread out, shocked by the sound of my own voice. I couldn't be in love this quickly. I barely knew her. I didn't even know her name.

"I don't love her," I clarified as my father's shoulders dropped. "But I won't hate her either. I can't."

"Then how do you expect her to live, Eric?" he asked. "They will kill her."

"I'll protect her."

"Like you protected Abby?" he asked, and his words punched my chest, broke my ribs, and sliced my throat all at once. He might as well have killed me with my worst memory, and the worst part was how right he was.

Knocking rapped against the office doors, and Urte shed his appearance as the doorknob shook. "Dear?" Mindy's voice floated through the wood. "Are you home? Your door is locked, and I thought I heard something."

"Eric and I are talking, sweetheart," he said, straightening his clothes. "We'll be done in a minute."

"We're done now," I said, storming toward the doors, but he blocked me.

"You can't do this, Eric; you can't be with her," he said, widening his brown eyes. "Tell me where she is; we'll protect her."

I stared into the eyes of the man who'd lied to me the most and pushed past him. "No," I said, leaving his office for the night.

THIRTY-TWO

H E WAS SLEEPING IN HIS CAR WHEN I FOUND HIM, AND HE looked worse than usual. His jacket was thrown over his torso, and his arms were wrapped around his backpack like a pillow. He was even drooling.

I cringed, contemplating leaving him to his sleep, but I couldn't walk away. I knocked on his window, hoping he wasn't the type of guy to get mad over a smudge, and he stirred.

"Eric." I knocked again, and he sat up only to fall back down. "Wake up. School's starting."

His eyelids opened, and he shot up, grasping his steering wheel. I jumped, but calmed when he turned to me. His mouth hung open, and he shook his head, slowly rolling his window down. "Jessica?" He practically groaned. "What are you doing here?"

I pointed toward our high school. "Class starts in fifteen," I said, and his brow furrowed.

He arched his neck, grabbing it with his hand, and surveyed the parking lot. It was full. "I guess it is."

I sighed. "Did you sleep here last night?"

He looked back at me and yawned. "It was more comfortable than home."

I frowned, looking over his washed out cheeks. "Do you need me to get a nurse?"

He straightened up, nearly breaking his Charger's seat.

"What? Why do I need a nurse?" He ran his hand through his hair and stared into the mirror as if he was expecting blood to trail down his forehead.

I rolled my eyes. "You look sick, Eric," I said. It was warm now, but I knew it'd gotten cold last night, and his engine wasn't running. He probably had a cold.

"I'm not sick," Eric said, fumbling with his car keys. "I'm fine."

"Are you sure?"

He stared. "Yes."

I put my hands up. "Okay. Okay," I said. "Just checking."

He turned away and rolled up the window before climbing out. With one hand, he threw his bag over his shoulder, and with the other, he rubbed his jaw. When he stretched his arm over his head, I turned away, remembering what he looked like shirtless. My cheeks burned.

"Why are you in the parking lot anyway?" he asked, yawning for the umpteenth time. He winked. "You were watching me sleep again; weren't you?"

"No," I said, crossing my arms. *Not for very long.* "My mom dropped me off, and I saw your car."

He leaned against the driver's door. "And you thought you might as well look into it," he said, smirking. "Even though I might have been inside the school already."

"You're always late."

His brow rose. "You pay an awful amount of attention to me."

"Don't flatter yourself," I said, turning away to walk toward the school. Why did I even try?

His footsteps followed, and he walked next to me. "Can I ask you something, Jessica?"

"I guess." I held my breath.

"It's about your parents—"

"I'd rather not talk about it," I grumbled, refusing to believe he'd pry into my life when he strived to keep his so private.

He whistled low. "The search isn't going so well, I'm guessing."

I stopped, cocking my hip. "Why do you care?"

"I'm sorry," he said, facing me. "I didn't mean to offend you; I was only curious."

"No offense," I said. "But I was planning on keeping the whole adoption thing to myself."

"Until our teacher ruined it for you," he said, and I glared.

"She wouldn't have ruined it if you didn't have a talent for eavesdropping."

He smiled. "You mean a hobby."

I groaned and stomped forward. I should've let him sleep through the day.

"Come on, Jessica," he said, running beside me. "I only have a few questions—"

I gripped my backpack's straps and dug my nails into the fabric. "What are you, five?"

"I think a five-year-old is more mature."

"I wouldn't doubt it," I said, barely glancing over. His hair was a mess. "Why would you want to know anyway?"

He didn't meet my eyes, and he shrugged. "I need to know more about adoption—for a friend."

I shook my head. "I'm not the only one adopted in Hayworth."

Abruptly, he stopped, and he leaned on his toes as if his momentum tried to push him forward. He raised his brow. "Do you know others?"

"No," I said. "But it's not exactly something people advertise."

His eyes flickered over my face, but he seemed to be somewhere else entirely. His green eyes were blank, and his mouth opened without a word to be spoken.

I stared. Why did he have to be so weird?

He sighed and dropped his shoulders. "There could be a lot, huh?"

I nodded, trying to figure out where he was coming from. "Yeah."

His jaw locked, and he jumped in place. He grinned and stepped in front of me. "Can I walk you to class?" he asked, and I tensed. "As friends, of course."

The warning bell rang, and I exhaled. "Sure," I said, wondering why my chest felt so heavy. I didn't want to talk about my biological parents to Eric, let alone to anyone, but it had happened, and I'd only been awake for an hour. Ever since reading the newspaper article, I dreaded digging deeper, but I knew I had to, and that was what unsettled me. Confessing my situation to Crystal and Crystal's mother topped my To-do list, but then what? I wanted to figure out who my parents were, but I already knew the truth. I'd only find gravestones.

THIRTY-THREE

"O F ALL THE THINGS YOU COULD'VE BEEN DOING WITH YOUR freedom, the last thing I thought you'd do is meet up with a girl," Camille said, spinning around in my computer chair.

It was after school, and she'd been with me—as Teresa—ever since. Leaving the house the night I'd admitted to knowing the third descendant did not sit well with my father. He was furious, and I was grounded. Although he didn't have much control on whether I left or not. I could transport out whenever I wanted to.

"Me neither," I admitted, throwing my stress ball at the ceiling. I'd used it since I was child, but it didn't do much for me anymore. I was surprised I hadn't dented the ceiling. "I'm amazed they even told you."

"Of course they did," she said, and the sickening smell of nail polish consumed my bedroom. Teresa was painting her nails. Again. "I'm your guard; I'm the one who should've told them."

"I know you're my guard," I said, and she sighed.

"I'm your friend, too," she said, and I could hear her scrape the brush along her nail. "You can talk to me."

"So you can tell my father?" I threw the ball again. "No, thanks."

She kicked the back of my bed, and it rattled. "I wouldn't," she said. "He still doesn't know about our deal. He has no clue how you snuck around without me knowing." I leaned back, and she smiled. "I didn't tell him that I knew you were out."

"But you already got in trouble once."

"Exactly why I didn't confess again," she said. Her nails were pink, for spring, and I had to turn away. I hated the reminders of spring's arrival. The Marking of Change was closer than I wanted it to be. "I told you I was your friend."

"And my guard."

"A guard who can keep a secret," she said, winking her blue eye. "Especially when it involves loveeeeee."

I rolled onto my side and stared at the blue light creeping beneath my desk. I couldn't help but feel conflicted about the word. I truly cared for the nameless shade, but I hated the idea of fate controlling my emotions. I wanted one piece of my life to belong to me, but the more I learned, the more I knew how much my life didn't belong to me. And her life wasn't hers. The Light was after her, and she didn't even know it. I wasn't sure what was worse: being oblivious or living within reality.

"What's she like?" Camille asked, leaning over to catch my eye. My stomach twisted as the girl flashed through my memory.

"She's—" I stopped. Logically, I didn't want to admit to anything, but emotionally, I'd been dying to confess to someone. Her smile was unforgettable, her power was startling, and her personality shook me. "She's stunning," I breathed, and Camille grinned.

"My little Eric—all grown up," she said, and I laughed.

"I'm not much younger than you."

"But you're like my little brother," she said, finishing her nails. She waved them through the air to dry. "How'd you meet her anyway?"

"She was by the river," I said, trusting Camille to keep the information to herself. "Same day as the Naming."

Camille sprang forward, and the chair squeaked. "I knew it. You were acting so weird that day."

I shrugged. "Can you blame me?"

"No," she sighed. "It's terribly romantic."

"And you're making me sick," I said, rolling my eyes at her. Sometimes, I forgot how much of a girl Camille actually was.

"I can't help it," she said, and she kicked her feet onto my bed. "You've been happier lately, but I couldn't figure out why. It's nice to know."

I looked at her and raised my brow. "I've been happier?" I asked, wondering how much I'd changed.

She smirked. "You actually talked to Mindy and Noah," she said. "It wasn't hard to figure out something had changed, especially considering your timing. It isn't exactly a time to get giddy."

I grimaced. "I'd rather not talk about my birthday," I said, knowing where the conversation was going: The Marking of Change. Camille couldn't let it go, and all I wanted to do was forget it.

"But this changes everything," she said, dropping her voice to a whisper. "A third descendant; who knew?"

"The elders," I said, feeling my anger rise again. "I still can't believe that they lied, let alone about her."

"I can," Camille said. "Think about it. If they told you the truth, you probably would've looked for her. You would've been emotional."

I frowned and laid my hands behind my head. "But their lies didn't change anything."

"It might have," she said. "If you'd followed the rules."

I met her gaze with a glare. "You can't blame me for this."

"I'm not," she said. "No one is."

I sighed, grasping my hair. "It feels like it."

She stood up, and my bed sank as she sat next to me. "I think you're blaming yourself," she said, and my jaw locked. "You can't let Abby's death linger like you have."

I gaped at my guard. "Who said anything about Abby?"

"I did," she said. "Because I know that's why you're beating yourself up. You always have, and this information makes it worse."

"No shit."

She tapped my leg. "She'll be okay, you know," she said, smiling, and I sat up, pressing my back against the wall.

"Abby's dead."

She rolled her blue eyes. "I was talking about your lover."

I opened my mouth to argue, but concentrated on her words. "You're the first to believe in me," I said, stretching my legs out. They were sore from training. "Everyone thinks the Light will find her, because of me."

Her gaze flickered over my face. "You must be somewhat scared for her."

I sighed. "Of course I am."

"When are you going to see her again?" Not, 'Are you going to see her again?' Camille knew I couldn't stay away.

"Soon," I said, and she breathed in.

"I'm supposed to follow you." She managed a small smile. "But you're going to tell me you're training, and I'm going to believe you."

I straightened up. "Seriously?"

"Tell me," she said.

"I'm going to train tomorrow night."

She grinned. "Have fun," she said. "But be careful."

I opened my mouth to thank her, but footsteps thundered toward my door, and rapping shook my door. "Eric?" Mindy's voice was high-pitched. "Your father wants to know if you're doing anything tonight," she said, opening the door, and her mouth opened. "Teresa. I didn't hear you come in."

That's because she transported in. She never used the front door.

Camille smiled. "I came in a few minutes ago, ma'am," she said.

Mindy blinked her round eyes. "But I was right by the front door."

"And you were so into your novel," Camille said, and her blue eyes flashed black. The air crackled with light energy, and I cringed, watching Mindy's red eyebrows furrow. Camille created an illusion, a power unique to the Light, and I knew Mindy would believe it.

"It was a good book," she said, touching her frizzing red hair. "Do you two want anything to eat? I just made lemon cakes." She'd even forgotten what she came to ask.

"I'm allergic," Camille said, and Mindy blushed.

"I can bake something else if you'd like."

"That's okay," she said, standing up. "We were just about to leave."

"*We are?*" I asked Camille silently, but she ignored me.

"Oh," Mindy's face fell. "You kids have fun." She turned to leave, but I stopped her.

"Mindy?"

She spun around, her face flushed. "Yes, Eric?"

"Can I take one of those lemon things to go?"

She hopped up, beaming. "Of course. I'll be right back."

She left, and Camille stared at me. "You really are happier."

I brushed her off. I didn't want to talk about it, but I knew I had to be nicer to Mindy. I'd partially blamed my father's marriage for Abby's death, since we'd been heading to the wedding when we crashed. But now I knew. Abby was murdered because of me. Not my father or Mindy.

"Where are we going anyway?" I asked, and Camille walked into the hallway.

"I'm going home," she said. "But I don't know about you."

I chuckled, shutting my door before I followed her down the hallway. Mindy popped up and handed me a cake, wrapped in a paper towel. "Here you go," she said.

"Thanks."

"You guys have fun," she said, grinning so widely I was sure her face would split.

I nodded, bounded down the stairs, and opened the front door. Camille and I rushed outside, and she stared at her old BMW, parked next to my Charger. She sighed. "I love that car of yours."

"Don't even think about it," I said, pulling my keys from my pocket. I knew she loved speed as much as I did. She'd crash it if I let her drive.

She laughed and strode to her car. "I'll see you later," she said, winking before she ducked inside. "Have fun training."

"I will," I said, waving at her as I got into mine. My car was perfect, my dream vehicle, but the reason behind the gift destroyed my ride as if it had a broken transmission. It was a pre-death present, and my father was lying if he denied it. He'd bought it out of guilt, nothing else.

I turned over the engine and bit into Mindy's lemon cake. It was sweet, moist and delicious. My taste buds tingled, and I shoved the rest of it in my mouth. *Not bad, Mindy. Not bad at all.* I had to warm up to her more often.

THIRTY-FOUR

S HE WAS IN OUR USUAL SPOT, AND I RUSHED TO HER SIDE BEFORE she'd sensed my arrival. "We have to get out of here," I said, grabbing her hand as she gaped at me.

"What?" she asked, dragging her feet along the grass as I led her away from the forest. My father had sent the entire force out to find her, and we'd be caught if we stayed close to the shelter. "What's going on?"

I pointed to the sky, and her purple eyes darted up. Streaks of green and blue soared against the blackness, and her grasp tightened. "What are those?"

"Shade energy," I said, lifting her into the air as I soared along the river. We were flying. "They found out about us."

"How?"

"I'll explain in a minute," I said, and the water flicked behind us as we passed over it. She steadied herself, let go of my hand, and flew by my side as we curved around the river bend. A cluster of trees—ones that I knew led to the school—hung over the edge, and she sped up, dipping into them.

She laid her feet on the ground, and the trees blew. I landed next to her, and the leaves waved between our faces. I pushed them away. "We'll be okay here."

"It isn't that far from our usual spot," she said, allowing her gaze to linger behind me.

I ignored her and wrapped my arms around her torso.

She squeaked, surprised by my sudden embrace, but leaned into my chest. Her hand tapped against my ribcage. "Shoman," she breathed. "What's wrong?"

"I'm glad you're okay," I said, laying my hand against her hair.

She leaned back, looking into my eyes. "I was worried about you, too."

"I'm okay."

She smiled, staring at her hand as she spread her fingers over my shirt. "I know that now."

I held my breath. Did she feel the same way about me? She had to.

"Are you in trouble?" she asked.

"They sensed our power," I admitted. "But I don't want you to be involved."

Her eyes widened. "They're looking for me?"

I nodded. "I'm not comfortable with it either."

Her hand curled into a fist. "Is it the Light?"

"No." *Not that I know of.*

Her brow furrowed. "Then what's the problem?"

I wanted to tell her that she was the third descendant, to explain the prophecy, but I couldn't, and she frowned at my silence.

"You can't tell me," she said, and I looked away.

"It's complicated," I said. "Did you use any of your powers?"

She shook her head. "Believe me, I took your word to heart. I haven't even transformed until tonight."

"Good," I sighed, knowing she could've been tracked. We both could be, but I could defend myself. "Are you feeling okay?"

Her shoulders dropped. "I've been exhausted."

"That's expected after activating your powers," I explained, knowing the descendant power came with faults. It completely drained me the first time.

"The descendant powers," she said, biting her lip, and I knew what was coming. "Did you figure out what I am?"

Yes. "Not exactly," I said. "But you aren't Darthon. You

don't have to worry."

She folded her arms and leaned into me. "But the war." Her words shivered through my chest. "If you're the first descendant that means you have to fight. You have to win."

"I know."

Her forehead pressed against my sternum. "How long do you have?"

"Less than a year."

She laid her hands on my hips and stepped backward. "But—"

"I won't be alone," I said, trying to calm her. "The Dark will be with me." Hopefully. It wasn't guaranteed. In fact, it was more likely I would be alone, but I couldn't tell her that. She'd be upset.

"I want to help," she said, and I froze.

"No."

She dropped her hands. "Why not?" she asked. "I have powers. I can help."

"You aren't going near the Light," I said, knowing her life was more precious than mine was. They could absorb her, whatever that meant, and her death would cause their success. I couldn't risk it. I wouldn't.

She folded her arms. "Whether you like it or not, I'm going to help. I'm here to stay, Shoman, or have you forgotten that?"

I sighed, running a hand through my hair. "It isn't that simple."

"Then make it that simple."

I can't. "You aren't fighting, and it isn't up for negotiation."

She dug her toes into the dirt and snapped a leaf off a branch. She fiddled with it in her hands and sat down, tearing it down the middle. "But I'm capable—"

I sat next to her. "I know you're capable," I said, sighing. "But it's too dangerous, and you're not going to get hurt because of my inability to fight."

Her mouth opened. "You're protecting me from something."

My shoulders tensed. "Why do you say that?"

The leaf sparkled purple beneath her touch. "I can read you better than you think," she said. "You aren't confident about defeating this Darthon guy, huh?"

I laid my arms on my knees. I had yet to tell her about Fudicia. "I don't know what to expect from him," I admitted.

She eyed me. "Or from yourself." I tensed, and she leaned against me. "I'm not trying to upset you," she said. "I'm just trying to figure this out, and it's hard when you don't tell me everything—or anything, for that matter."

My jaw popped. "It's better if I don't."

She was quiet, and her cold cheek pressed against my bicep. "I'm worried about you. I care about you."

My stomach churned. Was she supposed to love me, too? I didn't know.

"Don't worry about me," I said, fighting my emotions away. "I'll be fine."

"I can't lose you, Shoman."

I straightened up, and whiplash stung my neck as I turned to her. Tears pressed against her eyes, and my stomach twisted. "You're not going to lose me," I said, but she turned away. "Hey." I moved toward and leaned over. "Look at me." She didn't move. "Please look at me."

I touched her chin, lifting her face, and she blinked, pushing tears back. "You really think you're going to lose me?" I asked, and she almost nodded. I kissed her. She tensed, and I moved back, looking into her eyes. "You aren't."

"Then let me help," she said, and I grabbed her hand.

"I can't," I said. "You need to trust that. You need to trust me."

"And I do—"

"Then forget about the battle," I said, running my thumb over the back of her hand. "Please."

She bit her quavering lip, but she didn't nod. "I can pretend to," she said. "But I won't."

I sighed, opening my mouth to argue, but she placed a finger on my lips. She smiled, "I may not know all the details," she said. "But I know you're in trouble, and I don't want to see you get hurt."

I wrapped my fingers around her wrist and kissed her finger. I loved being near her. "We should talk about something else—"

"About how much I care for you?" Her voice was sharp, but her eyes were soft. My jaw locked, and she hugged her knees, laying her chin on them. She blinked, and the purple color glowed in the shadows of the trees. "I don't know how I can feel this much when I barely know you, but I do."

Her words explained everything I felt, and I knew I couldn't deny it anymore. I was falling in love with her, and she was falling in love with me. It was fated, decided before any of us were born, and I hated it as much as I loved it. I could barely stand it.

"I don't know either," I whispered, and she scooted closer, lying on my lap. I leaned back, placing my hands on the dirt, and she stared up at me.

"Do you think fate's possible?" she asked, and I stiffened.

Fate was a reality, but it wasn't a beautiful or angelic thing. It was a heart-wrenching nightmare. And we'd fallen blindly into it. We had no escape. It was happening, and it was up to me to guarantee our survival of it.

"Yes," I said. "I think it's very possible."

She smiled and pulled me down to kiss me, even though I knew she wouldn't if she understood the ramifications of it all. Her kiss could kill us, and my consent signed our death certificates, selfishly and without control.

THIRTY-FIVE

"If you put off dress shopping any longer, I'm going to write a nasty rumor about you in my column," Crystal said, sliding into the booth next to me. It was after school, and, for once, I'd taken the time to hang out with my only friends.

"I can't go tonight," I said. "I'm busy."

"Jess," she whined like a child. "You promised you'd go before prom, and it's two weeks away."

"Which means we have two weeks to shop," I said, drumming my nails across the sticky table. She glared at me, and I sighed. "I promise I'll go, just not tonight. Please."

Robb joined us with burgers as Crystal flicked her tongue over her lip piercing. "But I want to go tonight."

"I'm busy."

"With what?" she asked. "You're always busy, and you don't even tell me why."

I sighed. "It's nothing, really." Just searching for my parents and hesitating to ask for your mother's help.

"Then ditch it," Crystal said, and Robb groaned.

"Leave it alone, Crystal," he said, biting into his cheeseburger. "I'm sure Jess has good reasons. Right, Jess?" He winked.

I dropped eye contact. "Right."

Crystal sighed and picked at her fries. "Fine," she said. "But I expect you to go next weekend, no arguments."

"Deal."

Crystal reached over and grabbed the ketchup, filling her plate with it. "So," she began, twirling a fry in the mess. "Have you found a date yet?" she asked me, and Robb choked.

"No," I said, ignoring his reaction. "I'm kind of a go-single-to-avoid-drama sort of a girl."

"Good," Crystal said, munching on her food. "I was afraid you'd bring some random guy with us."

"It's not like I even know anyone else," I said, and Crystal rolled her eyes.

"For all I knew, you had a boyfriend from Georgia that was coming up."

My jaw opened. "Don't you think I would've mentioned that?"

"No," Robb and Crystal spoke at the same time.

I dropped my gaze. I guess I didn't tell them as much about my life as they'd told me about theirs. "Well, I don't—have a boyfriend, I mean."

"Do you want one?" Robb asked, and Crystal sat up, leaned across the table, and smacked his arm.

"You have Linda," she said, and he shrugged.

"Our relationship isn't defined," he said, and Crystal's eyes turned to slits.

"Would she say the same thing?"

He didn't react, and Crystal smacked herself on the forehead. "You're impossible, Robb."

"What?" he asked, and fries fell out of his mouth. "Prom is the best time to meet new friends."

"You mean girls," Crystal said, curling her lip.

"Friends," he repeated.

"I'm sorry, I didn't know friends sucked one another's faces off," she said, and he threw his hands in the air.

"I don't suck face with them," he said, stumbling over Crystal's diction.

She held her hand up. "Don't defend your raging teenage-boy hormones," she said. "I'm sick of it. You always bring girls around."

His brown eyes blinked. "I'm not bringing anyone to prom."

"Not yet."

"Come on, guys," I said, waving my hand between them. "Stop arguing."

"Easy enough for you to say," Crystal said. "You haven't watched Robb drool over every girl with two legs since you were able to walk yourself."

Robb sighed. "I'm not that bad."

Crystal flayed around. "You flirted with my cousin."

"So?"

"You were fourteen," she said, leaning on her hand. "And she was twenty."

I giggled, slapping my hand over my mouth. "That's pretty ridiculous, Robb," I said, and he grinned.

"You didn't see her cousin," he said. "She was hot."

Crystal banged her forehead against the table. "That's my family member you're talking about."

"Well, you have a hot family."

She groaned. "I don't even know why I'm friends with you."

"Lighten up, Hutchins," he said, chewing on his burger. "I'm only joking."

"Your joking is about to make me sick," she said, glancing up from the table. "And that cousin is an alcoholic stripper now."

Robb chuckled. "Explains why she was so much fun."

Crystal sat up to hit him again, but I pulled her back. "Relax," I laughed, and she groaned, leaning against me.

"Let's go do something else, please," she said. "This burger joint is too small, and I don't like where this conversation is going."

"Okay," Robb said, pulling his wallet out of his back pocket. The waitress darted our way.

He cursed, and Crystal's jaw dropped. "Don't tell me you forgot your money again."

He smiled. "Don't worry," he said, returning his wallet. "I

194

got this."

"Watch this," Crystal whispered as the waitress neared our table.

"Here's your check," she said, and Robb stood up, inches from her.

"Greta," he said as I recognized her from school. "I had no idea you worked here."

Her pasty cheeks burned crimson. "Yeah," was all she could manage.

Robb ran a hand through his thick hair. "I wish I'd known you worked here. I'd come in more often."

Greta lit up. "You would?"

"Definitely," he said. "I really enjoy talking to you in—math—er—history class."

"Art class," she corrected, tilting her head. "And I don't think we've talked before."

Robb smiled, leaning closer. "We should."

If I hadn't seen it with my own eyes, I wouldn't have believed it. He had this girl completely under his spell, utterly and pathetically love struck. She might as well have been hypnotized.

"So we should chill sometime," he said, flipping open his empty wallet "Let me write down my number." He stopped. "I don't have any paper."

She fumbled with the check and turned it over. "You can write on this."

"Thanks," he said, stealing the pen right off her ear. She shuddered.

Please.

"Call me tonight; we could do something," he said, handing it back to her as he stared into his wallet. "Or not."

"What's wrong?" she asked, and he revealed the emptiness.

"Looks like I can't afford it," he said. "I left my money at home."

"Don't worry about it," she said, laying her hand on his shoulder. "I'll take care of the bill. You can make it up to me when you can."

He raised his brow. "I can't let you do that."

"I insist," she said, and he nodded, smiling.

"Thanks, Greta."

"See you later," she said, bounding off to the kitchen.

Robb fell back in the booth and laid his arm on the back of the chair. "Told you I'd take care of it," he said, and I shook my head.

"I cannot believe you."

He shrugged. "I got you two out of your bill, too."

"It's the only reason I let him get away with it. I couldn't afford burgers without his charm," Crystal said, scooting out of the booth. "Let's get out of here."

I sprang up, ready to leave. I'd feel too guilty watching Greta walk around in her bliss. Robb would break her heart, and he probably wouldn't lose sleep over it. But he was my friend, and so was Crystal. My life was finally coming into place, but I couldn't feel more unsettled.

If I'd learned anything, it was how easily life could turn around. When everything was right, something was bound to go wrong. I could only hope it wouldn't be as bad as I was expecting.

THIRTY-SIX

I LOVED HOW SHE CURLED UP UNDER MY ARM, HOW SHE SEEMED TO fit into the space as if it was meant for her. Because it was. I'd ignored the reality of impending danger and replaced it with the comforting notion of significance. She was mine—my girl—and I actually cared about someone, even when I couldn't care about myself. To abandon her was impossible, but to stay was selfish. I didn't know what to do.

"Shoman?" She stretched her legs and looked up at me. Her purple eyes were illuminated, like stars against the night sky, but it wasn't midnight, and the night was dying. We had to leave soon. "Are you okay?"

"Perfect," I said, sitting up beneath the shelter of our crevice, yards from the main forest. I hadn't seen the force of shades my father had sent out to find her, but I didn't trust the silence. Shadows could be anywhere in blackness.

She bit her lip and sat up near me, holding her knees. "We should leave soon," she said. She knew the rules. We always had to return seconds before sunrise.

"I know," I said, grabbing her hand as I stood. I pulled her up with me. "But I wanted to show you something."

"What is it?"

"Wait," I said, leading us from the shadows and toward the grassy riverbed. I pointed to the sky, the clouds lightening with every moment. "Just watch."

She arched her neck, flicking her gaze over the mediocre spring shower. Thick raindrops fell from the sky, splashing against the water, and rain glittered against her hair. "I don't see anything," she said, turning back to me, but I pointed back up.

"Now you will."

Bats, hundreds of them, circled and dipped, dove and flew, twisting through the air as they collected their dawning breakfast. She sucked in a breath, and her gasp brought shivers to my spine in the same way the image of morning bats had when I first saw them as a child.

Every moment before a storm, especially between night and day, they came out, flying around the sky with a synchronized hunt. It appeared to be a dance, a game of sorts, but it wasn't. It was a life cycle.

I grabbed her hand, and she squeezed mine back. "How'd you know?" she whispered, and I shrugged, wanting to enjoy the moment rather than explain the reasoning behind it. My mother had shown them to me.

"They're beautiful," she said, and I nodded.

"*You are, too,*" I told her, diving into her mind with my voice.

She tensed, briefly turning away from the scene. "I'm not used to hearing your voice inside of me," she said, smiling afterward. "But I like it."

Her thumb traveled across my palm, and my heart thundered through the touch. I could feel her heartbeat; it was racing, too.

"I thought you'd like it," I said, watching the bats as they dissipated. The sunrise was coming. "I had—"

I stopped. Tiny hairs on the back of neck stood up, static electricity flowing through the thickening air. The warm wind seized, and the river quickened, sizzling beneath the sudden change in temperature.

I tensed, yanking her into the trees. She stumbled, falling against my chest, and I grasped her shoulders. She was rigid. "What was that?" she asked, and I shushed her.

I knew the feeling all too well. A light was near, and they weren't alone.

"Shoman—"

"Don't talk," I said, and her toes dug into the shredded leaves. We had to escape. *"Follow me."* I pulled her out, but it was too late.

Wind whipped around the valley, and the trees bent dangerously in half. Beneath us, the grass exploded, twisting into a whirlpool of green and black. I grabbed her, protecting the back of her neck with my hand, and closed my eyes. Suddenly, I was thankful for Luthicer's test months back.

I could handle the feeling, the ripping and burning of the electricity crawling across my skin. I clenched my teeth, put my back to it, and took the blow. It smacked against my body, and we fell to the ground, digging our knees into the dirt.

My vision spun when I opened my eyes, and I blinked, looking over the nameless shade in front of me. Her purple eyes were wide, and her already pale skin had drained to gray. Her mouth was open, but she didn't speak.

"This was much better than I was expecting," a woman said, and I turned, springing to my feet.

I knew that voice.

"Fudicia." Her name spat out of my lungs uncontrollably.

Her long, blonde hair was blinding against the dawning light, but her black eyes were holes, twinkling only when she dragged them over me.

"I was expecting someone else," she said, briefly signaling to the man beside her. "Thought I could train him with some real-life experience."

The boy was nowhere near the man I'd expected to see by her side, but I wasn't complaining. I could handle him. He was young and scrawny, and his different colored eyes signaled what he truly was, a half-breed.

"It's a little dangerous to bring him around me; don't you think?" I asked, steadying my feet as my girl clutched on my back.

Fudicia crimson lips spread into a grin as she leaned over

to look at her. "Who's this? A friend?"

My chest tightened. She didn't know about the third descendant. How was that possible?

"Let her go," I said, "and we'll deal with this ourselves."

Fudicia cackled. "There's no such thing as negotiation in war, Shoman," she said, cocking her brow. "Don't you already know that?"

I grabbed my shade's hand and tried to contain our molecules, but my body tingled. I hissed, grinding my teeth, and Fudicia continued to smile.

"You can't transport with our energy around," she said, stepping forward. "It'd only hurt you more."

We had to escape.

"Hold on," I said to my trainee, and her nails dug into my arm.

I shot up through the air, breaking off branches as I split the tree line. The Light energy burned, but I ignored the feeling, forcing our bodies through the suffocation. We flew, straight toward the forest, and I could feel them following. Their energy. The Light.

A blast of fire struck my leg, and the force knocked us from the air. She screamed as we fell, but I held her, feeling my muscles rip as we tumbled. I smacked the ground, and my chest heaved, forcing the air out of my lungs. I wheezed, but jumped to my feet. I'd felt the pain before. It was nothing.

"You're seriously running?" Fudicia asked, inches away as I pulled the third descendant to her feet. She was shaking. "That's weak."

The half-breed circled around us, and I glowered. "He's weak," I said, pointing at Fudicia's oblivious comrade. "And you're weak for using him."

"Like I care if he gets hurt," Fudicia said, waving her hands over us. "I have the first descendant in front of me."

The half-breed's eyes flickered. "What?"

"Don't worry," she said. "He can't hurt you anyway."

She spoke too soon. I shot forward, punching him across the face, and his jaw dislocated beneath my force. His face hit the ground, and I kicked at his ribs, but missed. A blast of purple mist collided with him, and he spiraled through the air.

The third descendant had attacked.

"Don't use your sword," I said, knowing she'd expose herself at any moment.

She blinked back, and Fudicia tensed, glaring at the girl behind me. "You." She pointed at her and moved closer, but I stepped in front.

"Leave," I said, but Fudicia raised her hand. I barely had time to turn to my trainee. "Run!" I screamed, and the attack struck the back of my head.

I bent over, regaining my composure, and watched as she fled, sprinting through the trees. Fudicia screeched, readying to chase her, but the half-breed was on his feet. "I got her," he said, and I reached out.

Fudicia's nails dug into my arm, and my blood boiled. Poison. She smiled, and her breath pressed against my cheek. "I didn't think you could care for anyone but the third descendant." Her words locked my jaw. "Don't you know?" she continued, rasping against my face. "I killed her a long time ago."

Abby's car wreck flashed, and I was there—bleeding in the car as I watched a young blonde lean in, surveying the damage. Fudicia was Abby's murderer.

I elbowed her stomach and shoved her sternum. She flew backward, smacking against a tree, and I didn't hesitate. I ran for the third descendant—the real one—and I didn't even cover my back as I did so.

I had to get to her.

Bursting through the trees, branches scraped my arms and tore my skin. Blood trailed out of my veins, revealing the reality of Fudicia's poison. She weakened my ability to heal.

My breath was rigid, and my heart was racing as I whipped through the shadows. Beneath the morning light, I was weaker, but the forest was blanketed with darkness. My power was rising.

"Shoman!"

The half-breed was standing above her, glaring as he

wrapped his hand around her hair. She screamed, kicking up dirt and leaves as she scratched at his wrists.

He didn't even blink.

He yanked her to her feet, and I shot forward, suddenly pulled backward. Fudicia latched onto my shoulders, tossed me to the ground, and pressed her boot into my neck. I grabbed her foot, but she didn't budge. "Back down, boy," she said, and I writhed beneath her.

"Let. Her. Go." My voice pressed against her weight.

She added pressure, looking up at the half-breed. "Give me the girl," she said, and the half-breed gawked.

"What?"

"Now."

He dragged her forward, and she stumbled behind him, staring at me the entire time. Fudicia, in a flash, wrapped her fingers around the girl's neck. She didn't move. "What's your name, shade?" Fudicia asked, but she didn't speak. "What's your name?"

My girl spit in Fudicia's face, and Fudicia seethed. Her hand lit up, and my girl's flesh burned beneath her grasp. She cringed, and a sickening smell clouded the air. "See if you survive that," Fudicia said, dripping poison into her veins as if it was her specialty.

"No!" I tried to move again, but my chest was heaving. I couldn't breathe.

The third descendant went rigid, her eyes widening, and Fudicia licked her lips, staring at the girl for a lingering moment before she tossed her. The nameless shade spiraled through the air, smacking against the ground, and the half-breed kicked her body down a ravine.

I couldn't stop myself—even though I knew the power would take everything out of me. My arm sprang out, as if it'd made the decision, and my fingers spread out. The Dark energy consumed me, and my body shook.

Fudicia jumped backward, nearly tossed by the wave, and her blackened eyes widened, consuming her expression. My sword began to form, and then she was gone in a flash of light.

The half-breed lingered, his face twisting from side to side as he surveyed the forest, and then he was gone, too.

They'd returned to their shelter—the Light realm, a place shades couldn't enter, let alone follow.

I sucked in a breath, and my energy collapsed. My chest was on fire.

If I had a name to call her by, I would've shouted for the third descendant, but I didn't. I scurried up, standing on shaking knees, and practically fell down the ravine. At the bottom of the hill, her body sprawled across the wet ground. Thunder rolled across the sky, and, as I neared her, my fears became a reality.

Her hair was no longer the slick black wave that it used to be. It was curly and brown, sticking to the dirt. Her porcelain skin was covered with dirt, and blood matted her forehead, covering an array of forming bruises. Her legs and arms were the same, but she was no longer a shade. She was a human, and she was unconscious.

I stiffened as I fell next to her, checking her pulse. She was alive, but I knew who she was and couldn't move. *This is not happening.* I shivered, pulling her into my arms as I tried to wake her. She didn't budge, and her head sank into my lap like it had so many times before, except she'd been awake then. She'd been a shade. She'd been a secret.

And now she wasn't. The third descendant was exposed.

THIRTY-SEVEN

I DRAGGED A WARM WASHCLOTH ACROSS HER TORN SKIN BEFORE tucking the covers beneath her. She didn't keep her bedroom as clean as I did, which wasn't surprising. I was only glad that I hadn't tripped over anything when I transported inside. The last thing I needed was her parents catching a shade in their daughter's bedroom. They didn't even know what a shade was. She'd told me that much.

I wiped the blood and dirt from her face, and then I stood up from her bed and walked into the bathroom. I rinsed the washcloth off and returned to her side, avoiding my reflection at all costs. I knew what I'd see, a mangled mess of bloody failure. It'd only be a matter of time before my father or Camille realized I hadn't returned at the normal time. I'd get caught—again. But I couldn't just leave. She needed my help; she was hurt.

The first thing I checked was the spell embedded into her neck. It was burnt and spreading, and so was mine, but I wouldn't use my remedy on me. It was hers as soon as she woke up.

I ran my fingers along her wrist, and she shuddered, her eyes flicking open. They were no longer purple.

Her gaze fluttered over me, but her brow furrowed. "Shoman?" Then she looked around, and her demeanor flipped. She shot up and covered her face with her hands.

"I know who you are, no matter if you cover your face now or not," I said, and she scooted against the wall. She couldn't even sit up without support. Her face was so pale.

"But—you can't know." Her lip quivered. "You're not supposed to know."

"It's done, Jessica," I said, forcing a smile. "I won't tell. Your secret is safe."

She shook her head and brought her knees up to her chin, hugging her legs as she had so many times before. How had I not realized who she was? Jessica did everything that the nameless shade had done. Because they were the same person.

I still couldn't believe it, even with her in front of me.

She swallowed and tapped her nails against her kneecap. "You know my name," she said, and I nodded. Could she figure out who I was? I didn't know.

"I can't tell you mine."

"I know."

My jaw locked. It was the only way I could keep myself from speaking. I wanted her to know.

"What happened?" she whispered, and I shook my head.

I didn't want to talk about it. We'd almost been killed, and it was my fault. If Fudicia hadn't thought Abby was the third descendant, Jessica would be dead, and it'd be my fault. It was always my fault. It always had been.

"Come here," I said, patting the edge of the bed next to me, and she leaned forward. I reached into my collar and pulled off my necklace, allowing my tree pendant to swing between us. "I need you to drink this."

She blinked. "Drink it?"

I twisted the top and pulled down the stump. The black liquid waved inside the branches. "It's a remedy," I said, handed it to her. "You were poisoned."

A gasp escaped her lips. "What do you mean?"

"Just drink it."

She pressed it to her mouth and tipped it back. Her neck moved, and she cringed, squeezing her eyes shut. She coughed and handed the necklace back to me. "That's disgusting."

"It's medicine; what'd you expect?" I said, draping the jewelry over my neck. As long as the leather was visible, Camille wouldn't know I'd used it.

She shook her head again. "That's the worst tasting medicine I've ever had."

"And it's saving your life."

Jessica bit her lip. "It's that bad?"

I nodded, and she grabbed my hand. I knew I had to pull away, but I couldn't.

"What about you?" she asked, and I shrugged. I'd been attacked too, but she didn't have to know. I could handle the pain. I'd been trained to. She shifted. "Thank you, Shoman."

I didn't respond. I didn't deserve the praise.

I stood up, moving away from her, and her bed creaked as she attempted to move. "You won't be able to use your powers for a long time," I said, briefly turning back. "The poison attacks your powers, so that medicine prevents the transition."

Her mouth opened. "How will I see you?"

"You won't."

"But—"

"Jessica," I sighed and leaned against her window. This was everything I'd ever dreaded. "I'm leaving," I said. "And I'm not coming back." Removing myself was the only way she could be safe. "Don't come looking for me either."

"What?" Her voice quavered, and she stepped off her bed. She trembled, and I caught her before she fell. Her body was too weak to stand.

I sat her down and tried to move back, but she dug her nails in my arm, grasping me. "Why are you doing this?" she asked, and I was unable to look away. Her eyes were watering, and I was breaking.

"I can't be with you anymore," I said, and her grip tightened.

"Shoman." She wasn't letting go. "You can't do this. You don't mean it."

Apparently, she was talented at telling if someone was lying to her. I forced myself to look away. "I do."

"Is it because I'm Jessica?"

No.

"Don't change," I said, and I forced my body to compress into shadows.

She grasped the air as I dissipated. "Don't leave me," she said, and then I was gone. She was safe.

THIRTY-EIGHT

Jessica

THE SCIENCE TABLE WAS ICE COLD AGAINST MY BURNING CHEEK and thundering forehead. I hadn't been able to sleep all night, not after what happened to me, not after Shoman left.

My eyes were sore and puffy, my cheeks blotchy and red, and I knew Crystal and Robb were worried. They'd realized something was wrong the minute they saw me in class, and they hadn't stopped trying to talk to me since I walked in the door. It'd only been two minutes, and class hadn't even started, but I felt as if they'd been interrogating me all day.

"Are you sick?" Crystal asked.

I feel sick. I shook my head.

"Did you get in another fight with your parents?" Robb joined in. "I hate that."

They don't even know what I am. I shook my head again.

"Did—"

"Nothing happened," I said, glaring before I realized I was doing it. They jumped, and Robb whistled low.

"We didn't mean to upset you," he said, and I bit my lip to keep myself from yelling at the only people I had left in my social life. Shoman was gone, and he wasn't coming back. He hadn't even told me why, and all I wanted to do was understand.

"I'm sorry," I managed, and Crystal leaned against my seat.

"I know what will make you feel better," she said, winking her dark eyes. "Dress shopping."

Robb groaned. "Come on, Crystal," he said. "Not now."

"Actually," I said, lifting my face. "I might be up for that." *Anything to distract me.*

Robb raised his brow. "Jess really is upset."

Crystal nodded. "I know."

"I can hear you," I said, and Robb cracked a smile.

"Just have fun tonight," he said, standing as the warning bell rang. Students rushed in, and Crystal stood, readying to go to their table.

"We will," she said, practically bouncing around.

"I'm bringing friends by the way," Robb said. "To prom, I mean."

Crystal smacked his arm. "You promised you wouldn't this year."

"It's just Zac," he said, stepping out of her arm's reach. "And Linda."

She cocked her hip and raised her brow. "Linda?"

"What?" He put his hands in front of him. "You like her."

"Says who?" she asked, and the two continued to bicker as they went to their table and sat down.

I sighed and drowned them out. I did not need more drama in my life.

"Hey, Jessica," Eric said, slowly taking his seat. He was further away than usual.

I stared at him. "Hey."

Clearing his throat, he pushed his backpack beneath his seat. He adjusted his headphones, took them off, and put them back on again. Then, he sighed and laid his hands on the table.

What was wrong with him?

"You look tired," he said, and his green eyes flickered beneath the fluorescent lights. He did too.

I shrugged. "I'd rather not talk about it."

"Why not?"

"Because of your witty remarks," I said, and his brow rose.

"Boy problems?" he asked, and I tensed.

How'd he know? Crystal and Robb couldn't even tell.

His lips pulled into a smile, but then it faded. "Don't act so surprised, Jessica," he said, unable to meet my eyes. "I've gotten to know you pretty well this semester."

"Not that well," I grumbled, and he whispered beneath his breath. I couldn't hear him, but the sinking expression on his face hinted to his thoughts. He believed he had. "You haven't," I said, and he leaned back.

"But I can read body language," he said, louder this time. His eyes flickered over my curling hands. "You really should be careful about that; you might give something away."

I glared. "To who? You?"

"I'm not trying to upset you," he said, repeating exactly what Robb had said moments before. Maybe I was being too sensitive. "I'm just saying that you might want to be careful. You wouldn't want to expose yourself to people you don't trust."

He was lecturing me, but I'd heard the lecture before. From Shoman.

I folded my arms and crossed my legs. "Don't trust anyone, no matter how close you are to anyone."

His brow furrowed. "What makes you say that?"

"My problem."

He paled, but placed his cheek on his hand. He hadn't moved fast enough to hide his expression. "You know, Jessica," he spoke against his palm. "I'm sure that whatever is going on between your guy and you, he has reasons for it," he said. "It'll work out."

"What makes you say that?" I asked, using his words against him, and his shoulders rose in a half-shrug.

"Because everyone hopes for the same thing," he said. "A happy ending." His hand dropped, and he managed a smile. "I'm a Welborn. I know these things."

I nodded, unsure of how to respond. I wanted to argue with him, but I couldn't. He was right. It was only hard to believe. Shoman cared about me, and I knew it. But he left me, and I didn't know about that.

I opened my mouth to respond, but the teacher walked in

and shushed the class. I kept my mouth shut as she began, and Eric didn't attempt a conversation again. Class seemed to end in a matter of minutes, and he left without a word.

I lingered in my seat, watched him leave, and waited until Crystal bounced to my side. "Let's just leave," she said, pulling me out of the seat. "Skipping will do you some good."

I nodded. "I'm ready whenever you are."

She beamed. "Then let's go," she said, and I strode out with her, willing to leave the day behind me.

————◆————

The shopping went great. If you consider sheer torture great.

Crystal had me trying on hundreds of dresses before I could protest. I wasn't even able to look in the mirror. She'd judged all of them the second I'd come out of the dressing room.

"No" became a word I heard so much that it lost its meaning.

She'd say it, hang the dress back up, and return with another one. The process repeated for three hours until she found the one. According to her, it was perfect, but I still didn't see it. I didn't care enough to argue either, so I bought it, and she drove me home.

I opened the front door, attempting to bolt upstairs, but my mother was in her usual place—the kitchen—and she appeared before I could make it.

"How'd the shopping go, Jessie?" she asked, and I peered through the banister.

"Good."

She beamed, and she flipped her blonde hair. "That's great. Did you have fun?"

I tried not to roll my eyes. "Tons."

"When can we see your dress?" she asked.

My father shouted from the kitchen, "Does it cover your knees?"

"Oh, shush," my mother said, rolling her eyes. I wished I hadn't held back. She smiled at me. "Ignore him. Are you going to try it on for us?"

"On prom night," I said, and her smile faltered.

"Oh."

I sighed, gripping the banister as I stepped up a stair. "I'm really tired, Mom," I said. "I just want to go to bed, but I'll show you tomorrow. Okay?"

She nodded, but she forced a smile that reminded me of bad Botox. "Good night, Jessie. I love you."

"Love you, too," I said, running away as quickly as I could manage.

When I got into my bedroom, I shut the door behind me and locked it, leaning against the wood for support. My legs were shaking, and I knew it was from Shoman's medicine. It felt like it weakened everything inside of me when, in reality, it was healing me. I was only glad my outer cuts had healed. Explaining those injuries would've been impossible.

I had to talk to Shoman again.

Throwing my dress over my computer chair, I groaned and collapsed on my bed. The mattress creaked against the old frame, and I twisted around, laying my head down. Beneath my pillow, a paper crinkled, and I pulled it out.

I'd left the article about my parents' car wreck there, and now it was wrinkled. The edge was torn, and my eyes watered. The only proof I had of them was practically ruined, and I only had myself to blame.

What was wrong with me?

The wreck, although I'd been a part of it, hadn't seemed real until I was flooded with emotions. I'd lost them—my beautiful family—and I'd lost Shoman and the Dark with him. Everything I was born with was gone, even though I was still alive. It didn't feel right. Without the only connection I had, I felt incomplete. I felt—abandoned—and I suddenly understood what Shoman meant about the Dark never accepting me.

I didn't know enough to stand on my own. I couldn't defend myself. I had known that the second Fudicia—whoever she was—appeared in front of us, ready to kill. I'd seen the commitment of danger in her eyes. She was dark—darker than the Dark could be—yet she was in the Light. The archetypal beliefs embedded in my everyday life, in literature and movies, were flipped, and my life was altered. It'd never be the same, and my parents' article proved it.

I flipped it over and slammed it next to my pillow. I refused to look at it. Not tonight. I couldn't stand it.

They'd betrayed me, not by death, but in death. They knew I was a shade, because they had to be shades if they birthed me. Yet they hadn't protected me with a will. They hadn't even bothered giving me godparents, a family within the Dark. Even I realized, they had been fleeing, because we would've been ostracized by the Dark anyway. I would've never known, and they knew all along.

How could they do this? I hated them. No. I didn't understand them. But I wanted to.

During shopping, I'd finally managed to mention them to Crystal. I didn't want to, but she'd kept pestering me about my depression, and I needed an excuse. I would've told her eventually. *Wouldn't I?*

I didn't know the answer to that, but it didn't matter. Crystal was too young to remember anything. When they died, she was a baby, too. At most, she said she'd ask her mother, but I sort of hoped she wouldn't and would at the same time.

I couldn't even tell what I was feeling, let alone cope with it.

I flipped the article over, but I didn't look at it. Instead, I closed my eyes and attempted to force my tears back. But I couldn't. They came, and my chest heaved, sour and tight, until exhaustion took over, and I drifted away.

THIRTY-NINE

TRAINING WAS NUMBING, AND, FOR ONCE, I WAS ENJOYING IT. She'd been crying—a lot. It was easy enough to tell in class. Her cheeks were blotchy, and her eyelids were red. It wasn't obvious to anyone else, she'd covered it with makeup, but I'd noticed it. I couldn't get the image out of my mind.

Other than feeling like a guilty fool, I was seriously contemplating stalking. It took everything in me not to follow Crystal and her to the mall. I knew the Light wouldn't be after her. Fudicia hadn't seen her human face. But I was consumed with severe, heart-wrenching paranoia that she'd be attacked, and I wouldn't be there to protect her.

What if the Light realized she was alive? What if Darthon found her?

I'd kill him, and until her existence had pushed me to do so, I never thought I could. It wasn't right, but I couldn't bring myself to care. I only cared about Jessica's life, and if Darthon threatened her, I had no problem taking his away.

My insanity begged for a distraction.

A target exploded, shattering across the floor, and I sighed. I was lying to myself if I thought I could quiet my thoughts. They were uncontrollable.

I twisted my fingers through my hair and shook my head just as it happened. A fire of pain split through my arm, and I fell backward. My back hit the floor, and I grabbed my scorching flesh.

What was happening?

I grinded my teeth, and my bones shook as if they were attempting to break away from my body. I squeezed my eyes shut, but the room spun, and molecules detached, reattaching at painful speeds.

I screamed as my body throbbed. A high-pitched ringing consumed my ears, and my jaw locked. I half-expected to bite my tongue off.

"Shoman?"

The door to the training room opened, and then the pain was gone, only a repercussion of exhaustion waving through my veins.

I exhaled, filling my lungs with air, and gripped my legs. Other than that, I couldn't move.

"Shoman?" Pierce circled around me. He was blurry. "Are you okay?"

I tried to nod, but I wasn't sure if my body moved.

"Pierce!" Urte's voice echoed a hundred times as the pain returned, taking over. "Get away from him." He shouted, but it was too late.

I exploded.

———◆———

I awoke to my screams, and my body tearing from the inside out. My throat ripped against my shouts, and my fingers dug into the bed where I was tied down. My wrists tore my restraints, and a man lay on top of me, holding me down.

"It'll be over soon, Shoman," he said, but I couldn't recognize his voice. "Don't move."

My vision spiraled, and I twisted my neck as he jabbed my arm with a thick needle. A dense purple liquid filled my veins, and it burned.

I was dying.

"Let me go." My words erupted on their own accord, but the man didn't budge.

"Breathe," he said as the needle struck a bone. "The more you squirm, the more it will hurt."

I shouted again, but the pain disappeared.

It was so abrupt, I hadn't moved. I was no longer fighting the man. Now I could see who he was, my father.

"Dad?" I croaked, and his blue eyes flickered over me.

The nurse tapped his shoulder. "You can let him go now."

He didn't move immediately. When he did, breath filled my lungs. I gasped, and my body shivered. Why was I so cold? I looked down, and my human body radiated beneath the light. I looked pallid and thin.

"Where am I?" I asked, and my dad collapsed in a chair next to the bed.

"A nursing center in the shelter," my dad said, rubbing his forehead. A nurse stood behind him with Luthicer hovering by his side.

"And so are Urte and Pierce," Luthicer said. "You nearly killed them."

"What?"

My dad held his hand up. "Not now, Luthicer," my dad said, and Luthicer's scowl deepened the wrinkles on his brow.

"Excuse me while I attend my other patients," he said, before he left.

My heart was racing, but it wasn't from the medicine. "What happened?" I asked, trying to sit up. I couldn't. "Where are Pierce and Urte?"

My father shook his head. "They'll survive," he said. "But only because Urte was there. He was able to block your powers."

I remembered the pain that consumed me. "My powers?" I hadn't activated them.

"You were poisoned, Eric," he said, using my human name as a scorn. After everything, I'd converted. I wasn't a shade in his eyes. "You couldn't control them, and it used them against you."

Fudicia. I raised my arm and stared at the cleared skin. The black slit was gone.

"You're lucky Luthicer could create another remedy so fast," he said, and I knew they'd seen my empty necklace. I didn't even bother defending myself. "When were you attacked, Eric?"

"Last night," I said, staring at the cement ceiling. "I didn't think it'd have that much of an effect."

"It's the Light, Eric—"

"It was Darthon's guard," I said, and my father went ashen.

"What are you talking about?"

"Fudicia," I said, turning to glare at him. He was still trying to lie. "I know who she is, remember?"

He folded his hands into his lap as if he was holding himself back. "How'd she find you?"

"I was being reckless," I said. "What else is new?"

"Eric," he growled. "This is not a time to be childish. You could've been killed. You're lucky you managed to get away."

I frowned, and my father stood above me. "How did you get away?" he asked, and I locked eyes with him.

"I had help."

His mouth opened. "You didn't—"

"I saw her again; okay?" I pushed my elbows against the bed and sat up. "I'm not proud of it," I managed. "But she's okay."

"Okay, Eric?" His voice rose, and the nurse stepped out of the room. "Okay? She's the third descendant. She could be dead—"

"Where do you think my remedy went?" I didn't yell back. I had no right to. "She's alive," I said. "And the Light doesn't even know it."

His crumbled brow rose. "What do you mean?"

"They still believe they killed the third descendant," I said, taking a moment to breathe. I wiped the sweat from my forehead, and my father blinked.

"Abby?"

I nodded.

He sank into his chair. "That's the only good news I've received out of all of this."

I stared at him. He looked much older than I remembered. Even in his shade form, his black hair was beginning to gray, and he was starting to develop wrinkles. His shoulders were bonier, and his chest was sunken in. I'd put him through hell.

"I'm sorry," I said, wondering when I had said it last.

He hung his head in his hands. "Don't be," he said. "You're a teenager; I can't really expect anything else from you."

"My age shouldn't matter."

"You'll understand when you're older," he mumbled and lifted his chin. "I should've known you'd go back to her."

I sighed. "I won't do it again."

"Don't lie to me, Eric."

"I'm not," I said, knowing the truth was more powerful than a lie could ever be. "I broke her heart, and that's exactly how it's going to stay."

FORTY

Jessica

PROM WAS TOMORROW, AND THE SCHOOL WAS REELING WITH EX-
citement. Students practically danced around the halls,
and it was only eight in the morning. The waxed, tiled
floor was covered in sparkles, and the main hallway was
draped with paper fans and fluorescent tissue balls. I'd spent
thirty minutes trying to figure out the theme, but I couldn't.
Hayworth High looked like the inside of an arts and crafts
store.

I didn't have enough coffee to deal with this.

I shut my locker just as Robb leaned against the one next
to mine. "Hey, Jess," he said, and my eyes darted to the boy
behind him. "I have someone I want you to meet—"

"I'm Zac," the other boy said, positioning his body between us.

He had thick black hair and eyes to match. He was taller
than Robb by a couple of inches, and his jawline aged him past
high school years. I could see why he made fakes for a living.
His clothes seemed to be pressed for intimidation reasons.

"Hi," I said, barely shaking his hand.

He waved over his button-up shirt. "Private school, right?"
He rolled his eyes, but I couldn't manage a smile. However, he
grinned, revealing a set of perfectly straight teeth. I bet he
hadn't even had braces.

"I didn't catch your name," he said, allowing his words to

linger.

"This is Jess Taylor," Robb said, and his brown eyes squint-ed. He knew I was uncomfortable.

I forced a meek smile. "Jess," I repeated, unsure of why I couldn't move. I didn't like him, and I hadn't given him a chance. What was wrong with me? I prided myself on being open-minded, yet I could feel judgment twist my gut.

"I'm coming to your prom tomorrow," Zac said, stepping away. He put his hands in his pockets, and I wondered if he'd felt my reluctance to meet him.

I cleared my throat and looked from Robb to him. "I thought only students from our school could go."

"Other students can with an outside date form," Robb said, and Zac shrugged.

"Crystal filled mine out," he said, "and Robb filled out Lin-da's."

I snapped my fingers. "I forgot you said they were com-ing," I said. "Where's Linda?"

Robb shrugged, but Zac's eyes lit up, showing the first sign of light. "You'll meet her tomorrow," he said. "She went to school today."

I raised my brow. "And you didn't?"

"Not yet," he said, winking. "I'm not really into those things."

Things. Like school was a choice.

I hugged my bag to my chest. "Yet you came here on your day off."

His smile widened. "I drove Robb," he said, and Robb shifted his weight from foot to foot.

"I'm getting my car cleaned for tomorrow," he said. "Couldn't exactly afford a limo."

"I think that's a little extreme anyway," I said, trying to en-courage him. For the first time since knowing Robb, he seemed insecure. I didn't understand.

"So what guy am I going to have to drag you away from to dance?" Zac asked, and heat rushed over my cheeks. *Had he just said that?*

Robb hit Zac's arm. "Come on, man."

"What?" Zac grinned, not even bothering to move his eyes away from me. "You didn't tell me the new girl was so pretty."

"I'm right here," I said, raising a brow, but his cockiness didn't subside.

"I know."

I stared at my feet. I was not in the mood. Not when Shoman was still missing.

Robb hit him again, with more force this time, and Zac swayed, laughing as he grabbed his arm. "Okay. Okay. I'll leave." He turned around and waved behind his shoulder. "See you tomorrow, Jess," he said, and I waited until he disappeared down the hallway.

"I can see why Crystal doesn't like you bringing people around," I said, and Robb sighed.

"Sorry about him," he said. "He's a nice guy; I promise. He's just a little forward."

"A little?"

Robb laughed and fiddled with his shirt. "That's actually why I brought him in here to meet you," he said. "I didn't want any surprises tomorrow, and I definitely didn't want him upsetting you." Robb's smile twitched. "It would make his day if you danced with him once—"

I rolled my eyes and groaned. "Robb."

"Please," he said, practically lowering himself to his knees. "The kid may seem confident, but I think he overcompensates."

"One dance," I said, trying not to smile. I had to admit that it was flattering. I only felt guilty for Shoman—a guy who didn't even want me. I knew I had to let him go eventually. But could I? I didn't know.

"Thanks, Jess," Robb said, cocking his head to the side as the warning bell rang. "I can walk you to class if you want."

I shrugged, and we started for my first hour English class. "Where's Crystal anyway?" I asked. "I half expected her to intervene at any minute."

"She would've if she was here," he said, chuckling, "but prom is a big deal to her. She stayed home to prepare."

I shook my head. "That's a little extreme."

"If you haven't noticed," he said. "She kind of is."

I giggled, thinking of my best friend. She was always in everyone's business, and she wasn't even hesitant about it. If anything, she reveled in it. I normally didn't enjoy people like her, but there was an innocence to her punk attitude she couldn't hide. She was sensitive, and I admired that. I could hardly open up at all, and it was nice to know someone who could.

"I'm actually looking forward to tomorrow," I admitted, wondering if my morning coffee had finally settled in my sleepy veins. I felt energized, and the decorations I had hated minutes before now seemed like a promise that everything was going to go right—even if it was only one night.

"Me, too, Jess," Robb said. "Me, too."

Maybe tomorrow would be amazing, and I'd finally let go of Shoman after all. I doubted it. But it was something I could hold on to.

FORTY-ONE

Eric

A S USUAL, SOMEONE KNOCKED ON MY BEDROOM DOOR THE MIN-
ute I'd arrived home and managed to relax. I was used to
the lack of privacy, but I'd learned to despise it.

"Come in," I said, not even bothering to get up. My door
was unlocked, and it opened quickly. I spun around and
stopped when my eyes settled on Jonathon Stone—Pierce's
human form. "What are you doing here?"

His thick glassed practically fell from his stout nose as his
one good eye wandered around my bedroom. "Our fathers are
talking," he said, leaning against the doorframe. It was Satur-
day, but the meeting didn't surprise me. Urte had been hovering ever since they were released from the shelter's hospital.

"I'm sorry about the other day," I began, but Jonathon
waved his hands.

"I was stupid enough to ignore Urte's warning," he said.
Jonathon had used his dad's first name—no matter what form
he was in—since he'd divorced his mother. His mother didn't
want him to be involved with the prophetic battle, and Urte
had refused. She left Hayworth. She was no longer a part of the
Dark, and Jonathon hadn't spoken to her since. But he still re-
sented his dad. We never talked about it, but it was understood.

"I'm still sorry," I said, and he shrugged.

"How's your arm?"

I shrugged back. "Still sore," I admitted. "But I have my

powers, which is a relief."

"Me, too," Jonathon said. "It's probably a good thing you didn't take your remedy. You'd be powerless for days."

I cracked a smile. "I guess Luthicer is good for something."

"Yeah; who knew?" Jonathon chuckled. "Are you going back to school Monday?" he asked, and I knew he'd noticed my absence. I could've gone. I just didn't want to, and my father hadn't made me.

"Unfortunately," I said. "Did I miss anything on Friday?"

"Just the usual collection of teen angst that prom brings," he said, shaking his head as he chuckled. "You should've seen how ridiculous people were acting."

I remembered last year too clearly, girls whining about the three D's—dates, dinner, and dresses. It was all so repetitive, yet I got a kick out of it. Although I'd never admit it. Prom wasn't my thing. It couldn't be. I was friendless.

"Are you going?" I asked, and Jonathon's brow rose.

"Are you joking?" he asked, waving his hands over himself. "I'm not exactly a lady's man," he said, grinning. At least he was comfortable with his different lives. "Now if I was Pierce— we'd be having a different discussion."

"You could get someone as Jonathon," I said, and he shrugged.

"I don't think I'd want to," he said. "I'd prefer someone who knows who I am—Pierce—not this guy."

Jessica flashed through my mind. Did she like me as Eric? I doubted it. I'd treated her horribly. I didn't deserve her.

"I'm sure she's fine," Jonathon practically whispered, and my shoulders tensed.

"What?"

He sighed. "I know when you're thinking about her," he said. "You mope, more so than usual." He smirked, but I didn't relax. "I'm sure she'll be fine at prom."

"Who said she went to our school?" I snapped.

"It's Hayworth," he said, fiddling with his glasses. "There's an obnoxiously high chance she does."

I took a careful breath, not wanting to sigh and give my

thoughts away. "I guess."

Jonathon opened his mouth to speak, but my door creaked open, and he stopped. Urte—as human George Stone—walked in, but my father lingered in the hallway.

"Jon, your brother is waiting for us at home," George said, laying his hand on his son's boney shoulder. Instead of his black hair, green eyes, and scruffy facial hair, he was clean-shaven and had long black hair. I wondered if he had the same insecurities as his son.

"We should go," George said.

Jonathon glanced at me. "See you later."

I waved, and the two were gone. I laid my hands on my knees and stared at my father, but he didn't move. He cleared his throat. "Are you resting like you're supposed to?" he asked.

"All day."

"That's good," he said, running his hand over his balding head. "George tells me it's prom night."

I nodded.

"Were you planning on going?"

"No," I said, but my body electrified. I could see Jessica tonight, and she wouldn't even know. I wouldn't be breaking any rules either.

I could drop by, make sure she's happy, and leave. I didn't have to talk to her or anything. I had dress clothes too. I'd been to enough funerals for that.

"Actually," I said, standing. "I think I am."

My father's brow rose. "But—"

I forced a smile, hoping he'd buy my lie. "Just to get my thoughts off things," I said. "Plus, it's probably better for my image. The Light wouldn't expect me if I started getting friends again."

His jaw rocked from side to side. "You think they'd pay attention to social events like that?"

"They might," I said, using Jonathon's logic. "It's Hayworth. It wouldn't be hard to cross people off the suspect list, and the first descendant wouldn't have friends."

"That insinuates Darthon wouldn't either."

I forced a grin and a nod. "I will look around to see who's absent," I said. "Maybe we can beat them to it."

He began to agree. "Okay," he said. "But be careful, Eric. I wouldn't want you to end up in the hospital again."

"I won't," I promised, believing I could avoid any more trouble as long as I was human. Just for one more night.

Forty-two

CRYSTAL TIGHTENED THE BLACK STRAPS OF MY DRESS AND smacked my back. "You're good to go," she said, and I turned around, lifting my shoulders. They stayed in place.

"Thanks," I said, and she winked.

"You look great."

"You, too," I said, and she ruffled the poofs of silver on her sleeves. Her dress was super short, unlike the average prom dress, and her stilettoes added five inches to her petite height. She loved it.

"If only I could wear this every day," she said, sitting in front of her vanity mirror. She pulled out eye shadow and applied it to one eyelid. Her dark eyes sparkled when she met my gaze in the reflection. "You know that car wreck you asked me about? That one where the young couple died?"

My heart stopped, and I sat on her bed, unable to stand. "Yeah—"

"I asked my mom about it," she said, finishing her other eye. "It was really weird."

I held my breath. My parents. "What was weird about it?"

"For one thing, their car was filled with all of their possessions, but they hadn't put their house on the market," she said. "My mom wanted the police to look more into it, but they figured the couple was moving." Her eyes flickered as she slicked mascara on. "Seemed really sporadic if you ask me."

She spun around and tied a ribbon around her wrist. "I mean, what kind of couple flees with a newborn without reason?" Her face flushed behind her heavy blush. "I think something happened."

My tongue was heavy. I couldn't say anything. They knew about the Dark. I was positive they had fled from it, but I didn't know why. It didn't make sense.

"Why'd you have me look into it anyway?" she asked. "Did you know them?"

"No," I lied. "My dad came across it at work."

Her brow rose, but she turned back to her mirror. She twisted her lip ring out and replaced it with a glittery one. "What does your dad do anyway?"

"I don't know," I lied again. He managed a small farming equipment company. He had no reason to find the article, except me, and I didn't want her to know that. "I just thought it looked weird, too."

"See?" Her eyes widened. "I want to know what happened," she said, standing up and adjusting her dress. It crinkled. "The article didn't even say what happened to their daughter."

I was adopted. "She was probably given to family members," I said.

"Probably."

"Crystal." Her bedroom door opened, and a woman with short dark hair walked in. She was Crystal's mirror image. "Your friends are here."

"Thanks, Lola," she said, and her mother left, not even bothering to say hi.

I hadn't even known she was home.

"Don't take it personally," Crystal said, grabbing her clutch off her table. "She barely talks to me, let alone my friends."

"Where's your dad?" I asked, and she shrugged.

"Who knows?"

I bit my lip, and we didn't talk about it again. Instead, she rushed out of her bedroom, and I collected my stuff, following quickly behind. When we hit the front door, Crystal burst out and shouted, "About time."

Robb and Zac stood outside, and I couldn't deny how well they'd cleaned up. Robb was in black, and Zac wore a white suit, bringing out the blackness of his hair and eyes. His hair was spiked up, the ends twirling in a hundred different directions, and his shoulders were broadened beneath his suit jacket. They looked good.

"Where have you guys been?" Crystal asked, and Robb groaned.

"I'm sorry," he said. "We got caught in traffic. Everyone has their parents' cars tonight."

They continued to bicker as my heels clicked against the concrete. I walked over to them, and suddenly Zac's hand was around my waist. He spun me around, and my vision settled on him when I stopped. My dress twisted. How had he gotten so close without me noticing?

He grinned. "You look great."

I stepped back but found myself giggling. The attention felt nice. "Thanks," I said. "You, too, Zac."

His dark brow rose, and he smirked. "You remembered my name?"

"I met you yesterday," I said. "It's kind of hard to forget."

He leaned in. "It's impossible to forget you."

I averted my eyes to hide my blush. *Was he serious?* Somehow, he didn't even sound cheesy.

"You two ready to go?" Robb asked, suddenly standing next to us, and I nodded.

Robb and Zac rushed to the car, hitting one another, and Crystal grabbed my arm as we followed them to Robb's Suburban. "Was Zac just flirting with you?"

"I—I think so."

Crystal bounced. "Good for you, Jess," she said, flickering her glittery eyes over me. "But I have to warn you. Linda is a little—oh, how should I say this—feisty."

"Feisty?"

"She's really protective of those two," she said, rolling her eyes. "More so toward Robb than Zac, but she doesn't like other girls around them."

When Zac opened the car door to the backseat, I saw her. Linda's golden hair glowed beneath the interior lights, and her diamond earrings sparkled. Her green eyes, like her jewelry, sparkled, too.

"You must be Jess," she said as she eyed me, and I stared at her dress.

It was crimson red and clung to her body like she was preparing for a model shoot. It was slick, long, and gorgeous.

I averted my gaze and swallowed my nerves. Why did Robb's friends have to be so intimidating? They weren't like the kids at Hayworth High; they were different. "Nice to meet you, Linda," I said as I got in to sit in the middle seat.

She shifted away and stared out the window even though we weren't moving. Crystal sat next to me, and Zac leaned over her. "Be nice, Linda," he said. "Jess is my dancing partner."

Linda's neck turned, slowly and methodically. Her thin eyebrows rose, and she smiled, tight-lipped. "Oh, really?" She was looking right at me, and heat sizzled over my skin.

"We are going to dance," I managed, and Zac chuckled, shutting the car door before he crawled into the passenger seat. No one spoke, but Crystal pinched my leg.

I jumped, looking at her, and she widened her eyes at me. Her message was loud and clear: don't mess with Linda.

I smiled at my best friend before focusing on the windshield. At least I'd be able to see where we were going.

"Is everyone buckled up?" Robb asked, and we nodded before he backed out of the driveway. The night wasn't looking as magnificent as I wanted it to be.

FORTY-THREE

W E'D BEEN AT THE DANCE FOR A FEW MINUTES WHEN ZAC dragged me onto the dance floor. He was forceful about it, almost too excited, but I did it for Robb. His friend wanted more friends, and I could sympathize with it. I only had Robb and Crystal, after all, and Zac wasn't a bad person.

He was handsome, but I wasn't attracted to him. He was too sure of himself, even worse than Robb's cockiness. I could handle Robb. Barely, but I could—but I couldn't handle Zac.

He was too domineering, and when he kissed me on the dance floor, I had enough. I pushed him away and stormed toward the doors without looking back. I didn't need to deal with him any longer.

"Jess," Crystal ran after me and latched on my arm. "What happened? I saw what Zac did—"

"I just can't, Crystal," I said, brushing her off. I didn't want Zac. I wanted—*Shoman.*

She spun me around, the decorative lights flickered over her face, neon and blinding. "Are you okay? I can talk to Zac if you want me to."

"No, no," I said, waving her intensity away. "I'm okay. I'm just getting air." I forced a smile. "I'll be back."

She frowned. "Don't be too long," she said, and I nodded, leaving through the back doors.

The dance was in the cafeteria, so I walked across the concrete patio we ate at during lunch. The spring air was surprisingly muggy, but I didn't care. I only wanted to get away.

My heels echoed over the thumping music, and I rushed toward the grass. I didn't even want to remember what shoes I wore. I kicked them off and circled a group of teenagers lingering outside. They eyed me, but I passed them, heading straight for the only place I knew would be close enough to the dance but far enough for an escape.

I climbed the steep hill, and the wet grass tickled my ankles. The willow tree waved, as if welcoming me, and I sighed, rushing to the stump. I leaned my forehead against it and breathed.

My heart was racing. My body was hot. I wanted to cry.

I held my breath, dug my fingernails into the bark, and exhaled. I stopped shaking, and I opened my eyes, allowing the night to wash over my skin. If only I could transform.

I groaned and stared into the top of the tree. It fluttered, flickering to one side and then the other. The green leaves somehow retained their color in the darkness, and it swayed, swishing against other leaves. The tree, in the mist of the prom's loud music, whispered. And I understood why Eric liked it so much.

It was serene, and it would be serene even after I died. I wouldn't be alive, yet it would remain, and it would live.

"Jessica?"

I knew that voice.

I turned around, and there he was—standing on the edge of hill. His brown hair waved like the tree, and his green eyes shimmered in the shadows. They were locked on me, but I couldn't look away. He was dressed up, wearing long, black pants and a pressed shirt. A black coat hung over his shoulder, and a black tie hung loosely around his neck. For once, his headphones weren't on, but I'd recognized him immediately.

"What are you doing here?" I asked, and Eric stepped forward, rubbing his chin.

"Are you okay?" he asked, and I threw my hands in the air.

His eyes widened, and I held my hands to prevent more gestures. "I'm sorry," I said, cocking my head toward the dance. "It wasn't going so great."

He lifted his hands and brushed the branches away as he stepped into the tree's space. "Why not?" he asked, sitting down before he leaned his back against the tree. He was so calm.

I shrugged, sitting next to him. He leaned on his knees and looked at me. "Same boy problem?" he asked, referring to the last time I'd seen him in class. He hadn't been there on Friday.

"Maybe," I said, wiggling my cold toes in the grass. "He isn't here."

"Why don't you dance with someone else?"

"I did," I said, and Eric shifted. "But I don't want to. Not anymore."

He nodded, but didn't meet my eyes. "That's understandable," he said, rocking his head from side to side. "But you shouldn't let him—or anyone else—ruin your night."

I fiddled with my dress. "I didn't say he—they—ruined my night."

He smiled. "But you're out here."

"You are, too."

This time, he chuckled and stood up. He stretched his arms over his head and breathed the night in. In seconds, he was staring at me again, but his smile had spread. "Come on, Jessica," he said. "Get up."

He offered his hand, but I didn't move. "What?"

He rolled his green eyes, stepped forward, and grabbed my hand. Pulling me to my feet, he only bent down again to pick up my shoes. "We're going to have fun tonight," he said, dragging me downhill.

"What does that mean?" I asked, unable to comprehend what Eric Welborn was doing. We were walking back to the dance. "Wait, Eric. You cannot be serious."

He responded with a laugh and only stopped at the school door. "You might want to put those shoes back on," he said.

233

I pointed at the prom. "We are not going in there."

"What?" he asked, raising his brow. "You don't want to be seen with me?"

"It's not that—"

"Then put on the shoes," he said. "We, my homeroom partner, are going to dance."

My face flushed, and I turned my face away as I slipped my shoes back on. He wasn't kidding. "Happy?" I asked, clicking them against the ground, and he nodded, opening the door.

"You are a difficult one, Jessica," he said, and I rolled my eyes at him.

"Coming from you, that's saying a lot."

"I know," he said, taking my arm as the door shut behind us. Wind blew against my bare back, and I shivered, not knowing if it was from the breeze or his touch.

He placed his hand on the curve of my spine and steered me through the flickering neon lights. I closed my eyes and breathed, and then I was against his chest, and the music changed. The thumping beat from before mellowed, and Eric leaned down to whisper, "Relax, it's just you and me."

I swallowed my nerves and placed my hand on his chest. He swayed to the right and then to the left. I followed his lead and breathed again. I expected my hands to shake, but they didn't. I was calm, and Eric was, too. For the first time all night, everything felt right—like the magnificent moment I'd hoped for. But it was with Eric.

He twirled me around, and my black dress flowed around my knees, swishing against his slacks when I stopped. His hand returned to my back, and my head rested on his shoulder. I hadn't realized how much taller he was than me until now, and I was in heels.

"Jessica?" His voice vibrated through my cheek. "Are you all right?"

I nodded, hoping he wasn't watching my expression. Even I could feel my smile crumble from my face. As much as I was happy with Eric, Shoman lingered. I liked him, and I still felt like I was betraying him. But hadn't Shoman betrayed me?

Shoman wouldn't ruin my night.

"What's wrong?" Eric asked, slowing down, and I glanced around the dance floor.

A few couples, if not all of them, turned away as I met their gazes. They had been watching. "Is it just me or is everyone staring?" I asked, and Eric chuckled.

"They are."

"Why?"

"Why do you think?" he asked, and I knew my question was already answered. Eric wasn't exactly the type to come to school, let alone dance with another student. Seeing us dance was probably the biggest event that happened since the prom king and queen were crowned.

"This is nice," Eric said, changing the subject, and I nodded. *Thud-thump. Thud-thump. Thud-thump.* My ears filled with a heartbeat unlike my own, yet my ear wasn't pressed to Eric's chest. It sounded so familiar—so calming and strong. I only wanted to hear it, not the music or the whispers around us.

"I'm glad I came," I said, and I arched my neck to meet his eyes. "You weren't going to, I'm guessing."

He chuckled. "Of course not."

I smiled. "I'm glad you came, too."

He returned my smile, but the corners twitched. "You don't mind dancing with me with that other boy on your mind?"

My fingers tightened on his jacket. "Of course not," I said, surprised by the truth. I was having fun, and it didn't matter that Shoman existed. He wasn't here, and Eric was. And I liked them both.

I lowered my face, hiding my blush, and forced my feelings into my gut. My stomach twisted.

"Not even a little bit?" Eric asked, and I giggled.

"Maybe a little," I said, gesturing to the stares around us.

He laughed, too. "Understandable," he said, placing his hands on my hips. We swayed to the music, but it felt like we were draped in a silence I didn't want to break. But I had to.

The question was lingering, and it had been since I found out, but only now could I feel it control my lips.

"Did you love her?" I asked, and his shoulders tensed.

"Hannah?" he asked, and I nodded, knowing the girl who'd been killed two years ago was his girlfriend, and, apparently, his reason for being antisocial. But he'd broken through that with me, hadn't he? I wanted to know.

He sighed, but he didn't speak, and I opened my mouth, "I didn't mean to offend you—"

"You didn't," he said, shrugging his rigid shoulders. He was trying to relax. "You're honestly the first person to ask, and I respect that," he paused, and we turned in a circle before he continued, "I suppose I did."

My eyes shot to the floor as if my heart had fallen there. Why was I so saddened by his honesty? I couldn't explain it, but I didn't want him to love her—the girl he'd dated all those years back—but his feelings weren't mine to decide.

Eric's hand moved away from my hip and met my chin. He lifted my face, and his green eyes lit up in the darkness. "Not in the way you think," he said, and his eyes flickered over mine. "I loved her, because she was the only person who understood who I was. I loved her like a best friend, not a girlfriend." He held his breath, and his chest rose beneath my hand. "I know that now."

I couldn't speak. Instead, I bit my quavering lip and laid my head on his shoulder. We remained like that, barely moving, and finished the mellow song in silence. When the song ended, Eric didn't move away, and I didn't want him to. I didn't want the dance to end.

He buried his face into my neck as we came to a stop on the dance floor. "You look so beautiful tonight, Jessica," he whispered into my hair, and his grip tightened before he let me go. His body heat disappeared, and chills covered my skin.

He stepped back, and I froze. Shoman managed to break through the moment and slice his words in half. Shoman's warmth, touch, smell, and words. Everything was flooding back to the instant when he left, and I couldn't force the memory away, even though I was looking at Eric.

"I wish I could stay longer," he said, shoving his hands in his pockets. "But I can't." He smiled, but his normally keen eyes were fogged over. He wasn't here any more than I was. "Have a good night, Jessica," he said, and, without another word, he walked past me.

He kept his head down, and his brown, shaggy hair covered his face. As he walked away, the entire dance floor followed his movements, watching him until he was out the doors. Then I felt their gazes on me.

I shivered, lingering in the last moment I'd seen Eric's back, lit up beneath the golden lights as he opened the doors leading outside. I pretended he was still there, I wished he'd come back, and I wanted to believe he hadn't left.

I felt as if I'd lost Shoman twice.

"Oh my God!" Crystal's voice shattered my thoughts as she grasped my arm. She was by my side, but I couldn't look at her. She pulled me off the dance floor, but her voice drifted past me until we reached our table. "Why—what—I don't even know where to begin."

"How about how Welborn was dancing with her?" Robb suggested, kicking back his chair as he crossed his arms.

Crystal waved her hand at him as if she could swat him away. "What was that about, Jess?" she asked, but I could only focus on Robb's darkened gaze.

"I didn't know Welborn and you had a thing going on," he said, and I shook my head.

"We don't," I said, but my entire body was hot. *Did that really just happen?*

"Ooo," Crystal whistled. "Defensive."

"We—" I tried to speak, but I could barely control my lips. "We don't," I repeated, but every piece of me was vibrating with nerves. *Why was I feeling this way?*

"You look sick," Robb said, but his voice sounded as if it was spoken through thick glass, foggy and contorted. I had to grip the table from falling over. "Jess?" Robb touched my shoulder, and his brown eyes were warm again. "Are you okay?"

I breathed, nodding, but I didn't have to speak. Linda ran up behind Robb and wrapped her arms around his torso. "We should ditch this dance," she said, but Robb didn't look away.

"Where's Zac?" he asked, and Linda groaned.

"He just left," she said. "He was upset about—" She stopped, and I looked up to meet her glare. She smiled and tapped Robb's shoulders. "We'll talk in the car. Let's go find him."

"Okay," Robb said, finally turning to his date. He grabbed her hand and turned toward Crystal. "Sorry, guys, but I think I should go. Can you get rides?"

Crystal nodded. "Just find Zac."

"Thanks," he said, and then they were gone, but I barely felt them leave.

Eric. His touch. It was familiar. And the way he'd spoken was too. Teresa—a girl who wasn't related to Eric—drove him around and watched him. Like a guard would. And Hannah had died. Like Shoman's friend had.

It couldn't be.

"Jess?" Crystal sat in a chair, but she leaned over, trying to catch my eyes. "Are you okay?"

"I have to go," I said, not even bothering to pick up my clutch as I turned around.

"What?" Crystal tried to follow me, but I stopped, turning her back around.

"I'm fine," I promised. "But I have to go," I said. "Don't wait for me."

My shout echoed behind me as I ran through the dance floor and out the doors—allowing the night to guide me toward the only boy I never thought I'd see again.

238

FORTY-FOUR

HE WASN'T BENEATH THE WILLOW TREE, AND I DIDN'T KNOW where to look next.

I leaned against the trunk and panted, looking over the parking lot and then the street. Nothing. Not a single sign of him.

I cursed my human vision and tried to conjure up any of my Dark powers, but nothing came. I was still blocked. *Keep it together, Jess.* My nails dug into the bark as my thoughts raced through my shivering body. Where would Eric go if he walked? Home. And I knew exactly what street would take him there.

I rushed down the hill, kicking off my heels as I sprinted across the wet grass. My dress tightened around my hips, but I didn't care if it ripped. I had to get to him. I couldn't let him get away again. I had the right to know, and if he was the kind of man I thought he was, he'd fess up.

The lampposts sprayed golden light across the pavement, and I stumbled as I leapt from the grass and onto the concrete. My arms flew out, and I caught my balance, continuing to race forward. Nothing was going to stop me. Not even my dress. Good thing Crystal didn't pick me out a gown like Linda's. My dress would be in shreds by now if she had.

The bottom of my feet scraped against the pavement, but I ignored it, pumping my arms and legs. My breath rushed through my throat and filled my lungs, and sweat beaded down my spine. My hairpins fell out, and my curls collapsed, waving behind me. I was running, and I wasn't going to stop until—

I saw him.

He was walking down the road, his hands still in his pockets, and his head hung low. He didn't even notice I was following him, and I hung onto the nearest lamppost, unable to run any farther.

"Eric!" My heart was racing as fast as my voice was loud, but he didn't hear me. "Eric!" *"Please hear me!"*

He spun around, nearly tripping over himself, as his hands lifted, readying for a fight. His green eyes glowed, flicking in the shadows, and my breath escaped me. How had I not seen it before?

His gaze landed on me, and his hands dropped as he jogged over to me. "Jessica?" He steadied me, taking us away from the lamppost, and he searched my face. "What's wrong? Are you okay?"

I slapped his arm away, but he didn't step back. His mouth opened, and tears sprung to my eyes. "How could you?" I screamed as all of my adrenaline—my anger, confusion, and desperation—rose.

He simply frowned. "How could I what?"

"You're him," I said. "This whole time you were him, and you hid it from me."

Eric's frown was replaced with a frozen blank stare. "I don't know what you're talking about," he said, stepping backward. "Look—I—I have to go—"

"Why did you leave me like that?" I continued, stepping toward him. He wasn't leaving without an explanation. "Why are you leaving again?"

He sighed, running a hand through his hair, and his shoulders rose. "I'm leaving right now, Jessica," he said, pointing over his shoulder, and he turned away.

My body simmered with electricity as I watched him walk down the street. My fingertips sizzled, and my heart thundered, adrenaline curling up my spine and through my hair. The curls straightened out, turned black, and then returned to normal. Everything about how I was feeling was changing into something more. My powers. They were back.

"No one calls me Jessica but you!" I shouted at his back, and my energy shot out, enveloping the street in a purple fog.

I didn't know if my words made Eric stop or not. Instead, my power disappeared, the purple flickered away, and a thick wave of air blew across the street. Hairs all over my body stuck up, and my stomach twisted against the familiar feeling. The Light was here.

A shadow surrounded Eric before simmering to his feet. His wavy brown hair was now black, and his skin was pale white. His blue irises were vibrant, even in the lamplight, and his jawline was defined. He was taller, broader, and his dress clothes were replaced with a plain black shirt and dark pants.

I was right.

Eric Welborn was Shoman, the first descendant of the Dark, and he always had been.

Before I could even comprehend what happened, in milliseconds an arm tightened around my waist and pulled me against a body. I squirmed, and Shoman stepped forward, but cold metal met my neck, and we froze.

"Don't move," the man said, and I knew what was against my throat, a knife.

I held my breath, trying to look up, but he grabbed my arm and twisted it behind my back. I whimpered, and Shoman—or Eric—pulled his sword out. The illuminated weapon stung my vision, and I closed my eyes as Shoman spoke, "Let her go, Light!"

"Put your sword away," my captor said, but Shoman didn't budge. "Put your sword away!"

Shoman's sword dropped an inch as his eyes flickered over me, but it didn't disappear. He was hesitating, and his hesitation was my punishment.

The blade left my throat, but sliced across a strap of my dress. I yelped as pain seared down my shoulder, and I reached up to grab it. But the knife returned to my throat, and the man's grip tightened. I gasped, fighting for breath.

"You misinterpreted a suggestion from an order," the man said. "Put your sword away, or it won't be her shoulder next time."

Shoman dropped it, and the glowing weapon fell into the shadows before it ever touched the ground. He winced, and I knew he'd absorbed it like I had when I first showed him—quickly and painfully.

"Let her go," Shoman said, shaking his head. He looked paler without his sword in front of him. "She has nothing to do with this."

The man lifted my chin, and I finally saw his face. It was boney, rigid and defined, and shadows crawled over his tanned skin. He had black pits for eyes, shadowed by elongated eyelashes, but his spiked hair was golden. He was taller than I thought and broader than Shoman. He looked stronger, too.

"I'm surprised to find a human here," he said, pushing my face back. I couldn't move. "I wanted another shade."

Relief shivered through me. He didn't know. My powers were obsolete, only returning for a moment, but he'd sensed me—not Shoman. I'd caused this.

I looked at Shoman, and I saw his shoulders drop. He was relieved, too, but he covered his emotions with a glare. "So let her go."

"But she's seen us," the man said, and the knife crawled across my skin. He was going to kill me. "And she knows something."

"I don't know anything," I managed, praying my voice wouldn't move my throat. I didn't have room to move beneath his blade.

"See?" Shoman said, barely stepping forward. "This is only between you and me, Light."

The man's grip loosened, but I felt his body tense. "I don't see why you'd defend such a useless being," he said, and the tip of the blade pressed deeper into my throat. "Unless she means something to you."

"The innocent will always mean something to me," Shoman said, and for once, I appreciated Eric's talents—or hobbies—for lying. I even believed his reason for defending me.

"You always were a better person than me, Shoman," the man spoke, and Shoman stopped.

"What's your name, Light?"

The man chuckled. "You already know it."

Shoman's brow scrunched as the man shifted me, holding me with one arm. With his free hand, he put the knife in his pocket, and stretched his fingers out. I squirmed as heat erupted through his hold, and I froze when a bright light expanded from his palm. It grew, doubling in size, and soared toward the sky. The beam shattered, and pieces of burning liquid dropped to the ground near my toes.

A sword, as wide and tall as Shoman's, had replaced his knife.

"Darthon," Shoman said, recognizing the descendant power as he'd done with me.

This man was the second descendant? The one Shoman had to kill?

"I'm not here to kill you, Shoman," Darthon said, watching his sword as he waved it from side to side. "Unless I get bored."

"Then what are here for?" Shoman growled, but Darthon grinned.

"I think you already know," he said and grinded his teeth. "I want the third descendant. I know she's alive," he continued. "Fudicia may not have, but I sensed two of you that night."

He wanted me.

"Let me go," I screeched, twisting against his hold. I scratched his arm, and I managed to stumble from his grasp, but he grabbed my hair and pulled me back.

Pain shot through my scalp, and I yelped as he gripped my arm. "You're lucky I'm keeping you alive," he said, shaking me, but I kicked him. I didn't care. I'd take my chances if it meant survival.

"*Don't fight him.*" Shoman's voice flooded my thoughts, and I froze.

"*But—*"

"*Not yet.*"

I stopped and fought the urge to look at Shoman. Darthon would know we were talking if I did that, and then he'd know I was a shade. I'd be dead.

Darthon's face reddened when he repositioned himself, holding my torso again. I half-expected the sword to go to my throat, but Darthon didn't move. He only glared at Shoman. "I know I'm right," he said, barely paying attention to his hostage. In his mind, I was human. I didn't matter. But he'd use my life against Shoman if he could. I was a pawn. "I think you'd be surprised at what I'm capable of."

Shoman forced an uncomfortable laugh. "And I think you'd be shocked at what I could do."

"I don't fear you," he growled.

"Even though I'm destined to kill you?"

Darthon tensed. "You won't be able to if I have the descendant."

What was he talking about?

"You won't be able to find her, Darthon," Shoman said, pacing from side to side. "I don't even know where she is."

"You're lying."

Shoman smiled. "Am I?" he asked, teasing Darthon's insecurities. Even I could see the second descendant was a boy— no older than Shoman himself. "It wouldn't make a difference if I was," Shoman continued. "She isn't here, and I still wouldn't tell you."

"You don't have to tell me," Darthon said, pushing his sword in front of us. "I traced your power; I could trace hers, too."

Shoman's eyes flickered over me, but he dropped his face, shaking it. "That's impossible," he spoke, but his other words filled my head. *"Forget what I said. Get away from him."*

"What?"

"Hit him; fight him. Do anything, but do it now!"

I didn't hesitate. I opened my mouth and sank my teeth into Darthon's free hand. He yelled, pushing me away, and I fell backward, smacking my head on a lamppost. My vision spun, but I scrambled to my feet.

It was too late.

Darthon grabbed my arm and tossed me. My body bounced off the ground, and I rolled over the grass next to the cement. I recoiled in pain, but fought through it, gripping the dirt to stand. I pushed myself up and felt his foot collide with my ribs. I spun over, and Darthon was standing over me, sword in hand. He lifted it, and I knew what he'd do—I was dead.

He struck the sword toward me, but a blast of black and blue exploded against him. His sword disappeared inches from my face, and his body was shot down the sidewalk. His torso bent when it smacked into a lamppost, and I blinked as Shoman appeared by my side, made of shadows.

"Jessica?" He could barely speak. "Are you all right? Can you hear me?"

I nodded, and that was enough. Shoman pulled me against his chest, and a shadow surrounded us as a beam collided with his back. His body lurched against mine, and air escaped his lips as his shirt tore from his skin. I smacked the fire on his shoulder, and blood crawled over his collarbone.

Behind him, Darthon marched toward us.

"Shoman—"

"Hold on," he said, placing his hands on my temples. "This won't hurt," he said, and his thoughts tore through me.

"Camille, I need help—now!"

I recognized the woman's name: his guard was coming.

"Run," Shoman said, his eyes flickering green, and then he was gone. He leapt over the brush and ran straight for Darthon. He pulled out his sword, and Darthon mirrored him. The weapons struck, and the ground vibrated.

I stood, ready to transform, but a woman appeared, splitting through a mix of shadows and light as she solidified on the ground. Her white hair was illuminating, but her expression was twisted with concern. *"Shoman."* I could hear her voice.

"Don't worry about me, Camille." Shoman's voice was rigid as he pushed Darthon backward. *"Get Jessica out of here; take her to my father."*

She spun around, and her black eyes landed on me. They widened. "Who are you?"

I didn't speak, and the woman mumbled, "Forget it." Latching onto my bruising arm, she forced me into her light.

FORTY-FIVE

I FELT EVERY SINGLE MOLECULE OF MINE REFORM, PULLING AND burning and twisting until I was whole again. I gasped as the light faded, and my vision returned. I was no longer in the grassy brush watching Shoman fight. Instead, I was standing in a golden office, filled with books, paperwork, and a man—one I'd seen before.

Eric's father leapt from his chair, and his glasses fell from his face. "Camille—"

"Eric's in trouble, sir," she said, letting go of my arm.

My skin was burned where she'd touched me.

"And I wouldn't have helped this girl if he hadn't ordered me to, but—"

Eric's father replaced his glasses with shaky hands. "Jess?" His brown eyes were slits. "What are you doing here?"

"Hi, Mr. Welborn," I squeaked, and Camille's jaw dropped. "You know her?"

"She's Eric's—uh—"

"Forget it," Camille said. "We have to get the others. Eric's in trouble."

Mr. Welborn looked between us. "What kind of trouble?"

"I'm not sure," Camille said. "He's fighting a light."

"He's fighting Darthon," I corrected, and Camille gaped at me.

"You can't be—"

247

"The third descendant," Mr. Welborn said, and I threw my hands in the air.

"What does that even mean?" I shouted before I realized I even had the energy to raise my voice. Darthon had said it too, but Shoman told me that didn't exist. He lied.

"He never told you?" Mr. Welborn asked, and I shook my head.

"I don't think that matters right now," I said.

Camille nodded, grabbing my arm—again. "Let's go."

Before I could protest, my body ripped apart and reformed. I thought I was going to puke. I hunched over, catching my breath, and a man's hand landed on my back. "It's hard the first few times," he said, and my head spun.

At first, I thought I was looking at Shoman, but I wasn't. The speaker was an older man, with the same thick black hair and striking blues eyes. Eric's father. Of course he was a shade, too. It was genetic.

"If you guys are so capable of transporting, why didn't Shoman just transport us both out?" I managed to speak through my nausea and confusion.

Camille's face fell when I looked up. "He can't when there's a light around."

I understood now. She was a half-breed. She could've saved him instead of me, but she hadn't. She listened to Shoman.

"We're in the shelter," Camille said, forcing me to sit on the floor. "You're safe here."

As she spoke, a thick black smoke clouded the air, and four men fell out. One was my age—tall, strong, and overly buff—but the other three were older.

"Bracke," a man with green eyes and a short black beard spoke first. "What's happened? Why is there a human here?"

I glared back. "I'm not entirely human."

A white-haired man—a mirror image of Camille—allowed his eyes to trace over me. "The third descendant."

"We've gone over this," I said. "I think we need to concentrate on Eric."

Everyone gasped, and Camille kneeled by my side. "How do you know his name?"

"I figured it out," I said, leaping to my feet. "So can we go help him now?"

"He's fighting Darthon," Bracke—Eric's father—said, and the four men spun toward him.

"But The Marking of Change is eight months away."

"I know."

"I'll go after him," the green-eyed man said, and the boy my age took his side.

"We both will." They were obviously related.

Bracke waved, and the two men turned to Camille. Her dark eyes lit up white. "He's in the forest," she said, and they were gone.

I coughed as their fog disappeared, and the shortest man stepped forward. "How could this happen?"

"I don't know, Eu," Bracke said, shaking his head. "But I'll go too."

"You know you cannot," he said. "It's too risky."

"He's my son," he said, and then Bracke was gone.

Only Camille, the half-breed man, and the shortest man remained, and all of them looked at me. "I'm going, too," I said, trying to activate my powers, but Camille suffocated the air with Light energy. My entire body burned.

"Don't," she said, smiling quickly. "There's a reason why Shoman protected you. We'll explain later."

The half-breed elder nodded. "You have to stay here— uh—"

"Jess," I said, and the others tensed, unsure of how to take my name. Identity was everything, but it seemed I never had one.

"Luthicer," he introduced himself. "Does Darthon know who you are?" he asked, and I shook my head.

"He definitely didn't think I was this third descendant."

Luthicer flinched. "You don't even know what you are," he said.

"Eric never told her," Camille whispered, and Luthicer's

brow rose.

"He's protecting her."

"I am right here," I said, crossing my arms, and Luthicer acknowledged me.

"That's an unfortunate thing, Jess," he said, opening the nearest door. "You need to stay in here; it's a safety room. Eu will protect you—"

"I'm tired of being protected!"

"You don't have a choice," Luthicer said, reaching out to grab me, but I pulled away.

"Promise that Eric will survive," I said, and he hesitated. Even I knew he couldn't promise something out of his control, but I wanted to hear it.

"I promise."

"Then I'll stay," I said, storming into the room.

The others didn't move, but I pulled the door shut. I breathed, and they dissipated, leaving Eu outside my room. But I could transport now that Camille was gone. And they couldn't stop me from saving Eric, too.

FORTY-SIX

ARTHON SWUNG HIS SWORD, AND A WAVE OF BRIGHT LIGHT-ning shot across the ground. It tore through a tree, and I leapt over a log, dodging the blow by my feet. I returned the attack and missed his body by inches. He was stronger, but I was faster. It had been that way since I'd managed to get back to the forest, retreating in a calculated battle. My thoughts were even faster than his were.

A knife stuck the bark above my head, and leaves shattered around me. Or not.

I sucked in a breath and pulled the blade out of the tree. Having the heavy weight of my sword in one hand felt offsetting with the knife in my other, but I didn't allow it to affect my focus. I watched Darthon's every move—his legs, his arms, his torso—as he paced to the side, glaring through the dark. I knew he couldn't see as well as I could. It was a light's weakness. It was his weakness.

"How's that shoulder doing?" Darthon asked, his voice straining against his throat. He was wearing out.

I winced at the reminder. My left shoulder muscle was torn and obliterated. It was painful to even hold the knife with my hand. I could feel the pain increase with every movement. "I'll live," I said, steadying my stare.

I hated to admit it, but I was wearing out, too. My entire body burned, inside and out, and I knew his attacks had inflicted more damage than my adrenaline allowed me to register. I was hurt, but I'd fight through it. No matter what.

"What'd you do with the human?" Darthon asked, taking deep breaths. "I always enjoy seeing them fall—and so easily, too."

Urte was right. Darthon wasn't like me. He was born evil.

"She ran," I said, hoping he wasn't playing a game. He could've lied about seeing Camille take her away, but I doubted it. She'd come and gone so quickly, I'd barely registered it in the midst of our battle. "I don't know where she is."

Darthon glowered, and his black eyes expanded. "She's a shade; isn't she?"

"I assumed she was a light."

His upper lip curled. "Why would I hurt my own kind?"

"I wouldn't put it past you," I said, and he grinned. His teeth illuminated like his hair. "You've used Fudicia before."

"She's easy to use," he said, and I tightened my grip on both of my weapons. I couldn't let him relax forever. I had to strike.

I lifted the knife, ready to throw it, but Darthon's eyes lit up and so did the blade. It turned into fire, and I gasped, dropping the scorching metal. My concentration faltered, and my sword disappeared, zipping through my veins.

Darthon ripped through the air, his sword before him, and flew straight for my torso. I leapt back, but I hit a tree. It was too late. I was as good as dead.

Inches in front of my face, a cluster of shadows smacked into his feet, and Darthon flipped over himself. His sword, before shattering into the darkness, sliced my stomach, and I curled over as he collided into the trees behind us.

Urte and Pierce stood in front of me, and Pierce grabbed my shoulder, picking me up. "You okay?"

"Fine," I grumbled, but my spilt blood spoke for me. It dripped over my fingers, and I grasped my torn abdomen, trying to catch my breath. The wound was deep, but not deep enough to kill me. Yet.

Pierce stiffened. "Shoman—"

"I'm fine," I repeated, and then the air warmed.

Bracke, Camille, and Luthicer were here, too, and they didn't hesitate. They rushed through the woods, dodging flying debris as Darthon shot energy their way. He was strong, but I didn't know if he could take us all on his own. He was outnumbered.

The ground shook, and I stumbled, grabbing the tree as Darthon's energy exploded against my father's. A man of the first descendant bloodline was stronger than the others.

"Let's go," I said, leaping past Pierce before he could stop me.

I yanked out my sword, and my feet left the ground. I flew over the forest floor, flickering in and out of the shadows, and I was on the frontline. Even though I couldn't see Darthon through his illumination, our swords struck, and the power vibrated across my arms.

My feet pushed backward in the dirt, but I shoved back and gained my ground. My skin felt like molten lava, and breathing hurt worse. I held it, drowning the pain, and pushed until my shoulder couldn't hold up any longer.

I tumbled backward, rolling over myself before standing up. The dirt stung my stomach, and my vision spun, but I remained standing. I couldn't lose. Not now. Not ever. My sword was intact, and so was my body—sort of.

The glare died, and Darthon's black eyes met mine. Blood trickled through his blond hair and down his forehead. He licked his lips and tilted his head before I ever saw them coming.

Camille and Luthicer rushed past, and the others followed. Darthon lifted his palm, bloody and torn, and fire blasted against their bodies. Eu and Pierce smacked into a tree, but my father held up his arm, and it flew over him. Next to him, Urte was unharmed, and the half-breeds were unfazed.

"Give up, Darthon," my father said, but the boy locked his expression and stance.

He wiped his fire-covered hands on his pants and spread his fingertips apart. The ground melted around Urte's feet, yanking him toward the dirt. It molded over his arms before he could react, and my father followed.

I jumped away, but Darthon hadn't even tried with me. Instead, he laughed. "I should've assumed you'd bring friends into this," he said, and his eyes fluttered over Luthicer and Camille. Chains—as bright as his sword—wrapped around their limbs and tied their bodies together. They collapsed, wiggling against the metal as it cooled, but they couldn't break them.

I was on my own.

"I thought you liked other people to be involved," I said, trying to kick the dirt away from my father, but it didn't budge. His blue eyes widened, and I blocked an attack Darthon shot toward him.

"Only when I want a challenge," he glowered, and I shot forward, hoping his attacks would be concentrated on me—and only me. I didn't need the others to be hurt.

"I didn't know I was a challenge," I said, and he took one step forward. Sweat spread the blood across his face.

"You're not," he said. "Alone."

As the words left his mouth, a black silhouette flashed behind him. The arm wrapped around his neck and twisted. His neck snapped, and he hit the ground before I could even breathe.

The shadow formed, and I recognized her for the first time—her black hair, her pale skin, her purple eyes. Jessica. "What are you doing?" I asked as she ran toward me, breathless.

"I had to help," she said, and her stare widened as she took in my injuries. "You're hurt."

"I'm alive," I said, and she spun around, reaching for Camille and Luthicer.

"Don't touch us," Luthicer said, wincing as his body smoked. "It's made of Light energy. It'd only hurt you."

"But it shouldn't hurt you—"

"He can hurt his own kind, too," Camille managed, and I grabbed Jessica before she ignored their warnings. We couldn't help them.

"Get out of here," I said, but she glared.

"It's safe," she said. "He's dead."

SHANNON A. THOMPSON

But he wasn't.

Darthon groaned, standing up on shaking knees. Jessica froze, and he grinned as he met her stare. "Didn't they tell you?" he asked, cracking his neck into place, crunching the skull against the spine. "I can only die by Shoman's hands."

I yanked her back as the information struck me. Did that mean I could only die by his? I didn't know, and, by the other's reactions, they didn't either.

"I would ask for your name," Darthon said, marching forward as he gained his composure. "But I'm guessing I already know who you are—"

She pulled out her sword, and it was over. He knew who she was.

"Jessica, no!"

She shot forward without me, attacking despite the illogical reasoning. She couldn't kill him, even if she tried.

Darthon, at the last second, pulled his weapon out, and the two collided, flipping over one another. I leapt toward them, but fell when a hand wrapped around my ankle. It was my father's.

"Get me out," he said, and I threw my hands in the air.

"I can't!"

"Use your sword."

I followed his orders and dug the blade into the ground. It waved, and the mud slashed, smacking my father in the face. He shook his head, covered in muck, but stood. I released Urte, too.

We stumbled over one another as we ran toward the explosions, dipping in and out of the darkness. Darthon and Jessica were fighting, but she was pushing him backward. She was stronger.

I twisted around the last branch and squinted against the light as I neared them. Urte lifted his arm, but he continued with my father. All three of us got to her side, and Darthon's eyes widened behind his weapon's glare.

I maneuvered around them, attempting to get behind him, but he swung his sword around. He broke through branches, bushes, and split trees with his force. Beads of sweat curled over his face, and his arm was sliced, numerous times and deep into the flesh from Jessica's attack.

His black eyes blinked rapidly, as he turned his torso, lifting his skinned hand. My father grabbed Jessica's shoulder, and they shot to the side. The blast missed them by centimeters, and I struck Darthon's leg before he could do it again.

He radiated, and my dark energy sucked to my feet. My knees sank to the ground, and the others collapsed, falling against the sinking forest. I clenched my teeth, expecting Darthon to strike with his sword, but he folded in half and disappeared.

The power that defeated us was the Light's realm, and Darthon couldn't use it against us, even if he was leaving. He'd given up.

I gasped, and air pierced my lungs, freezing the molten blood in my veins. I shivered, and my sword disappeared. It was over. He was gone.

"Shoman." My father stumbled to my side, and I looked into his eyes. His normally unreadable face was contorted. He opened his mouth, as if ready to speak, but then his arms wrapped around my shoulders, and I grabbed his arm. He was shaking.

"He's gone," I said, and my father leaned back, sitting on the ground. Even his knees were trembling, and his blue eyes flickered between brown and blue. He could barely hold his form together.

"For now," he said.

"We have to go," Urte said, walking over, and Jessica rushed behind him.

She was the only one not bleeding. "What happened?" she asked, but I doubted she was asking about Darthon. Her eyes were focused on my injuries.

I managed to stand, and she reached for my arm but pulled away, biting her lip. "I'm afraid to touch you," she said.

"I'll be okay," I said, and the others shattered through the darkness, bringing shadows and light. Their restraints had disappeared with Darthon.

"Let's go," Camille said, and her white aura enveloped our crowd.

I clenched my teeth as my molecules shattered, whirling into an abyss. We landed in a white corridor, filled with shades. Two rushed forward, grabbing Pierce and Eu as they collapsed. They were hurt.

"Help them," my father barked, and he sat on the nearest bench. His appearance was faltering, but no one paid any attention.

Nurses dragged Eu, Pierce, and Urte away, while Luthicer and Camille stood around. Their burns were already healing, and I stared at my own injuries. They remained.

"Shoman?" Jessica was the first to notice. "What's wrong? Why aren't you—?"

My knees hit the floor, but pain didn't follow. I fell backward, and Luthicer was over me, his white hair dangling across my face. "What hurts the most?" he asked, and I opened my mouth.

I couldn't speak. I couldn't feel anything.

Luthicer paled, and he yanked Camille down. "Lift him up," he said, and my vision fogged over. I was aware of Jessica's screams, but I couldn't hear anything else. I only saw red— blood covering Luthicer's hand as he lifted it.

He shouted again as my shade form ripped. My skin tore apart into a human as I lost all control, and the blackness consumed my conscious.

FORTY-SEVEN

HE WASN'T SHOMAN ANYMORE. HE WAS ERIC.
Feet away, men held him against a bed as Luthicer poked and prodded his bleeding body. From the hallway, I could see his brown hair plastered to his hot cheek, his continuously bleeding shoulder, and paling skin. His screams were getting louder and louder. I could barely stand it.

I closed my eyes and shivered beneath my torn dress. I was human, too, but I wasn't hurt. I didn't understand.

"Take this," a boy said as he draped a thick blanket over my shoulders. He was the younger one, with green eyes and black hair, but his arm was wrapped up. He'd gotten injured, too.

"Thanks," I managed, grasping the cloth as Eric screamed again. I trembled.

"He'll be okay," the boy said, and I realized I had been biting my lip.

"What's wrong with him?"

"Darthon's sword struck him," he said. "It's imbedded with poison just like any Light weapon." He smiled, but I didn't know why. Poison was serious, wasn't it? "Luthicer will get him back to normal in a matter of minutes."

I dug my nails into the cotton blanket, fighting my nausea, and Bracke left Eric's room, shutting the door behind him. Eric's screams mellowed, but I knew they were just as loud behind the closed doors.

"Jess?" Bracke gestured his neck toward the nearest room. "Come with me," he said. "You don't need to hear this."

"But—"

The boy sighed and pulled me to my feet. "Follow me," he said, and he dragged me. I was too exhausted to pull back.

We walked into the room, and Bracke shut the door behind us—adding another barrier between Eric and us. He was the only thing I could concentrate on. "He'll live, Jess," Bracke said, and I sat down.

"How's he doing?" I asked, and the older man took a seat across from me.

"Okay," he said, and the door cracked open.

Camille—the white-haired woman—slipped inside, and I wondered if she was who I thought she was. Teresa Young. She had to be.

"You asked for me, sir?" she asked, and Bracke nodded.

"Watch after Jess with Pierce," he said, and I looked at the younger boy, comforted by the knowledge of his name.

The two replied instantaneously, "Yes, sir."

Bracke's eyes glanced over me one last time, and he dismissed himself, returning to Eric's side. I held my breath, watching Camille as she walked across the room. She didn't sit, and Pierce thumbed his fingers across his leg.

Neither of them spoke, but Camille's dark eyes glided over me. She opened her mouth, sighed, and closed it again.

"What?" I asked, and she finally pulled a chair in front of me and sat down.

Her gaze flickered over my face. "Jessica, right?"

"Jess," Pierce corrected, and I jumped, blinking at the green-eyed boy. He knew my nickname, the one everyone called me except Eric.

"How'd you know?" I asked, and he chuckled.

"Hayworth is a small town, Jess."

I squinted at his facial features, trying to tear them apart, but he was unrecognizable. "I've never seen you before," I said, and he shook his head.

"Shades don't exactly walk around school like this."

"Pierce," Camille hissed, and I knew he'd given away his information.

He threw his hands in the air. "It's kind of obvious if you ask me," he said, but Camille's glare didn't shift.

I smiled, hoping to defuse the tension. "Well, it's nice to meet you, Pierce."

He nodded. "Just wish it was under different circumstances."

My eyes dropped to my lap. Eric. I'd caused the attack, but I felt as if I also saved them. Darthon had been beating them—destroying them—and he could've killed Eric if I hadn't shown up. But Darthon wouldn't have been there if I hadn't followed Eric in the first place. I didn't know how to feel about it, but I definitely felt guilty.

"I'm sorry," I said, and Camille groaned.

"This isn't your fault," she said, and I stared, unable to comprehend how her words could be truth. "You didn't know, and neither did Eric," she said. "The elders hid everything. Their decisions caused this, and they know it."

I blinked, and Camille sighed, dropping her head. She grabbed her scalp, stomped her feet, and met my eyes again. "He really didn't tell you anything, did he?"

"He told me a third descendant didn't exist," I said, and Pierce chuckled.

Camille smacked his leg, and he waved his hands in front of him. "Sorry," he said. "It's just sort of ironic if you ask me."

"No one asked you," she said, and I curled my legs beneath me.

"I will," I said, turning away from Camille to look at Pierce. "What's going on?"

His shoulders rose, but he didn't speak.

"Are you explaining this one?" Camille asked, and Pierce shook his head.

"I'd probably screw it up," he said. "I'm still confused."

I looked at Camille, and she rolled her eyes. I couldn't believe how light-hearted they could be when Eric was suffering one room over. I wanted to ask how they could be so calm, but

Camille began spewing out information. I bit my lip to prevent speaking.

She explained the prophecy—the entire prophecy—and didn't hesitate about my part in it. "Eric left you to protect you," she finished. "Even though his idiocy got him there in the first place."

I couldn't speak. Eric Welborn—Shoman—was supposed to love me? He was destined to find me? And I was his weakness?

"He's kind of lucky," Pierce said. "I wish I had a girl lined up."

Camille smacked him again, and his green eyes widened. "What?" he asked. "It's true."

"And it came with a price," she snapped, and I dug my nails into my legs.

"So my existence hurts him?" I asked, and the two quieted.

"It's not as bad as it sounds," Camille spoke through her frown, but I knew it was a lie.

It was that bad. We could love each other, but we could die because of it. And the Light. They wanted me, and they could find either one of us if one of our identities were revealed.

"What do they want with me?" I asked, and Camille shook her head, the whiteness of her hair glittering in the room's dim light.

"It's referred to as absorbing, but we don't even know what that means," she said, leaning forward to lay her cold palm on my arm. "We only know it could alter the ending."

"So Darthon would win," I said, and Camille hesitated. She didn't have to confirm my thoughts. She'd already told me.

I exhaled a shaky breath, and Pierce leaned his chair back. "Too bad Shoman's the only one who can kill that son of a bitch," he grumbled. "You would've solved all of our problems tonight if that wasn't the case."

Camille's lips pressed into a thin line. "And we only learned that tonight."

"You didn't know?" I asked, and she played with the ends of her hair.

"No," she said. "But they did."

"So they know more than we do," Pierce added.

"Which isn't a good thing," Camille said.

I stared at the floor. It was made from stone. The air was musty and smelled like dirt. I knew we were underground, but I didn't even know where I was. Were my parents worried about me? I didn't have my cellphone, but I was afraid to ask them for a phone. I doubted the Dark would be too excited about my adoption.

"Did Shoman ever give you a liquid to drink?" Camille asked, and I looked up at her.

My heart skipped, but I nodded, remembering Fudicia's attack—something that seemed like child's play compared to Darthon's. "It took away my powers," I said, and Camille leaned on her hand.

"Do you know why he did that?" she asked, and my body tensed as I remembered his words from the night he left me.

"I was poisoned," I said, staring between the two. "Just like he is now."

"See?" She grinned and lightly kicked my chair. "He'll be fine, too."

"At least no one will get caught in his explosion this time," Pierce grumbled, and my neck whipped around. I gaped at him.

"He what?"

"That was so unnecessary, Pierce," Camille said, rubbing her forehead before she explained. "He was poisoned that night, too, but he used his remedy on you."

"So he took his powers out on me," Pierce said, but his face lit up. "I was almost killed."

My jaw dropped, and Camille stood, slapping the side of Pierce's head. "That's nothing to be proud of," she said, rubbing her hands together like she'd hurt herself.

He shrugged. "It's not a big deal now."

"And Eric's current injuries aren't either," Camille said, desperately trying to comfort me. She pointed to the door. "He'll walk through there any minute."

"He'll walk out? On his own?" I could barely manage the questions. Everything seemed so unreal—so supernatural—and I had to remind myself that is was. We weren't human. We never were.

"He wouldn't heal so quickly if he'd let it attack his blood-stream for a day," Camille said. "He was unconscious for a while last time."

I sat up, nearly dropping my blanket. "He was unconscious last time?"

This time, Camille was the one to laugh. "If you're going to be one of us, Jess," she began. "I suggest you toughen up."

Be one of them. The words finally brought me the comfort I'd desired since moving to Hayworth: I was one of them—a shade—and I reveled in it. I could finally accept what—and who—I was. The third descendant, someone of power, of reason, of capability.

"Thank you," I said, and Camille started to speak but stopped.

"I think you have a visitor," she said, winking, and the door opened.

Luthicer and Urte were the first to appear. Eu and Bracke followed them, but the one I cared about most was in their shadows.

Eric's brown hair was pressed against his forehead, dried to his skin from sweat, and his green eyes were fogged with drowsiness. His clothes were in bits, and his face was scratched, but he managed a smile when he met my eyes.

I leapt up, pushed through the crowd, and I was in his arms again.

He stumbled backward, but gained his footing and chuckled. "Hey," he whispered, laying a hand on the top of my head.

As much as I hated to admit it, I started to cry. I sobbed, harder than I had in the past few days, and right in front of the ones I wanted to impress. I didn't even care. All I cared about was Eric's health, and he was fine—he was alive.

"I'm okay," he said, and his hand stroked the back of my neck. "You're okay. Everything is okay now." He moved his hand to my chin and lifted my face to meet my eyes. He wiped my tears away with his thumb. "It'll be all right, Jessica."

I managed a nod before laying my cheek against his chest. My cold tears pressed against his clothes, and I sniffled to catch my breath. Eric's hold tightened around my torso, and I could see why.

The others were gaping at us, unable to move or speak, and I realized what I hadn't thought of before. The prophecy said Shoman would love me, but they hadn't witnessed it. Now they had.

"I think it's time I introduce Jessica," Eric said, and a few managed an uncomfortable smile.

"You're lucky she isn't dead," Luthicer muttered, crossing his elongated arms. "You're lucky you're both alive."

"I know," Eric said. "Thank you for your help, Luthicer. Really."

The man's eyes widened, but he didn't speak.

"So now what?" Pierce asked, breaking through the tension. "What's next?"

"Everyone will have to stay here tonight," Urte said. "Darthon left, but we don't know where he is, and it's too dangerous to leave until we're sure he's not coming back."

I interjected, "But my parents—"

"Think you're at Crystal's house," Eric said, and I stared at him.

"How?"

"Don't worry about that," Luthicer said, and I turned in time to witness his grin.

"He's a half-breed, like Camille," Eric spoke to me in silence. *"He can create illusions. Your parents will never know."*

"Eric." His father's voice was full of scorn.

"Sorry," Eric muttered, but he continued to speak to me.

"My father can tell when we're using telepathy," he explained quickly. *"He thinks it's rude."*

I blinked, trying to process the abundance of information, but it seemed impossible. I'd learned so much, and I'd expected none of it.

"But we have to figure out what to do with—er—Jess," Eu said, flushing as he used my name. I imagined using someone's human identity didn't come naturally within the Dark's walls.

"We have to do something," Urte agreed. "She can't stay here forever—not when the Light could break in at any moment."

"We can't even train her here," Luthicer said. "It'd be risking too much."

"I can already defend myself," I said, and the others froze. They weren't used to my input.

Eric rubbed my arm. "She's stronger than Darthon; that's for sure."

"That doesn't mean we need to egg him on," his father said, and Eric's grip tightened.

"So what are you saying?" he asked. "She has to go? Because I can't imagine that anywhere would be safer than here."

Luthicer grabbed his chin. "We really have no solution."

"But Darthon doesn't know my identity," I whined, feeling my acceptance disappearing.

"He could figure it out, Jessica," Eric said, and his heart beat against my back. "He saw you as a human, too."

"But he didn't know—"

"We can't rely on that."

I froze. Eric was right. I'd made a mistake. Big time. And there was no coming back from that.

"What if I wasn't a shade?" I whispered, and Eric's eyes widened.

"What are you talking about?" he asked. "You can't just change your genetics."

"You said they stripped abandoned shades of their powers," I repeated some of the information he taught me and turned back to the others. "If I didn't have my powers, I'd be useless, Jessica or not."

Bracke's jaw popped like his son's. "But what good would that do?" he asked. "You wouldn't be able to defend yourself if he found you."

"Unless even I didn't know who I was," I said, listening to

the pieces fall into place before I recognized them. "If you can create an illusion for my parents, you can do it to me, too, and, even if he came after me, I wouldn't be anything. No matter what absorbing means."

I exhaled, and Camille crossed her arms. "She'd practically be human."

"I don't know about this," Pierce said, and Urte agreed.

"You wouldn't want to do something like that anyway, Jessica," he said, and I shook my head.

"If it meant keeping everyone safe, then I would."

The others blinked.

"I'd do anything," I said, and the room was enveloped in silence.

It was a solution, and everyone knew it. If I didn't have powers, I wouldn't transform, and if I didn't have a memory, I wouldn't want to. I'd be a human, unable to slip even in the most emotional times, and Darthon would be unable to trace my powers. Even if he came after me, I'd no longer know, and I'd no longer be powerful. I'd be useless to his cause, and the others wouldn't even have to protect me. I'd be safe and so would they.

"It's risky," Luthicer finally spoke. "But it isn't impossible."

Urte, Eu, and Luthicer erupted into arguments, and the room vibrated with anger. Their voices bounced off the walls and died against the floor until Bracke lifted his hand. Everyone silenced as Eric's father stepped forward, looking only into my eyes.

"We're capable of what you're offering, and I think it's our best option at this point," he said, pausing to choose his words. "But there are some issues we need to address."

His blue eyes flickered up to Eric, and Eric tensed against me. I knew what his father would ask, even before the words were spoken, "Would you be able to give up my son so easily?"

I leaned back and caught Eric's eyes. They were resigned, shadowed beneath his furrowed brow, and his jaw clenched. He wasn't talking, and I knew why. He'd realized what everyone else had.

"I wouldn't have to," I said, unable to look away from him. "I wouldn't remember him."

Eric turned his face to stare at the wall, and my hands curled into a fist on his chest. I could feel his heart pound. After everything—after all the tears, words, and kisses—he'd return to being Eric Welborn, the guy who sat next to me in homeroom. Nothing more. Nothing less. And he wouldn't even try to rekindle the relationship. It had to be over for our plan to work.

"There's no point carrying out this plan if Eric continues to see her," Luthicer said, and Camille agreed.

"And it'd be too risky to mess with his mind," Camille said. "He might forget his training."

"We don't have a solution," Urte said, and Eric shook his head.

"Yes, we do," he said, wrapping his hand around my fist. He met my eyes, but they were no longer fogged over. They were bright, aware and driven. "I can stay away this time," he said. "My mistakes could've caused—" *death.* He wouldn't say it. Instead, he ran his free hand through his hair. "I won't make them again. I can't."

His father raised his brow. "I don't know—"

"I can do it," Eric said, and his father stepped back. The forcefulness of Eric's tone even made me jump. I hadn't expected it, but the others hadn't either. Eric wasn't lying.

"Then we'll do it," his father said, looking at Luthicer.

The half-breed elder shook his head. "I can't do it now," he said. "I'm too weak. I need time."

"How much?" Bracke asked.

Luthicer breathed in, and his chest sank. "I'd want to wait two months," he said. "I have to practice. I haven't done something that big in a long time, and I don't want to hurt her."

I swallowed my nerves, knowing what he meant. His powers could potentially affect my brain. I pushed away the thoughts as they came. I didn't want to think about the others who'd been hurt in order for Luthicer to figure out he could do harm.

"If that's our only choice, we can wait for the memory loss," Bracke began. "But I'll block your powers tomorrow," he said, pointing at Eric and I. "And you two can't see each other—not in public anyway."

Eric straightened up. "You'll let me see her at all?"

I was like him. I had expected to be banned completely and immediately, but Bracke sighed.

"I think we can allow it for now," he said.

"But—" Luthicer started to argue, and Bracke glared at him.

"Let the two have a few days of normalcy," he said. "It's our fault they got into this anyway. It's the least we can do, and I'll take full responsibility on guaranteeing it's appropriate." The words came out in one breath, and I grasped Eric's hand.

"You mean it?" I asked, and Bracke nodded. No one interjected this time.

"Thanks, Dad," Eric said while the others started for the door.

"Let's get to bed," Eu grumbled, obviously disapproving. "I can't handle any more of this tonight."

"Me neither," Luthicer agreed, leaving with the others.

Only Eric and I remained, and he didn't hesitate to lift my face. "Mind if I kiss you as Eric?" he asked, managing a smile, and I kissed him as an answer.

He tensed, but relaxed, and I leaned against his chest, taking him in. We were together—finally—and I loved it, even if it wouldn't last forever. One moment of true happiness was worth all the moments of pain.

FORTY-EIGHT

Jessica

T HE FIREWORKS WERE BEAUTIFUL. REDS, BLUES, AND GREEN GLIS-
tened against the darkening sky, and sparklers glittered
in the valley below us, reminding me of every moment
I'd used my powers. The powers I no longer had.

"How are you feeling?" Eric asked, leaning into the shadows beneath the willow tree. It was the only time we'd been in
public together. We were still hiding and I couldn't be more
grateful. At least we had one night, one instance of freedom.

"Tired," I admitted. Ever since Bracke had blocked my
abilities, I didn't feel quite right, but I was adapting to the feeling. I was started to feel like my old self—the girl who was
oblivious of everything to come.

"That's expected," Eric said, and I nodded, knowing we
repeated the conversation every time I managed to see him,
mainly at his house and only when Teresa—or Camille—
deemed it safe enough to pick me up. I wasn't even allowed to
drive my own car over.

"I spend every Independence Day up here," Eric said, and
we sat down.

I pushed my dress beneath me, loving the hot air summer
brought. It was nearly suffocating, but I'd been cold for so long,
I embraced the humidity entirely.

"I can see why," I said, taking in everything, even though I
knew I wouldn't remember it the next day. I grabbed his hand

and tightened my grip. "Do you think it will hurt?" I asked, and Eric's green eyes peered through the shadows.

"It shouldn't," he said, running his thumb over the back of my hand. "It'll happen when you're sleeping, so you won't even know."

I forced a nod, mustering up the courage to ask the question our three months together hadn't allowed. "You're planning on fighting Darthon without me; aren't you?"

He straightened, dragging his fingers through my curls. "What do you mean?" He was avoiding the answer.

"You turn eighteen in December," I said, crossing my arms. "And you're not going to bring my memory back until afterwards. I can tell."

His expression didn't move. "That was always the plan, Jessica," he said, and I knew he was telling the truth I'd denied to myself.

"I don't want you to, Eric."

He sighed. "Jessica—"

"Why don't my feelings matter?" I asked, and he tilted his head, nearly smiling.

"You know they do," he said. "Especially to me. But—"

"But what?" The closeness of my memory being erased was causing me to panic. Had I made the wrong decision? It didn't matter. There was no turning back from it. Luthicer had already placed the illusion.

"But your presence would only make things worse," he said, the voice of reason. "And you know that."

"What if he kills you?" I asked, tugging on his shirt when he didn't respond. "What if he wins, Eric?"

"I'm not going to die, Jessica," Eric said, and he sat up, pulling me into his lap. He poked my side, and I giggled, fighting him. I didn't want to laugh.

"Stop it," I said, sticking out my bottom lip as he leaned over me, his brown hair hovering over my face.

"Then relax," he said. "I said it'd be fine, so at least attempt to believe in me."

I sat up and kissed him before lying back down. "I do."

His hand brushed my curls off my face, and he laid his palm on my cheek. "I don't want this any more than you do, but it has to be this way," he said. I didn't bother nodding. He knew I agreed. I'd offered, after all.

"I love you," I said, and his fingers dropped from my face. He didn't say anything, and I sat up, my heart racing. I hadn't said it before then, and he wasn't saying it back. "What's wrong?" I asked, and he grabbed my hands, lacing his fingers through mine.

"You know I feel the same way," he said as his green eyes held mine. "But I want to say it when you'll remember it. Not now. Not when you may never get the memory back."

He reminded me that Luthicer had erased every memory of Shoman, the Dark, and anything that could trigger it, but he'd done it with hesitation. He wasn't sure if I'd get every moment back, even when he removed the blocks.

I bit my quavering lip, and Eric leaned forward, kissing me. His hand waved through my curls, resting on the nape of my neck, and he held me against him. Beneath the willow tree, we remained like that for minutes, until I needed to breathe and pulled away.

"I still love you," I said, and he chuckled, knowing my love wasn't something I gave expecting it back. I loved him, and because I did, I knew how he felt. If he needed more time to express it, then I accepted it. I wanted to.

"I am sorry," he said, pulling me under his arm as an array of fireworks burst over the night sky.

"Me, too."

His shoulders rose. "What are you sorry for?"

I swallowed my nerves. "In case anything happens," I said, hesitating to elaborate. "In case, I date someone else—just know that my heart belongs to you."

His jaw tightened as if the thought hadn't occurred to him. "I forgive you already," he said, and he rubbed his hand over my back, although he was the one who probably needed comfort. "We'll get through this, Jessica. I promise."

I brought Eric's hand up and kissed it. His eyes widened,

and I leaned back, yawning for the first time. My face fell into a frown, reminded by the upcoming sleep that would trigger the illusion, and Eric didn't bother to hide his grimace either.

"I'll be back before I know it," I said, and he tilted his head to the side.

"It'll be a blink for you," he said and smiled before I could talk about his reality. "This won't be the last time I hold your hand," he promised with a kiss.

I agreed and hoped it was a promise we could keep, despite the future ahead of us.

Acknowledgements

ANY MOON CYCLES AGO, A FOURTEEN-YEAR-OLD EXPERI-enced an array of terrifying nightmares—many of which felt too realistic to have only been dreamt. These nightmares continued for one year, and the only solace resided in a singular boy who appeared in them to discuss a magical and unfamiliar world. Without explanation, the dreams ceased, but the girl's memories continued to captivate her, eventually becoming the inspiration for The Timely Death Trilogy.

In the decade following, The Timely Death Trilogy was written, and with the support of many talented people, those dreams became a reality when The Timely Death Trilogy was published. For that reason, I want to thank my teachers—Mrs. Metcalf, T.L. McCown, Megan Kaminski, and Dr. Valk—for showing me a literary world full of possibilities. I also want to thank all of my dear friends who've gone beyond themselves to help with this novel, including Kirsten Moore, David Flores, Alex Villers, Tyler Gravenstein, Raul Diaz, Kyle Pettey, Cassie Barker, and Atheil Barker. A special thank you also goes out to the dedicated team at Clean Teen Publishing for believing in the world of the Dark with eager determination to share it with readers. Another thank you is for all the Members of the Dark—book bloggers and reviewers—who supported this trilogy through many trying times.

Without all of these passionate people, this novel would not be possible.

To all of you mentioned and beyond, I owe the greatest gratitude.

Stay Dark,

Shannon A. Thompson

Join the Dark and visit www.ShannonAThompson.com

ABOUT THE AUTHOR

Shannon A. Thompson is a twenty-three-year-old author, avid reader, and habitual chatterbox. She was merely sixteen when she was first published, and a lot has happened since then. Thompson's work has appeared in numerous poetry collections and anthologies, and her first installment of The Timely Death Trilogy became Goodreads' Book of the Month. As a novelist, poet, and blogger, Thompson spends her free time writing and sharing ideas with her black cat named after her favorite actor, Humphrey Bogart. Between writing and befriending cats, she graduated from the University of Kansas with a bachelor's degree in English, and she travels whenever the road calls her.

Visit her blog for writers and readers at
www.shannonathompson.com